BLEAK SCAR

J C Bligh

Copyright © 2022 J C Bligh

All rights reserved

The characters and events portrayed in this book are fictitious. Any similarity to real persons, living or dead, is coincidental and not intended by the author.

No part of this book may be reproduced, or stored in a retrieval system, or transmitted in any form or by any means, electronic, mechanical, photocopying, recording, or otherwise, without express written permission of the publisher.

ISBN: 9798801093116

I dedicate this book to my friends and family who challenged, encouraged and supported me every setp of the way.

To my wife, for spending countless hours being my soundboard and discussing the undead, demons and dragons in the middle of the night.

To my son, for inspiring me to put my imagination into words. I hope that one day you can read this book and enjoy reading it as much as I enjoyed writing it.

Thank you all for helping me on this journey.

PROLOGUE

Kruul, The Clan Lord, a position earned by mortal combat and held by those same traditions, sat in the hut of The Eight. The Eight were seers, wretched and putrid females chosen at birth to give their bodies and souls to entities beyond in exchange for the power of The Sight. This was their responsibility as advisors and seers to the clan lord. Kruul sat hunched, his huge scarred and tattooed frame almost reaching the ceiling of the small hut as he looked down on them, waiting. They sat around the fire chanting and swaying in rhythm around him. The sound of their moans, the rattling of small bones and the squealing of a swine filled the room as much as the intoxicating fragrance of strange herbs burning. Kruul hated being here, he hated relying on the knowledge of old crones and their unknown powers to guide the clan but it was tradition. He waited.

The crones all suddenly stopped swaying and chanting at the same instant. All seemingly reaching a mutual climax, snapping Kruul's attention from the small fire in the center of the room. The eight screamed in unison "We must flee! The evil comes from the mountain! We must flee! Flee to the North!"
Their eyes were bulging and their green skin had turned a pale sickly white colour. They were visibly shaking. Kruul's brow furrowed as he said with authority "Nae! We 'dunnae run from invaders. If we go North, the humans will slay us all. There are too many of them and we have children and elderly in the clan. I 'cannae risk a war we 'cannae win."
Louder than before The Eight screamed almost hysterically making his ears ring.
"This is no mere invader we run from. This is a darkness deeper than those between the stars! We must flee!"

At that moment Kelregg, Kruul's head scout, came bursting into the hut, letting in daylight and with him, clarity from the hazing smoke in the room. Trying to catch his breath he rasped "Chieftain Kruul! From the mountain..." he doubled over to catch his breath.
"What is it, Kelregg?" Kruul barked.
The Eight began to wail as tears of blood streaked down their sickly pale cheeks. Kelregg swallowed and looked his chieftain in the eye.

"A darkness I have never seen before, the scouts are gone. I am the last." He dipped his head in shame "It's coming this way".

CHAPTER 1 - MARKET DAY

A stunned young man stared out from beneath a market stall that was propped up against one of the oldest buildings in Cornwalk. His breathing was quick and shallow, panicked. His mind had blocked every sense but sight, desperately trying to process his father's violent death. His only vision was the blurred image of his father through the heavy rain bent backwards over the seat in their familiar old sturdy wagon. His father's lifeless gaze looked directly at him as the horses silently galloped away in terror flicking sprays of wet mud high into the air, the arrow still protruding from his chest. Pelts and meat, brought to market that morning falling from the wagon as his image grew smaller.

In the calmer recesses of his brain a voice ordered

him to take action. Closing his eyes in a slow deliberate blink, his vision focused on the tears and rain water caught in his eyelashes, red with blood, he wiped it away with the back of his hand. His senses started to come alive again as the numbness of watching his father die drained away in favour of self preservation.

The deafening hissing sound of heavy rain all around him was, at first, overwhelming. Then his sense of smell sparked to life as he took a deep shuddering breath. He could smell mud, rain, smoke, wood and tobacco from Mr.Thomlin's market stall which he was hiding under. The strongest smell was the metallic smell of blood. More strange sounds became clearer to him as he focused on his surroundings. The pounding hooves of his father's horses in the distance, Nell and Bessy desperately fleeing from the village of Cornwalk as they dragged his father's body away. Each second the sound became more and more distant. More sounds, distant and muted by the rain; fire, shouting and slaughter. Another much clearer and much closer sound. *Was it crying?* And another. *Heavy grunting? From where?* Somewhere off to his right beyond the cold wet stone wall of The Fallen Cow Inn blocking his sight.

He forced a second deep breath. More senses returned, the bitter cold of the wind whipped through the woollen throw on the stall above and around him. To his left, the tap tap tap of cool water coming through the woollen throw above in the heavy rain and onto his shoulder. A tight ache in his knuckles. He looked down to see his belt knife gripped so tightly, his hand trembled. His knuckles were white as his hands shook with terror and adrenaline. He didn't remember drawing the blade in the frantic moments leading to this point.

He took a final deep breath, this time opening his mouth to breathe out slowly. He could taste mud, tears and what he now realised was his father's blood on his lips.

He crawled out from under the stall and suddenly felt exposed from every side. His sense of reason screamed at him to keep moving. Get to the forest outside of the village. Get home. He took several sluggish paces in the thick wet sucking mud as he came around the corner towards the bridge leading North out of Cornwalk. There, to his right, behind The Fallen Cow Inn was the source of the nearby noises.

A green-grey skinned muscle-bound creature was hunched over something thrashing around, it was sky blue and the large creature was struggling to control it. His haze cleared more and he understood what he was looking at. The orc had its back to him and the flailing blue thing below it was Lilly Cooper, Mayor

Cooper's daughter. The orc was oblivious to his presence and obviously too distracted to hear anyone stalking up behind him. The young man's knuckles ached again as he found himself, against his logical brain which was telling him to flee, walking towards the hulking figure. His head pounded with the rapid beat of his heart furiously pumping adrenaline. He held the knife in both hands and drove it into the back of the creature's neck. He felt skin, muscle, tendons and bones against the knife's edge which, although sharp, was barely longer than his finger. He put all his weight into it and released his grip reeling back. Only when he stumbled back awkwardly in the mud to witness what he had done did he realise he was screaming.

The orc gave a short sharp spasm and started to rock to one side, one arm awkwardly trying to reach for the tiny blade. Its massive body struggled to cooperate as the spinal cord was slashed. Before its gnarled meaty hand could touch the hilt, a smaller slender hand reached and grabbed it and tore it to one side using the blade to cut the knife free, tearing open the creature's thick neck. The brute fell on its back, its eyes bulging in pain and horror and its ugly fanged mouth uttering terrified silent questions. Its body didn't move but its desperate eyes darted around looking for answers. Lilly picked herself up, never taking her eyes from the creature's. Looking down at the massive orc as it looked up at her in a futile emotionless stare, as though she was going to make things better in its final moments. She did not, she viciously kicked and screamed at the orcs face as blood sprayed into the air from his neck. She didn't stop until she had exhausted her anger, sadness and frustration.

When she was done, breathing heavily, she turned and wiping the wet sandy blonde hair from her pale blue eyes she gasped "Thank you, Kaln."

Lilly ran into him with a desperate hug, their wet clothes making a thick slapping noise as she nearly knocked him off his feet.

Hearing his own name was enough to break what remained of his stupor. He held her.

They both stood there in the embrace, shaking with shock and cold in the rain. Kaln, looking over Lilly's shoulder at the rising plumes of smoke from beyond the nearby buildings towards the village center, loosened his grip.
"We need to move." Kaln whispered as he took his arms from around Lilly. As soon as he broke contact with her, he suddenly felt desperately alone, more tired and cold. There was an almost magical quality to her touch that took the edge off this brutal reality.

He watched her as she gathered herself, closed her eyes and took a deep breath. Even covered in blood, mud and wet top to toe she was beautiful.

"If you had not come when you did...well... I may have lost something I could never have retrieved. Praise the moon you were here Kaln. Thank you." She said awkwardly but with the fullest of sincerity and forced herself to smile briefly. Her eyes glittered. She looked at him for a moment longer and after a sharp breath through her nose, as though snapping herself out of whatever scene was playing through her head, she said "Yes, lets go. My father will be in the village square."

She grabbed Kaln's hand and started towards the village center.
Kaln used her momentum to spin her around and grab both hands, forcing her to look him in the eyes again. Somewhere beyond the Fallen Cow Inn, the cries of a dying man rang out between the burning buildings and the rain almost as if on queue.

"Lilly, you know he's dead. You know there is nothing we can do for any of them. If we go back there we both die." Kaln said in a clear firm voice, streams of bloodied water running off of his chin.

Lilly stared back at him but his grey eyes were

unwavering with conviction. Before she could argue he tightened his grip on her cold delicate hands and with a slight nod of his head, he all but whispered the words "We have to run, come with me." knowing what he was asking her to do meant to her.

The small woman stood there in silence for a long moment. Kaln knew that Lilly was intelligent enough to know he was right but passionate and desperate enough to argue with his logic. As her internal conflict raged, Kaln stood there stoic as a beacon of light in the darkness of her inner turmoil with a patient and reassuring look waiting for her to make her decision.

Her eyes welled again and she sobbed into his chest whimpering weakly "No, no... no..." Logic had won the battle.

In as soft a voice as he could muster he said "I know." and held her closer to him "There will be time later, Lilly, when we are away from danger. Stay close and I will get us to safety."

Another long moment passed and with a sharp sniff, she wiped her eyes, pulled her hair back into a ponytail and nodded.
"You'd better have this back then." she announced with a meek smile. She wiped the blade on her dress and passed him the whittling

knife back. He gave her a small smile in return and holding her hand tight they fled towards the bridge to the North away from the sound of slaughter, away from the mud and blood and away from Lilly's home.

CHAPTER 2 - RAINFALL

Kaln was a huntsman, one in a line of huntsmen. These were the Black Rock Woods. His forests. Once they had broken the treeline he was confident, even with the dying light he could get both of them to the house where he and his father lived. Where they would be safe.

The two ran and Kaln quickly realised that Lilly was struggling to keep up, her smaller legs and large water soaked dress hampering their speed.

"A little further and we should be out of sight!" he shouted to her through the heavy rain. She gave him a nod as she grimaced into the downpour.

Lilly stumbled where the thick mud met the

cobbles of the North End bridge and almost pulled Kaln down to the ground with her. As he turned to help her to her feet, a violent whistle ripped through the rain and a red hot pain blazed in his thigh. He heard the arrow clatter off the far side of the bridge and noticed the arrow would have been in the center of Lilly's back had she not stumbled.

White terror washed over him and he all but lifted Lilly off her feet as he helped her up and placed himself between her and the archer somewhere back in the ravaged village, hidden by the rain and shadows. Turning to her, Kaln shouted over sudden rolling thunder "Run as fast as you can! Get to the treeline! I will meet you there!"
She glanced at the blood running down Kaln's leg and gave him a quick questioning look, her face illuminated by a flash of lightning some miles off. Only concern was dancing on her features, not fear. Kaln answered the look with a grin of defiance and a quick nod. She turned and ran. As he watched her flee, he noticed the even deeper clouds beginning to blot out what was left of the fading light.

Kaln was exposed on the bridge with nothing but a pocket knife against the hidden archer. He knew he didn't have much time before the next arrow flew. Sheathing the knife and looking around him, he saw the scattered pelts and meat that he and his father had brought to Cornwalk which had fallen from their wagon as the horses fled in panic. He crouched low and grabbed the largest haunch of meat he could find and a thick bear pelt. Throwing the pelt over the slab of meat, he held both to his back and stayed as low as he could while trying to run. He made for the vague blue shape of Lilly's dress heading for the treeline.

Thunder boomed again overhead as Kaln sploshed through deep pools of water covering most of the road.

He made it maybe twenty paces before something hit him hard from behind and he heard breaking bones. He winced, hoping the meat had taken the arrow and adrenaline wasn't numbing his broken ribs as he staggered and regained his footing at the far side of the bridge. Not daring to look back he saw Lilly disappear into the forest.

Now that she was safe all he needed to do was get to her. Holding his makeshift shield as best he could over his shoulders, he broke into a standing sprint, his height gave him an advantage when closing short distances and he used all of it. As he pushed off, his thigh flared with hot complaints and he gritted his teeth, his pace faltered.

A further forty desperate long paces and another blow that felt like a punch to the back hit him. He staggered and fell to one knee by a sapling tree no higher than his waist. In that momentary pause, between deep shuddering breaths, he could feel the arrow tips protruding through the meat and pressing against his back. The plan had worked but he had stopped moving. He was close to the edge of the forest now.

The light was all but gone with the sudden thickening of storm clouds and the rain had become even heavier. He had to hope the archer could see as little of him now as he could see of the archer after the first arrow missed Lilly. He was exhausted and had no idea if his make-shift shield could take another arrow, he had to change his plan. With his next stride he placed the makeshift shield against the sapling, exposing himself and relieving him of the weight, he made a break for the nearby treeline. An arrow struck the sacrificial sapling and it collapsed under the blow but Kaln had disappeared into the trees. He couldn't help but feel smug as he darted between the welcoming naked branches of the blackbarks.

Once he was deep enough into the forest that he was confident a stray arrow couldn't hit him he doubled over catching his breath, his thigh and his lungs burning. Something touched his back and he barely stopped himself striking Lilly with his elbow in pure reflex. She flinched and looked up at him with her big blue eyes looking scared, cold and desperate. She held his hand. In it was

a torn piece of the pale blue dress she wore. She knelt and with surprising expertise she checked and dressed the wound on his leg with the makeshift bandage. Kaln gave a sharp intake of breath as the makeshift bandage was tightened. He closed his tired eyes for a moment and smiled in thanks to Lilly. She returned the smile.
"It isn't deep. We have to keep moving." Lilly said softly before Kaln could and nodded, telling him to take the lead.

Kaln found his grip on her hand and moved at the fastest pace he thought Lilly could handle. The light was almost completely gone and with it, the warmth of the day. Although his footing was sure and his direction true, the trees without their leaves whipped and lashed in the cold rising winds of late autumn. Positioning himself in front of Lilly his cold hands and face were clawed and scratched by the writhing forest as it danced to the tune of the storm's howling winds. He drew his cloak around him and realised the rain had stopped now, a small comfort when you are wet and the winds are just as punishing. They pushed on for what felt like an eternity, into the darkness and rough terrain. The sounds of the forest getting closer between the howls of wind which made his cloak whip violently around him. In the dark he lost his footing and as he slipped down a steep slope, he had the presence of mind to release his grip on Lilly so as not to drag her with him. He fell, watching the world tumble around him. Distantly he felt himself hit a gnarled tree stump hard in his ribs, knocking the wind from his lungs. Consciousness washed away from him, leaving only peaceful, warm darkness.

Kaln came-to with Lilly, knelt over him. For a moment, moonlight pierced the clouds and made the tears on her cheeks sparkle. Her eyes widened as she realised he was alive and able to move.

"Praise the Moon!" she gasped looking up to the peeking moon between the clouds and helped him to his feet.

"How long was I out?" he groaned, holding his head and side with a wince.

"Long enough for me to climb down here and stir you... I thought I'd lost you!" she blurted and put her arms around him. In that moment Kaln realised how cold she was, she wasn't wearing travelling clothes, she didn't have a cloak or even sensible shoes. She was wet-through to the bone and only slight of build. A pang of guilt wracked him as he realised how selfish he had been and while she held him, he removed his cloak and wrapped it around her small frame. She was shaking and didn't refuse the cloak.

Guilt thick in his voice, Kaln said "I'm sorry Lilly, I...We aren't far now and we can get warmed up and some food... But first I need you to get on your knees..."

Her head jerked back with a flash of defiance and horror on her face. Before she could say anything Kaln raised his hands and whispered with a careful smile "Trust me".
There was a pause and she did, keeping her eyes on him as much as she could in the patchy moonlight. He knelt down with her, drew his knife and cut the heels from her boots making them more suitable for traversing forests in a thick late autumn storm. She realised what he was doing and let out a small giggle of relief. That sound made Kaln's heart melt, even in this bitter cold. He understood how cold, scared, hungry and tired she must be and yet she stayed strong and kept moving without complaint. *A strong woman,* he thought to himself as he looked at her with a new respect.

The sound of her laughter drew him back to summer, like it was the first day he had noticed her beauty at the market, her in-elegant giggle caught his attention that day and hadn't lost it since. He stood and pulled the cloak around her. Kaln clenched and unclenched his fingers a couple of times in hopes of getting warm blood to his hands.
"Stay strong Lilly." Kaln said with an earnest smile, took her hand and led her further down the slope. He didn't think the orcs would or could track them this far but he left the broken heels

of her shoes on the steep slope and walked them through a stream which the rainfall had swollen leaving it ankle deep, in hopes it would disturb their scent. The cold air and branches in the darkness gnashed at his hands and face. Holding his open palm out in front of his face he pushed into the scraping branches in the darkness following the far side of the stream north.

The light got less and less as they approached the base of a cliff edge which blocked out a lot of what little moonlight remained between the dense storm clouds. Kaln pushed a thick bush to one side that hid the base of a hidden track leading up the cliff and Lilly stepped through with a whimper of relief to be stood on solid stone and more steady footing. Lilly noted Kaln putting the brush back behind them after he passed through. The path was crafted, carved, used and smooth. It was practically invisible from the ground and especially in the dark. Kaln would know, he used it most days with his father. A pang of sadness hit him as they began to ascend up the slope but weariness beat the emotion back down. It was steep and twisted several times but always wide enough for a wagon. At the top it levelled out to an outcropping two thirds of the way up the cliff. There, perched on the outcropping was a hut made of stone in the moonlight pressed against the cliff wall to avoid some of the elements.

Lilly gave Kaln a hopeful look and he nodded as he limped behind her. She was now moving faster than him and she picked up pace towards the house.

"Lilly!" Kaln shouted over the winds in the valley below. She turned still pacing backwards towards safety. There was a shimmer of moonlight as Kaln threw her the key, which she caught and turned towards the house.

"Turn it three times." he said as he tried, and failed to keep pace, not sure if the winds had drowned out his words. By the time she had fumbled long enough with the somewhat overly secure door and managed to unlock it, Kaln had caught up to her and collapsed through it as it opened.

Kaln fell in front of the fireplace in the center of the small building. It had three openings, one for each room. The largest of which was the kitchen where they entered. He shifted to sit on his knees with a grunt and grabbed the flint and tinder that were on the fireplace. His hands were shaking with cold and exhaustion.

As he prepared to light the fire he said "Lilly, can you go into each room and close the shutters? Make sure they are closed tight so the wind doesn't open them. They should stop the light of the fire giving us away to anyone looking."

He turned to find she had already closed the door, locked it and had started closing the shutters.

He smiled to himself as he lit the kindling and watched the flames slowly spread to the wood he and his father left ready for lighting when they returned from the village.

"Can smell a storm commin' lad, better get some wood ready for't fire cus I don't wanna be fetching none in a storm. Thas ow ye get struck by lightnin'." he remembered his father saying before they left for market. His father was rarely wrong in such matters.

In one of the smaller rooms he heard Lilly moving around. Then, at the far side of the fireplace in his bedroom he saw her bare feet pad across to the shutters and close them. She padded back as the fire had grown enough to give out heat and both of them paused in silence to appreciate how good it felt.

Another moment passed, "By the moon, I may yet feel my toes again!" the pair of feet said through the fireplace and her toes wriggled in the heat before she headed to his father's room to close the shutters.

When the last shutters were closed the little house creaked and groaned for a moment as it settled down into the wind pushing against it, then fell silent. Kaln heard Lilly's small footsteps coming towards him as he suddenly felt too weak and tired to tear his eyes away from the dancing flames that mesmerised him. He felt her place a hand softly on his shoulder and lean down.

"Food?" she whispered, as not to disturb his daydream. He raised a hand vaguely at one of the cupboards and leant back against the base of his father's arm chair. Like he had as a child after finishing his chores. His father would sit there watching the fire and smoking his pipe while Kaln played with whatever toy his father had brought from his latest trip to one of the nearby villages. A life-time ago.

Through weary and bleary eyes he saw bread and cheese on his lap and felt a hand in his hair. For a moment he had forgotten the day's events and was about to playfully bat his father's hand away. Then reality came crashing down on him again and how alone he was now... No, not alone. The hand belonged to Lilly and she was here going through the same thing he was. He turned to her as she took a seat in the chair behind him.
"Thank you Lilly, thankyou for being strong".
She looked back at him eating mechanically, her eyes looked hollow.
She lowered the food and whispered with an air of numbness to her voice, "I'm not strong." Tears streamed down her face. She quietly curled up in the chair and lowered her head to rest on Kalns shoulder with her arm around his neck and the two sobbed until their eyes could stay open no longer. Their worlds destroyed in a day.

Kaln woke with a start some time later to the

sound of the chimney whistling in the wind as though the little house sat idly watching on the cliff edge and was mildly impressed with the force of the storm. The fire was almost out, giving a low amber hew to the lower half of the three rooms it illuminated. Lilly had drooled on his shoulder where she still slept. He attempted to move and every muscle, scratch, bruise and arrow wound on his body screamed at him. He winced, took a breath and slowly rose. Suddenly feeling light headed, he grabbed the back of the chair to stop the room from spinning and he took another breath. Lilly stirred but didn't wake, she merely curled up into a tighter ball. She looked so peaceful.

He lifted her up and she murmured something from a far off distant dream as he walked across the small kitchen into his room and laid her down in the bed. Kaln smiled as he tucked her in and turned to add wood to the fire. He noticed her high boots were by the fire, drying from their wade through the stream earlier and looking worse for wear. He piled the wood in the glowing red embers and blew lightly until the flames took root in the logs and started to engulf them. Then paused to watch the flames again, he was hesitant to move his seized body but knew he needed rest.
I could watch the flames a little longer, he allowed himself.

Until he heard whimpering noises from Lilly behind him on the bed which made him rise and ignore the flash of pain his body screeched at him. Going to her, she was still sleeping and obviously having some kind of nightmare.

He stroked her hair and whispered "It's just a nightmare, Lilly" then paused staring through his bedroom door at his father's empty chair. It took everything from him and he slowly sat on the edge of the bed and began to sob quietly.

"No, it isn't just a nightmare." He whispered bitterly to himself.

He felt Lilly stir and she put her arms around him, pulling him into the bed with her. "No... no it isn't Kaln, but I'm here with you." she whispered. For the second time that night, the two cried themselves to sleep in the low firelight as the wind continued to crash and tear at the cliff walls below.

CHAPTER 3 - A BREATH OF FRESH AIR

Lilly rose before Kaln, he was in a deep sleep and Lilly had decided he'd earnt as much as he needed. She climbed out of bed without disturbing him, noted how sore her muscles were, how her feet were blistered and also that daylight was beaming through the cracks in the shutter door's edges and catching the last wisps of smoke from the fire in the air as she inspected the bottoms of her feet with a wince. The fire was out but the beginning day's warmth after the storm meant that it wasn't needed. She went to the kitchen and opened the shutters. The brisk morning air on the cliff edge washed over her and cleansed the scent of wood smoke from the little house. The smell was fresh and cool as she took a deep breath and felt her lungs tingle. She adjusted her eyes to the daylight bathing her and the sight in front of her. A vast vision of a late autumn forest stretched as far as her eyes could see and although the trees were not green at this time of year, the strong reds, deep oranges and vibrant yellows that still clinged to the trees looked beautiful. This was her favourite time of year.

She stood there for a long moment admiring the view then turned to see the interior of the small house in daylight. Not the dim refuge she saw last night, but a home. A deep smile spread across her face as she saw the hand crafted, well maintained and well used furniture. The thick blankets draped over the chairs. The strange fireplace was cleverly designed to heat all three rooms. The arrows, bows and blades used in their craft lovingly placed on a rack on the far side of the room under the antlers of some monstrously large stag. Thick strong door frames and doors, same with the window frames and shutters. The kitchen was designed like the rest of the house; solid, functional, comfortable and most of all, wholesome.

She glanced through the bedroom doorway at Kaln, laying on the bed in the deepest of sleep. Lilly had known of Kaln since they were both much younger. She had always looked out for him when he and his father came to the village to trade their wares. They lived in the forest so only came to market when the weather was fine and this far north, that was rarer than she would have liked.

She liked his gangly awkwardness as a boy and the way he blushed when she caught him admiring her. That felt like a lifetime ago when they were still children and care free.

They had only ever exchanged small talk with each other at the market in years gone by but only now, illuminated by the new dawn, she saw him for what the latest winter in the forest had turned him into.

He was tall for sure, as a child growing up he had always had hands and feet that looked too big for him and had shoulders too broad for his slender build. It would seem puberty had finally finished its work on the boy, now he lay there as a man with a muscular chest that filled out to meet his shoulders, his gangly long arms and legs had also filled out to match his large hands and feet. He looked strong and healthy in a way that only someone who lived off the land could.

Working and living off the land was obviously good for a growing young man, she found herself admiring. His thick dark hair and strong stubbled jaw-line framed a handsome face with dark eyes. He carried his father's contagious smile that was always surprising from his quiet demeanour. She hadn't seen him in over a year, but now she did.

She stood between the kitchen table and the collection of knives, hatchets and bows under the great antlers. Along with oils, cloths, sharpening stones, feathers and other paraphernalia. She picked up a blade, to feel the weight of it, to check its edge was as sharp as it looked. It was. As she jerked her finger away and put the wounded finger tip in her mouth she noticed the blade had something itched in the side.
"*BRIE*" she whispered to herself, confused. Lilly put the knife back on its rack and noticed a hatchet had an engraving on the head, "*FETA*". Another had "*CORNIE*" - a local cheese. One of the bows had the engravement: "*ENGAVA*" , a soft cheese and a delacy of Whitebluff to the far north. All of them were named with different cheeses. After marvelling at the different tools and weapons and their engravings she stepped back to see herself in a tiny mirror nailed to the doorframe of the front door at the far side of the house.
She looked down at her dress, it was covered in rips and tears. Stained with mud, blood and the moon knows what else. She used a basin of water to bathe herself as best she could. This outfit is most troublesome in a forest, she thought as she picked pieces of twig out of one of the loose threads struggling to hold the garment together.

Looking around it didn't take her long to find a needle and thread. *A practical tool for practical men* she thought while threading the needle. Her attention was drawn to Kaln's room as if remembering something.

CHAPTER 4 - THE INEVITABLE NEXT STEPS

When he woke, Kaln was surprised to find it was still dark, the only light coming from the small fire in the large fireplace. His body was stiff and sore and he suddenly had an overwhelming urge to get out of the clothes he'd slept in. He swung his legs off the bed and pushed himself upright. As he sat there in his small room he noticed three things amongst the low crackling fire that gave off little light; First, the storm had ended, he could no longer hear the winds at his shutter doors. Second, his other set of riding leathers were piled at the end of his bed, not where he kept them. Third was a beautiful sound, the sound of Lilly humming to herself.

He used the water and basin in his room to clean himself off as best he could. He cleaned his wounds and redressed them. Lilly was right, it was only shallow and the others were mere scratches. His bruised ribs would heal. He took off his dirty clothes and threw them against the back of his bedroom door as he changed into a different set of leathers. Once dressed, he used what was left of the water to slick back his long dark hair, pocketed his whittling knife and peered out the window. *How long have I slept? An hour? Two?* He wondered as he peered out of the shutters to see a quiet, cloud filled night sky. He noted how quiet the night was in that silent moment, even Lilly's peaceful humming had stopped.

As his room door creaked open he winced. *I really should oil those hinges,* he thought as he crept into the kitchen to find his small table had two plates set. One with bread, cheese and an apple. The plate closest to Lilly had a few crumbs.

His eyes scanned to her and he noticed something had changed. Instead of the ruined blue dress she had on earlier, she was wearing what looked like his old clothes. Clothes he'd outgrown in his last growth spurt over the winter but hadn't got around to getting rid of. If they weren't his own he wouldn't have even noticed the subtle adjustments Lilly had made to them. She wore leathers on her lower half, obviously brought in on the waist and legs. They looked very good on her, he had to admit. Even if that look wasn't the latest fashion amongst the women. On her top half she wore a thick linen long sleeved shirt, she had rolled the sleeves up and the laces down the chest of the shirt had been left loose to accommodate her womanly curves, which Kaln allowed himself a moment to appreciate. As he did, he noticed her necklace. A deep green stone with golden veins which seemed to move and dance in the firelight like lightning in a thundercloud. The stone wasn't cut, but seemed to be a broken piece of something much larger. The trinket was held there with a simple leather binding. On her lap she had one of the pelts Kaln's father had decided not to take to market and was obviously in the middle of making a cloak out of it when she had fallen asleep in his father's chair. He took the cloak from her, covered her with a blanket and sat to eat and drink. She truly was stunningly beautiful as she sat sleeping across from him, her blonde hair looking golden in the low firelight. It had dried from the rain in loose ringlets which fell to frame her features, a delicate nose, high cheekbones speckled with freckles and full lips. Her pale blue eyes always looked like she was smiling and when she was actually smiling, it was a smile that was so cheeky that she could get away with anything.

What comes next? He wondered to himself as he finished his meal in what was almost a frenzie, hunger had crept up on him.

He turned to the half finished cloak and could see that she had skill with the needle and thread and set to work finishing what she started. Hours later, once the cloak was finished, he sharpened his blade and checked his weapons on the rack then finished the job he had started on Lilly's boots. Making them more practical, if less fashionable. By the time he had done all those things, the sunlight was peering through the shutters in the window. Morning had arrived.

The light from the window had settled on Lilly's face, stirring her from her sleep. She stretched like a cat, limbs splaying in all directions joined with a deep satisfied yawn. Kaln had replaced the food on the plates just as she slapped her lips together and wiped the sleep from her eyes looking up at him.
"Morning handsome!" She beamed and Kaln's cheeks blazed red as he sat down and busied himself eating breakfast.
"Mornin'. I finished the cloak you started. Why don't you try it on?" Kaln said. He was shovelling food down his throat and taking big gulps of water from his tankard to hide his blushing cheeks caused by the sudden compliment.

She stood and treated herself to another stretch starting from her upraised fingers and ending with her on her tiptoes then relaxed with a satisfied sigh.

"You know you slept for over a day? You obviously needed it" she said in sleepy tones. She padded over to the cloak and whirled it over her shoulders.

She adjusted the fittings and looked up at Kaln with a bright smile "Perfect!" she giggled. "What do you think?" grinning and giving him a twirl in her new ensamble.

"You look perfect." He echoed before his brain could engage, then quickly went back to eating to cover his renewed blushing. Lilly went to open the shutters and took a deep breath with a smile, then left to open the shutters in the other rooms. If his comment embarrassed her, she didn't show it.

Had I slept that long? He thought. *No wonder I was so hungry.*

It wasn't long before the two were sat across from each other eating their meagre breakfast. A silence had fallen over them as they ate until Kaln noticed Lilly was staring at him, her mouth full and eyes wide.

"Is that where you get your family name from? Grey." Crumbs and partially chewed cheese falling out of her mouth as she spoke. She waited expectantly.

Kaln shot her a quizzing look and he swallowed his mouthful.

"Eh?" he grunted and went back to chewing.

"Well, I know most names come from what the family is known for. Generation after generation of fletchers will be called Mr or Ms Fletcher. I only just realised your eyes are grey." She leaned over the table with a sandwich in hand causing Kaln to lean back a little in surprise.

"Not pale green or off-blue, but grey." she murmured as she inspected his eyes. With a shrug of her shoulders that gave finality to her research, she sat back.

"You see, my family name is Cooper. I think it's because my father's father used to make barrels, and his father mind you." She explained as she finished her sandwich.

"I'm surprised you aren't 'Kaln Hunt' or something similar." She wiped a hand across her mouth and took a deep gulp of water.

"Father had eyes just like mine... I guess you're right. I never met his father but I think he was a hunter too." Kaln said as he realised she was right.

A silence fell over them again, it wasn't an awkward silence but a comfortable one.

Kaln was the first to break it, "I don't know why the orcs attacked, I mean, our people and theirs keep out of each other's way. No need for us to venture into their mountains as much as they don't wonder about our lands. I know we aren't

exactly in trade negotiations with them but for them just to attack Cornwalk out-right like that… It didn't make sense, even for orcs. They must know the other settlements will retaliate."
He was thinking out loud. He realised his words had hung in the air and now there was a different kind of silence, like the kind before a storm. He had an idea what was coming.
Lilly took a deep breath before saying "I want to go back."
She had looked him in the eye and said it in a way that let Kaln know she wasn't asking.

Kaln cleared up the plates and turned to lean on the small worksurface in the kitchen facing Lilly. "Aye, figured you would… Well it has been a couple of days since the orcs hit Cornwalk. Can't imagine they would still be there." He said as he allowed himself a stretch and cracked his knuckles. He sagged his shoulders back into a relaxed position swinging his arms.
"Lets get some things together and go then, I know telling you 'no' isn't an option but please stay close to me." She smiled and stood up, full of enthusiasm.

The two gathered their things, and were making their way into the valley by midday. The day was bright and cool as all the finest autumn days are. There was a rich earthy smell as they made their way down into the canopy of the trees. The sunlight coming through the autumn canopy gave the forest an almost magical hue as Kaln led them back towards Cornwalk. Lilly watched him as he navigated his way through the forest, his dark hair and powerful shoulders giving him a top-heavy gait. *Almost a lumber...* She smiled to herself as she managed to keep pace much more easily in her new ensemble.

"You know, you walk a bit like a troll Kaln." she called over the sound of crunching leaves under foot. Kaln raised a hand over his shoulder to present a gesture usually reserved for beggers, buggers and miscreants. Lilly barked a laugh and the two pushed into the forest. An hour or so later they found themselves at the main road leading South back to Cornwalk. The amber hews of the dead leaves lining either side of the dirt road and the low sun in the early afternoon made the road almost picturesque. It felt good to have the sun on their faces as they made their way south.

Lilly probed Kaln about his life in the forest, what he did for fun. Kaln answered her and returned the favour in kind, equally as mystified by the idea of living around so many people. Spirits were higher than they deserved to be as they talked. Lilly snorted with laughter as she recalled the weapons she had seen, "Well there's one thing we certainly don't do in Cornwalk Kaln. I've never owned a butter knife with a name. Especially one named after a cheese!"

Kaln simply laughed, he knew how ludicrous it sounded. "My pah let me name my first knife," Kaln replied and continued in a caricature impression of his father's voice *"Yer knife is the most important tool tha'll 'av lad, tha' should name 'er, treat 'er with respect and maintainer 'er. She'll look after ye in kind."*

He had a sad little smile as he passed Lilly the pocket knife that had saved her couple of days before. It had been cleaned and sharpened since and smelled of oils that Kaln had explained protected the metal. Badly etched with wavy lines was the word "*CHEDDAR*" along the side of the small blade.

She looked at Kaln expecting an explanation. Instead, he shrugged and said "I was eight... became a tradition after that."

They both began to giggle and Lilly nudged into him, an unspoken "Thankyou." for sharing.

It wasn't long after this when they came upon a crucifix cross at the side of the road. The smell of blood carried on the wind made them aware of it before they saw it. On a huge crudely made cross was a man, stripped bear. Stakes driven through each limb. Blood covered his body and pooled at the base of the cross. Some smaller woodland creatures had obviously taken their fill of the old man's lower flesh. Kaln's stomach whirled as he realised the man was Mr. Thomlin, one of the farmers from the outlying lands around Cornwalk. The orcs must have pushed North and he got caught in their wake. Kaln took a few breaths to steady himself with hands on his knees. He looked up to see Lilly stood by the man. She reached up on her tip-toes and closed the old farmer's eyes and he could see she was praying for him. Kaln didn't intervene, he just listened to her calming words and hoped that some-how Mr.Thomlin could hear them too. Hopefully, at her request, he passed on in peace. He forced himself to look once again at the poor man's figure, something niggling at the back of his mind told him that this wasn't the orcs doing, from what he knew, orcish culture would view this as dishonourable. But what did he know of orcs? He stood silently checking the treeline, up and down the road to make sure whoever did this was gone. Somewhere deep down he knew whoever did this, were long gone. He knew the busy work he assigned himself was a way of processing what had happened here, he also knew there would be more to come when they got to Cornwalk.

The two walked down the road in silence for some time after that. The beautiful Autumn scene somehow felt nowhere near as warm and pleasant as before.

CHAPTER 5 - AN ELF WITH A ROPE

It was another half an hour before the two saw anything on the road. With the exception of the idle autumn winds playing with the dead leaves, the roads were quiet. Eventually, they did see a burnt out cart with no horses to be found.

For a moment Kaln's heart sank when he saw the cart but approached and could tell from the wreckage that it was once a very valuable and well made cart. Not the sturdy but basic cart he and his father had made. Kaln also noticed that its contents were missing. As he stood there looking for clues he could hear a very quiet, subtle tearing noise. He wouldn't have caught the sound if not for a lull in the wind.

As he searched around the cart, Lilly eventually became impatient and began to walk away from the cart. "There's nothing here Kaln. Come, let's move before it gets dark. We don't want to be out here after nightfall, do we?" She said as she turned to Kaln with exasperation and nervous trepidation plain on her features. Kaln turned towards Lilly and said agreeably "Yeah, you're right. Nothing here."

Lilly's expression was that of utter confusion as she suddenly noticed something above him. They stood in the middle of the road, there was nothing above him. He wondered what she could possibly be looking at and glanced up to see a wiggling rope. A fine silken rope. A rope which seemed to be dangling off the ledge of nothingness about ten foot up in the air. He watched as the rope slowly lowered down to the ground beside him. Now that he was looking he could tell this is where the subtle sound was coming from. He took a step back towards Lilly, prepared to draw back an arrow and watched. When the rope had lowered to around a couple of feet off the ground, a pair of shoes, trousers and the lower half of a cloak appeared at the top of the rope, where there was still nothing but autumn sky. Kaln's heart raced and he shot Lilly a glance, she gave him one back and she came to his side with Cheddar in hand. They watched as more of the man was birthed from the sky just above the road with grunting and profanities caught in the autumn breeze. Rather awkwardly the man climbed down and a little overdramatically dropped the last foot with the grace of a man who wasn't used to physical activities. He had his back to the two. Kaln could see from where he stood that the man was a Dark Elf, slight of build, taller than Kaln, dark grey skin, black hair and the finest clothing he had ever seen. They were made of various materials in various shades of dark reds. Half lowering the bow he stuttered "C-Can we help you, sir?"

The elf was in no rush to turn and greet them, he slowly began working his way through a series of stretches. Like a man who had sat in a small box for several hours or was preparing to outrun a bull. Kaln and Lilly traded looks and watched, dumbfounded. With his hands on his hips leaning to one side in a stretch, the elf grunted "I bloody well hope so, I've been hiding in there for far too-" He finished his final stretch "-long." and turned to the two. Holding out a perfectly manicured hand adorned in jewellery in a gesture of formal greeting, the elf said in a regal tone "My name is Vodius Crimsonguaarde. Of *the* Crimsonguaarde family." He paused long enough to realise they were not aware of the family name, lowered his eyelids in disappointment and continued.

"As I hope you have gathered by now, I am a sorcerer. It is yet to be seen if it is indeed a pleasure to meet you." The grey skinned sorcerer had the thin lanky frame and the high proud features you would expect from any elf. His features were angular but danced somewhere between pretty and handsome. One perfectly sculpted eyebrow sat perpetually higher than the other in a vaguely inquisitive state, leaving him looking roguish. He had long slicked-back hair that was arrow straight and without a single stray hair. He also carried a small devilish smile that never seemed to leave his face. Like he was in on a joke the rest of the world didn't know about. Strangely the smile made the venom of his words somehow lesser and put the two at ease, contrary to what he had said, he seemed likeable.

Kaln lowered the bow further and Lilly stepped forward and reciprocated the greeting gesture. "I'm Lilly and this is Kaln." She beamed. Vodius took her hand, smiled the way you would expect to smile at your peers in the king's court and said in a pur "My, even for a frumpy human, you are quite divine." and kissed the back of her hand with a quick bow of his head. Lilly, not knowing how to take the backhanded compliment, giggled. "And what glorious laughter, quite infectious. Like when goats make bizarre sounds and you simply can't help but laugh." he chuckled. Lilly stopped giggling but continued to grin. He lowered her hand with a light squeeze and a twitch of his smile and looked to Kaln.

His smile grew as he held out his hand to Kaln "No need for the bow my thick shouldered bulk of a man! I come in peace." Vodius grinned as he took Kaln's free hand and patted him on the arm with his other. "My! You have the build of an ogre. Did you know your parents well?" He jested. Kaln found himself unable to take offence from the comment. It was subtly evident the elf meant no offence.

"Ma' died when I was young and my father died but a couple days ago." Kaln said numbly.

It was still stunning to him when he said it aloud. This didn't seem to phase Vodius and without missing a beat he said, as though giving someone a job offer "Ah, well that is terribly shit my brutish looking fellow. Regardless, I am in need of help and I believe you might just be capable enough to assist me." He flashed Kaln an appraising look, the way a man checks a bull before purchase.

Kaln found himself somewhat at a loss for words as he looked at the elf in his fine clothes, still wearing his disarming smile. Kaln noted the elf smelled of almonds. That told him one of two things, either he was wealthy enough to eat almonds or he was indeed a sorcerer. A tell-tale sign of magic. While both were probably true, the latter seemed more probable as he had indeed just climbed out of the sky.

Lilly stepped forward and said "I'm afraid he is currently in my employ." Her eyes flicked to Kaln and back to Vodius. A look of deep disappointment flashed briefly across the elf's face. "I'm sure whatever need you have of the man, my needs are -" his words halted suddenly as the dying autumn light glimmered on Lilly's necklace. "Where did you get that?" He managed to stop himself from snapping but with a tone of voice that demanded an immediate response. Lilly took a step back, not sure what Vodius was talking about.

Before she could speak he reached out with surprising speed and grasped the necklace from her. Almost as quickly, Kaln's hand was around the wrist of the elf. Vodius didn't even seem to notice. "Answer me. Where?" Vodius' voice was bordering on anger, almost. Though Kaln could tell already that anger was not an emotion Vodius was comfortable with. "My father gave it to me, a gift from my mother before she died when I was a babe." Lilly said, gaining her footing and grabbing the leather strap holding the necklace. Her expression had changed from surprised to irritation and finally anger in a heartbeat. The tiny pocket knife glistened almost un-naturally in the amber light as she gripped it tightly. Slowly she said, looking Vodius in the eye, "Take your hands off me...now." and took a step towards him. Somehow, her tiny frame looked menacing. Again, Vodius didn't seem to even notice the threat but held the amulet more loosely in his hand pointing to the golden veins in the stone with his other hand.

The three clustered around the necklace stood in the dead leaves by the side of the road leading to Cornwalk. Kaln and Lilly were tense but Vodius was not. In a tone he would take explaining something to a child (or his peers) he whispered "I believe this is a Rehlk Stone." Then looked at them both as if expecting a gasp. There were no gasps to be had as they looked back at him blankly. The elf's expression of excitement dropped as he took a deep breath and said, "This is the reason I am here, these stones imbue powerful magic. The scriptures even suggest that they can bring upon prophecies." His eyes never left the stone as he rolled it around in his hand. Still holding Vodius' wrist, Kaln said "It's just a stone, let go. " His tone was calm like the quiet before a storm. Vodius barked a laugh, shaking his head he chuckled "No, human, it is not 'just a stone'. I assure you."

As he did, the knot holding the leather together at the back of Lilly's neck came loose and the stone fell from Vodius' hand and tumbled towards the ground. All three flinched to catch the falling stone but Kaln was quickest and held it in his hand. The Leather wrappings had fallen around his wrist and as he held it up all three

watched as the leather wrapped itself around his wrist multiple times and knotted. Kaln leapt back and tried to unknot the thing around his wrist in panic. Lilly fell to her knees, Vodius visibly deflated as he watched Kaln try and fail to force or cut the binding. Kaln strained against the thin leather binding with all his strength and grunted "Get it off me!".
"It isn't going anywhere my fellow, it has chosen you." Vodius said with a hint of sad contentment in his voice. "I think you had better help your friend to her feet..." he said in his normal dismissive tone as he inspected the burnt cart with sighs of further disappointment.

Kaln realised at that moment that she was on her knees and breathing heavily. He ran to her and helped her stand. He brushed her blonde hair from her face. As he touched her skin the feeling of being scared, tired or alone was destroyed. Only comforting warmth filled him as he helped her to her feet. That same feeling he missed when his touch left hers a few days before in Cornwalk. He didn't understand what it meant. Lilly looked up at him with a knowing smile. "I understand now!" she exclaimed with a look of peace on her face and tears in her eyes. Kaln's eyebrows furrowed in confusion. "Are you ok? You understand what?"
Somewhere beyond the ruined cart Vodius' voice said, quite flatley "She won't be able to explain

it, my meatbound fellow. One does not easily explain magic. Especially when it first awakens." Vodius approached the two with soot from the burnt cart on his hands. With a vague look of irritation he wiped his hand on Kaln's cloak as he walked and continued past them "I think it wise we head for Cornwalk before night falls. There is only space for one at the top of the rope I'm afraid." Waving his hands as you would casually usher sheep to their pen he started walking toward Cornwalk. Confused, Kaln fell in line with Vodius and Lilly as they walked South to Cornwalk. The trio walked silently as Kaln desperately attempted to work out what had just happened. Looking down at the stone tied to his wrist he noticed it was heavier than it should have been for a pretty piece of glass. The stone shimmered as it had when he had seen it around Lilly's neck that morning only now the veins of golden light were quite clearly hollow and empty and the rest of the stone took a darker lifeless colour of pale grey. Still, he noticed it felt good to have it around his wrist, though he could not explain why.

"Why are you coming to Cornwalk, Vodius? You should know there is nothing there but destruction." Kaln said to the back of Vodius and Lilly. Kaln watched Lilly's body language tighten at the comment. Vodius didn't turn to speak to Kaln but said wistfully, "I would dare to assume you want more answers. I hope I am right." He picked at a finger nail and said half distracted "Regardless, I have a use for you both which we will discuss once we are somewhere safe."

Kaln sighed, "Right, but if I don't like the sound of what you have to say, you are on your own from Cornwalk...You must know now that Cornwalk will be a place of ruin. Do not expect a warm meal and a comfortable bed. It was attacked two days gone by orcs." Kaln said as a matter of fact as possible.

"Ah-ha!" Vodius stopped and turned to Kaln and Lilly with an excited grin. "I knew it! My spell was correct!" he said with a self righteous smile as though expecting praise. Instead, Lilly lunged at him "Moon watch over me, if you have anything to do with the attack on Cornwalk and my father's death I will slay you where you stand!" she screamed, the knife suddenly in her hand again as she closed in on Vodius. Vodius took a step back with a look of displeasure the way someone might if a stranger's muddy dog tried to jump up you for some fleeting attention. His upper lip turned up into a vague confused sneer as he realised what Lilly was so angry about. "What? Your village? No, no, no. My spell simply lead me here. More specifically, to you. Trust me darling I have very, very... very little interest in your village." he said shaking his head dismissively. Lilly and Kaln exchanged glances and Lilly sheathed the blade. The sun was beginning to set on the three. "We need to pick up the pace." Kaln said peering at the skyline. Kaln said with a tone of finality "Answers when we get somewhere safer than here. Quiet on the road until we get to Cornwalk. We don't need to attract any attention." Vodius gave a mock salute and the three walked in silence, the remainder of the way as the sun set.

CHAPTER 6 - CORNWALK

Just as the last of the day's light faded and night took hold of the sky, the small group caught the scent of burnt flesh thick in the air. Vodius' nose scrunched up as he held a handkerchief to it. "Oh my that is truly offensive" he gasped. Lilly scowled at the elf as she said "That smell is my family and friends. I suggest you have a little more respect". Almost as though he hadn't heard, he retched.

The group turned the corner and could see the husk of Cornwalk at the bottom of the hill. There was little light coming from the village, though there were the last dying flames in the destroyed buildings. Kaln gestured to the others to keep quiet, keep low and follow him. He led them to the bridge where they had fled two days earlier. Some of the pelts were still strewn across the floor. The meat was gone.

They passed the corpse of the orc they had killed, tucked away behind the inn, its face still staring desperately towards the sky beneath the flies. Kaln and Lilly glanced at the orc and at each other as they passed. Vodius said under his breath "Most vile. I do hope this was not one of the friends you mentioned." a look of disgust plainly on his face.

Kaln shot Vodius an impatient glare that told him to be quiet as the group crouched down by the stall Kaln had hidden under. They paused to listen as the light from the burning buildings couldn't be seen from where they waited. Nothing, a moment longer just to be sure... Still Nothing. Just as Kaln stood to move to the village square, he heard and felt a heavy thud somewhere beyond The Fallen Cow Inn. He froze, holding out a hand to the others to stay where they were. He forced himself to listen past the sound of his heart beat thumping in his ears. Something heavy was moving through what sounded like thick tar. Kaln held his breath, distantly he heard the sound of clicking, like the sound of thick bones rattling together mixed with the intake of a deep breath of a huge creature. The sound shuddered between the ruined houses. Loose debris, roof slates and tiny shards of glass falling to break the following silence. White fear washed over the faces of all three in the group. Suddenly, some distance away at the far side of the square a loud metallic sound clanged against the cobble stones. Less than half a second later the huge creature thundered in the darkness moving towards the origin of the metallic sound in a handful of heavy strides followed shortly by the sound of thick liquids hitting the ground in its wake. The group took that moment of distraction to peer around the corner.

There was very little light illuminating the market square from the waning fires in the husks of buildings. In the center was a pile six feet high of what could be identified as burnt corpses from the smell of burnt flesh, blood and the sound of buzzing flies, even from this distance. Engraved into the cobblestones under and around the corpses was a blood filled symbol, the air tingled their noses with the acrid smell of almonds and sulphur.

Kaln heard Lilly take a sharp intake of breath but his attention was beyond that, at the blacksmith's shop. There was light coming from within The Old Horseshoe, the building looked untouched by the chaos. The sickly yellow light created a silhouette of at least part of the creature they had heard as it loomed in the shadows. The sight they saw didn't make sense. The lower half of the creature's three legs seemed to be clawed, even from this distance

Kaln could see this was no natural animal. The rest of the creature was hidden in the darkness of the night, the weak light of the blacksmith's doorway shone no higher than seven feet. The creature stood eerily still, seemingly watching the building.

As Kaln stood there not knowing whether he should run or charge, he saw a figure appear in the doorway of the black smith's. A small figure, smaller than an orc.. Smaller than a human. Kaln's heart skipped a beat in disbelief as he whispered "Is that a-" before he could finish there was a flash of light and a thunderous boom from across the market square. The blacksmith's was engulfed in a plume of gold and deep red flame as the small creature was launched into the air trailing an oily streak of smoke towards Kaln, landing somewhere in the pile of bodies on the side closest to the group. The creature reared back and let out a roar that sounded like falling rocks and tearing flesh as it staggered back. There was a pause as bits of burnt flesh fell out of the night sky with thick wet slaps all over the marketplace courtyard. The goblin's bulbous head with over sized ears and a large mouth appeared out of the pile of bodies with a stupid, delirous but strangley proud toothy grin on its face. Wisps of smoke still whirled from the top of its ears, it wiped the blood from the goggles and was looking directly at the group frozen by the edge of the firelight. "'Ello! You should run! Not safe! Legsy mad!" the goblin shouted as he climbed out of the pile of bodies. Seemingly unphased by its grim surroundings.

It had a stupid grin on its oversized head that bobbed side to side as it trotted down the pile and towards them. As the goblin reached the stone floor the three-legged monster had found its footing and was now thundering towards the goblin, and the group. Its horrific shuddering scream tearing through the broken buildings. Only when the goblin waddled closer with clinks and clanks of paraphernalia hanging from its body did they realise its mad grin had a matching giggle.

The goblin leapt with surprising speed and agility directly onto Kaln's face. Kaln reeled back in shock and horror, knocking himself and Vodius to the ground in a tumble of muffled profanities. The goblin didn't seem to mind, he was pointing enthusiastically Northward from his position on his newly found steed "Run!" waiting to be carried to safety as Kaln frantically tried to prise the little green creature off his head and Vodius tried to push the two of them off his back. The frantic scramble was stopped by the booming footsteps which now stopped upon them as a silence rang out. The goblin's ears drooped and with slumped shoulders he said dejectedly "Too late."

The huge creature, directly above them in the darkness that low light couldn't pierce, stood silently again as if watching or assessing the group. A few eerie moments passed that felt like an eternity as the group looked up into the pitch black looking back at them. The only sound was the creaking stones giving way under the weight of the monster. Then, a small voice could be heard "By the moon, by my father, by my friends and my home. You will not harm these men." Lilly stood over the prone men and repeated in a louder more fierce voice "By the moon! By my father! By my friends and my home! You! Will not! Harm these men!" She stood bellowing into the black abyss with her arms either side of her waist, her fingers curled up as if tearing up some invisible heavy mass. The smell of almonds was palpable in the air as Kaln, the goblin and Vodius could only watch. They all felt the creature shift its weight and all three of the claws dug into the stone flooring as it prepared to lunge. It roared a horrific scream as before only more intense and around ten feet above them. They saw tendrils emerge from the darkness above and a wash of hot air bathed them before the sound of rattling bones and rushing air rained down over them and there was a sudden jerk of movement as the monster plunged down at them. A dome of light flashed into brilliance over the group and the hideous toothy maw of the creature rebounded off it with a scream and staggered back. Lilly was holding the dome with her hands shaking, straining to hold the force in place.

She brought her hands together in front of her as though pulling up on two heavy invisible ropes and pushed the energy in the direction of the staggered creature. The dome of light curled back on itself like the petals of a flower closing into a sleek teardrop shape held in Lilly's open hands. The point facing skyward. She let go.

The pale white teardrop streaked into the blackness and struck the monster hard. The sound of sliced flesh followed by thick gushing fluids hitting the ground could be heard. It crashed into one of the few still standing buildings and writhed horribly like a wounded spider in the rubble. The monster found its footing and leapt into the sky like a giant three legged frog before the group could clearly see its shape. A moment passed and a distant boom could be heard some way off followed by another then another until no more could be heard. The three lay on their backs looking up at Lilly as she stood listening to the night. She stood there silent, the only sound was her heavy and ragged breathing until the monster could no longer be heard. Then she fell to the ground.

The goblin began to sing a song of victory in goblin tongue, an unpleasant sound even if it was sung surprisingly well. Its ears were flopping up and down as it bounced from one foot to the other. Vodius swiped the smaller creature off his chest and sat up with a groan as Kaln scrambled over to Lilly and cradled her head. She was breathing but unconscious. Whatever she just did to save them, took everything out of her. He let out a sigh of relief. Scanning the market square there were only two buildings still standing that they could use to take refuge: What was left of the smithy - The Old Horseshoe or the Mayor's home, Lilly's home.

Kaln lifted her in his arms and to his surprise, she was almost weightless. He had felt her weight before and even if she was small and slight of build, how she felt in his arms now, shocked him. Maybe she had always been this light and the last time he carried her, he was exhausted. This was not the place for questions. He rose to his feet as dust and rubble fell from them both and made his way to the house. He grimaced as he passed through the pile of corpses and symbols engraved on the floor. The smell of smoke, blood and gore rich in the air. The only sounds he could hear were the distant flames and excited footsteps emphasised by clanking trinkets, pots and pans behind them. Somewhere further back in the direction of their hiding place some vague complaints from Vodius as he brushed himself off. Kaln tried not to pay attention, tried to keep his mind on the house on the corner of the square as he trudged through the remains of the villagers. Forcing his eyes straight ahead and trying not to breath through his nose Kaln fought off the light headedness that suddenly washed over him as fingers crunched under his boot. At that moment Kaln saw his worst nightmare. His foot snagged in the pile of limbs and bodies. He staggered and looked down to see his own father's lifeless face in a sea of lifeless faces staring up at him. His world spun and the last thing he heard was his own panicked breathing as blackness took him.

CHAPTER 7 - A BROKEN HOME

Kaln woke in front of a warm fireplace. He took a deep breath and bolted upright searching for Lilly. His abrupt awakening had obviously interrupted Vodius and the Goblin, bickering over something as they turned to look at him. He scanned the room and quickly found Lilly on what was left of a damaged couch. The floor of the room was covered in destroyed or damaged portraits, vases, crystal decanters and other expensive furniture.

"Rise and shine noble steed!" chirped the goblin in a high pitched nasally tone. Vodius, shaking his head, said "It would appear this creature has a name. Kaln, this is-" He was rudely interrupted by the goblin as it held out a wiry hand in Kaln's face and shouted "My friends call me Gleb. Nice

to meet ya!" in a tone of voice that someone with no friends but liked the idea of it very much, would use. Half paying attention to the goblin, Kaln shook his hand and asked Vodius "Where are we? Is she ok?"
Vodius shrugged his shoulders as he picked up an overturned chair and sat down with a book in hand and began reading. Distractedly, he said "Dear ogre, I'm not a medic, nor a priest. As far as I can tell, she is asleep."
Gleb softly prodded Lilly in the forehead with a lanky finger and turned with a beaming smile "She sleeping, I checked."
"I lit some incense burners we found to try and take the edge off the smell of death. You're welcome. Do try and stay with us this time. Dragging people about in the middle of the night through piles of bodies is certainly not my forte, shall we say." Vodius said whilst thumbing through the book.
"I 'elped!" Yapped Gleb.
He raised a finger and scurried behind the couch and after the sound of smashing glass and heavy items of value being thrown, presented Kaln with his own boots. Kaln gave the goblin a confused nod and took the boots. Gleb grinned and watched with intense fascination as Kaln tied his laces. The goblin stood with his hands behind his back, attempting to resist the need to get involved with the act.
"I thought you said they were yours now?"

Vodius said, raising an eyebrow but not looking away from the book.

"He not dead so he can have them back." Gleb gave an approving smile and a little nod as he watched Kaln finish tying his laces, seemingly content with the quality and technique of the knot.

Kaln stood and found himself fighting the urge to pat the goblin on the head as Gleb looked up at him for a fraction of a second longer than was comfortable and padded off into another room, dragging his backpack with him.

Kaln rolled his shoulders and started to look around the Mayor's house. Finding a bottle of Black Beck still intact, he poured two drinks. He turned over another chair with stuffing hanging out of it and sat by vodius at a small table. Sliding the second drink across to him, the chair creaked. To the sound of pilfering and giggling coming from the other rooms in the house, he watched the flames in the fireplace and dared to let himself think of his father. Vodius picked up the drink and continued to read without so much of a nod of acknowledgement.

An hour or so later Lilly stirred, stretched a thorough stretch and sat up smacking her lips and rubbing her eyes. She looked dulley around the room for a moment then her eyes widened with a gasp. Kaln sat down next to her and passed her a glass of Beck. He didn't say anything

but his eyes were bloodshot and puffy.
"Quite invigorating, is it not? The power." Vodius asked, peering over the book he was reading. With a numb look on her face, Lilly nodded and took a swift drink.

"You will learn to control it. Or, more likely, it will kill you. I'm no mentor but I would suggest trying to control the flow somewhat next time. It's like turning on a tap, the more you open the valve, the more you use. Thus, the harder it is to control. Although, I must admit you did quite well today. I would not have liked to find out exactly what was lurking in the courtyard." He closed the book and put it down, his features looked drawn and tired. Then he refilled his glass and put his feet on the table. He picked up another book and started to read.

Lilly noticed Kaln was snoring quietly next to her, she pushed him lightly so he was laying down and lifted his legs onto the couch. Taking a deep breath, she wandered around her ransacked home taking in one painful sight at a time. She found her father's torn cloak, sat on the floor by the fire and wrapped herself in it. Then she closed her eyes and let the flood of memories, that being inside that house had revived, wash over her. One painful wave at a time. *Thank god for father's Black Beck.* Lilly gazed at the label of Black Beck and let herself be distracted for a moment by the artwork of a lonely soldier looking down from atop a cliff over a bloody battlefield from a great height. "Bottled bravery." She pondered numbly as she read the label aloud to herself. Slowly she swirled the thick oily liquid around in the bottle.

There was little sound in the house, bar the distant snoring from the other room where Gleb had tired himself out, the occasional turning of pages from vodius in the corner with his growing pile of books and the occasional crackle of flames in the fireplace as the two drank Mayor Cooper's Black Beck and eventually fell asleep.

CHAPTER 8 - DAWN AND CROWS

Kaln laid on the couch with his eyes closed, he could hear crows cawing outside. Morning, he thought. As he prepared himself to open his eyes he could hear a muted growling sound like that of a hungry belly, though he knew it wasn't his own. It was close by. He listened. Again he heard the sound of a rumbling belly and he opened his eyes to find his face inches away from Gleb's. "Am 'ungry." Gleb grinned and on queue, his stomach growled a third time.

Kaln sat up and saw that the fire had gone out, Lilly and Vodius were asleep and pale sunlight was beaming through the window leaving everything else in deep shadow. Kaln went to stand but accidentally put his weight on a damaged picture frame. It gave a loud crack as he stood and the others stirred.

"They awake, let's eat!" Gleb squealed and ran into the kitchen giggling, arms flailing with excitement. Shortly after there was the sound of a small tornado tearing through the kitchen as pots and pans flew. Meanwhile, the group woke, gathered themselves and stretched just as Gleb came running back into the room with a variety of foods, some grossly decomposed, others edible on a platter held above his head. Gleb didn't seem to mind which he ate and devoured what the others didn't want with glee.

"Before we do anything, I think that we all need to have a discussion." Vodius said whilst attempting to eat stale bread and shooting a look of contempt at the Goblin.

Kaln grunted in agreement as he ate a slightly over ripe apple. The group ate the meal and Gleb stashed the platter in the now bulging sack he carried.

After preparing for the day and cleaning the blood, dust and soot off themselves as best they could, they gathered around the small table where vodius had spent the night. Now there was only one book, it was open. Vodius cracked his long slender fingers and looked at the other three. Gleb was barely able to peek over the edge of the table, his head bobbing up and down on his tiptoes.

Vodius took a breath and, putting his hand on the open book, began. "As you know, I spent most of the evening making myself useful." he shot Gleb another look of contempt who grinned back, oblivious to the implications as he continued to bob up and down.

"After reading your father's diary amongst other-" Lilly snapped "You did what?!"

Vodius rolled his eyes and sighed, "If you would let me finish. I read your father's diary in addition to other books he had been researching. I believe my assumptions are correct on the stone." His gaze went to Kaln's wrist where the stone glimmered momentarily in the morning sunlight.

"Shiny..." Glebs eyes widened as if noticing it for the first time. Kaln shot the goblin a look and said "You dare take another thing of mine while I am living and I swear I will put your bag of goodies somewhere you cannot reach." The words had an impact on the little goblin as his eyes snapped to Kaln and his ears drooped in shame.

"I no take..." he whispered in a pained voice, hurt that they thought he would steal from them, while they were alive. Kaln gave Gleb a playful nudge and the goblin resumed his gormless grin, bobbing up and down again.

"As I was saying," Vodius continued with less

patience in his voice "That stone is a Rehlk Stone, one of two ancient pieces of The Tear of Celuna, goddess of the moon."
Kaln noticed Lilly didn't seem surprised by this, this must have been what she meant when she said she understood.
"These stones are widely considered a myth. I was using magics of my own to attempt to find them, that is what led me here, to you. If the scriptures I have read are to be believed, These stones have great powers. They can bless those without power with magic and other gifts, twisting fates and fortunes. They do so with purpose as each has an agenda of their own. As I said, there are two, each representing humanity as Celuna does. The stone of Celuna's mercy and the stone of Celuna's wrath"
Vodius began to pace, his fingers steepled as he contemplated "I believe the stone we have here is the Rehlk Stone of Mercy. From my own research and indeed, that of your father's, it fits the description closest. Further to this research, seeing the gifted abilities you now have, this would lend itself to my theory." Nodding as if approving his own theory now that it was said out loud.

Kaln held up his arm, the small stone dangling from the leather bindings. The pretty stone twirled around displaying its almost mystical intricate veins and refracted light. "This?" Kaln wondered as he admired the stone. He noticed how the colours dancing in the stone seemed to have returned if much reduced from when Lilly had worn the amulet.

"You can try and cut it off your wrist again if you would like, that worked so incredibly well for you last time." Vodius said with a flat expression. "The stones are said to have the ability to bend fate and arrive in possession of precisely who they mean to." he gestured to the bindings around Kaln's wrist "Although, if they are in the wrong hands they can be used in the will of their owner. Thus, they were hidden or locked away. Becoming stories of legend and myth."

Kaln lowered his arm looking at Vodius, "So why is it attached to me?" Vodius sighed and leaned on the table with both hands. "To be honest with you, I don't know but there must be a reason. Things are in motion that are beyond our control."

Frowning, Kaln sat down at the table and asked "So what is this job you have for me?"
Vodius raised an eyebrow "Do you think it is a coincidence we are all here in this village with the stone? Even him..." Vodius gestured to Gleb's still bobbing head as it momentarily appeared over the edge of the table with a toothy grin on his face. There were blank looks from all three. Vodius paced to the window and said "Do you really think that outside is the orc's doing? They

are physically powerful tribal creatures but even so, they are smart enough not to play with blood magic and demons" shaking his head. Kaln rose to his feet "Whoa! Who said anything about demons?!"

Vodius rubbed the bridge of his nose "So the three legged monster last night was a fifteen feet tall lame pony?" Kaln closed his eyes tight and ran his hands through his hair. Some naive part of him wanted to believe that it was just a nightmare. He leant back in the chair and rolled his neck, his eyes resting in the window and the pile of corpses being picked at by the crows. He forced himself to look and amongst the feast was movement. His chair slammed into the fireplace as he leapt to his feet, Vodius stopped pacing, Gleb stopped bobbing and Lilly looked up from her father's diary, a tear down her cheek as Kaln grabbed his blade and ran for the door. The rest shot each other a look and followed, gathering their things on the way out. Kaln scrambled up the pile of bodies and the crows dispersed leaving a rain of black feathers as he reached the top of the pile. Kaln drew the knife and started cutting. By the time the rest had got to the top, he had cut the man free from his bindings. Most of his skin had been flayed, his teeth torn out, his flesh had been picked by crows and his fingers removed. His eyes bulged wildly in agony and locked on Lilly.

She fell to her knees, "Father!" her hands shook as

she tried to hold him without causing him more pain. Kaln had no idea how Lilly even recognized him. There was barely anything left of him.
Through torn lips he whispered to her "Do you have the stone?" Lilly wiped the tears from her eyes and replied, "Yes pa, why?" in a shaky voice. Suddenly, his voice turned calm, there was a smile in his words "Good, keep it close. It's very special. Your mother really wanted you to have it. I didn't tell them you had it sweetheart." his bloody hand brushed her cheek and what was left of his eyelids closed for the last time.

"Nooooo!!!" Lilly screamed, breaking down into a sob as the crows waiting to continue their meals watched from the rooftop of the Mayor's house. "He was here alone all this time! They tortured him! For what?!"
Vodius stood with his hands behind his back looking down to the market square floor. "They were looking for the stone." he said bluntly.
Kaln looked up at him. "The orcs? They did all this for a stone?"
There was a hint of bitterness in Vodius' voice as he snapped back "No, oaf, do you not listen? I told you orcs are wise enough not to toy with blood magic. Whatever the orcs were running from did this. We need to get down from here." He started making his way down the hill. "If I must explain in layman's terms, up there is 'bad juju' and from what little I know of this type of magic it was

probably the only thing keeping that man alive. Now that you have disturbed the spell it will become unstable. Move. Now." he reached the bottom and Gleb followed, humming to himself taking big leaps down like making jumps from one stone to another in a stream.

Kaln stood but Lilly didn't move, she just held her father's body and wept. Kaln put a hand on her shoulder and whispered "There's nothing we can do. We should move."

At that moment, the great mound of bodies moved, it swelled and shuddered. There were loud tearing and crackling sounds of the spell breaking down around them. Kaln was on his feet beside Lilly. He could see down below Vodius and Gleb looking up. Vodius, moving to stand behind Gleb, who only came to his waist, raised Gleb's cloak up in front of him and shouted up at Kaln "Get down from there fool! The spell is collapsing!" Meanwhile, Gleb didn't seem to notice or care that Vodius was standing behind him. With his big grin looking up at the pile, Gleb pulled down his goggles from the top of his head and with clenched fists shaking like a child watching fireworks he waited with anticipation.

Kaln didn't understand what was happening but he grabbed Lilly and threw himself down towards the ground. As he pushed off, he felt the mound convulse again and tried to turn in the air to land on his back and cushion Lilly as they fell.

Time seemed to slow as they fell and he noticed two very distinct things happen. The first, was that there was a heavy, deep and dense boom that came from behind them as they fell, coming from the corpse pile. He felt the shockwave hit him and he stopped falling downwards and instead changed to a more lateral trajectory. The second, was hitting the unforgiving wall of the mayor's house. Though he had succeeded in cushioning the blow for Lilly, white pain washed over his back and prickly white stars danced at the back of his eyes for an instant accompanied by the sound of his ear's ringing before a thick liquid washed over them. Then they hit the ground. After a dazed moment, he wiped the dense fluid from his eyes and looked up. The great mound of bodies was completely gone. The village square was entirely blackish red, washed with the same liquid that covered him. Every cobblestone, every wall facing the square and every inch of the statue of Ron'lo in the center village square was covered in thick slime. Looking over at Vodius and Gleb, Vodius looked mostly untouched by the explosion as he dropped Gleb's cloak with a wet slap. Gleb, however, was entirely covered front and back with the stuff. He spat and lifted his goggles. Only his big pointy toothed grin and his eyes, still brimming with amazement, left him identifiable as Gleb. He let out a triumphant yelp of excitement pumping one fist into the air and spattering Vodius with the liquid. Vodius flinched and his lip curled in disgust as he darted away from the celebrating goblin.

There were no bones, no innards or eyeballs splattered around the square, only liquid. The Liquid itself did not taste (noted Gleb) or smell or feel like blood. It smelled acrid and made the sinuses tingle painfully. Its colour was black marbled with deep reds and never really seemed to quite stop moving. There was a strange tension across the square as the group scraped and flicked the fluid off themselves.

Vodius, standing back so as to not get caught by stray flicks of the black ichor noticed that around the square, more specifically, around the group there were areas where the liquid gathered. In deeper pools at first, and quickly into mounds. The mounds began to rise. There were half a dozen and as Vodius whispered "Look!" in a harsh rasp as they continued to grow. The group looked on in horror as each of the mounds grew to the size of a large dog with a similar shape but made of sinewy flesh from the pools of ichor. Within the constantly swirling liquid ripples of their flesh were deep set eyes that did not look like a hound's eyes, they almost looked human. Below the haunted hollow eyes, as its maw extended out, pointed teeth like hundreds of human fangs stretched out from beneath the layers of liquid flesh as they stood dripping and snarling at the group. "Gore hounds..." Vodius gasped.

Suddenly a high-pitched hissing noise came from over in Gleb's direction. His goggles were down and his grin bigger than ever as he aimed the sights of a crossbow far too big for a goblin. On the crossbow bolt was a cylinder with a small fuse with sparks flaring out of it. He giggled as he loosed the bolt with a heavy - ***thunk*** - knocking the goblin back a few paces. The bolt flew into the side of one of the hounds, it staggered and snarled, seemingly not feeling the pain of the bolt plunge deep into its side. Gleb dropped the crossbow with a heavy clatter. The group and the other hounds all looked at the hound which had been shot. The hissing fuse came to an abrupt end and a silence drew out as everyone looked at eachother. Gleb didn't break sight on the hound; instead his grin grew as he bobbed up and down on his toes in anticipation. Suddenly a dull - ***thwump*** - noise rang out as the hound exploded. Kaln's ears rang as his skin was covered in a fine dark red rain. The remaining hounds recoiled and howled a howl that sounded somewhere between vomiting and choking. The hound closest to Gleb pounced at him. He was ready. Screaming a shrill battle cry with daggers drawn, he lunged to meet the hound in the air with all the ferocity of a small dog. The hound latched onto his shoulder and Gleb latched onto the hound's neck, he dug the daggers in the creature's sides and wrapped his legs around the creature as the two went down screeching, scuffling and snarling.

Vodius stepped to help the goblin as another hound leapt at him, he jumped back and as he did he slashed his hand in an arch with his palm facing down and shouted "Flammeus Nocturnus!" There was a flare of heat and a wash of the smell of almonds. The hound never landed, instead its leap led the hapless creature straight into the wall of flame Vodius had just summoned between them. As it breached the flame, only thick acrid smoke emerged from the other side in the vague shape of the hound. The flame was out within an instant and the hound was nothing but streaks of oily smoke.

Kaln flipped the dagger so its blade was facing down and took a low stance, bracing for the two incoming Gore Hounds. They came at him from opposite directions and he managed to strike one with the pommel of the dagger as it leapt, causing it to tumble. He took the opportunity to dive on the staggered creature and plunge the dagger deep into the chest of the monster. The small blade pierced the heart of the hound and its physical form all but ceased to exist, turning back to the black-red ichor from which it was born. He took a breath, his face hit the slime as the second hound landed on his back and tore at his shoulder.

Lilly stood further back from the rest; she hadn't moved or spoken since the pile of corpses exploded into ichor. Her hair was covering her face, she was breathing heavily with fists clenched. She didn't seem to notice, or care that the hound was closing in on her. Its head was low, its maw wide in a grin of pointed vicious teeth as it paced closer with its claws scraping on the cobblestones beneath the ichor.

Kaln pushed upwards and managed to throw the hound off his back long enough to turn over. The hound recovered quickly and was back on top of him again, pinning him and preparing to lunge at his throat. There was nothing Kaln could do, the monster had him pinned. He closed his eyes tight as he saw the hound lunge at his face. A moment passed and he opened one eye, squinting. Beyond the snarling hound's open mouth was Vodius, he was around ten feet away but his hands were writhing as though they were holding the hound's mouth open and stopping it from tearing out Kaln's throat. Vodius grunted, his hands clenched tight as he wrangled the invisible force holding back the gore hound "You might...hmph" he found steadier footing "want to.. Kill the blasted thing!" but Kaln couldn't move, the creature weighed too much and had him pinned. It was only a matter of time. He could feel the powerful creature fighting against

Vodius' magic and its claws digging deeper into his chest for purchase. The dagger had been knocked from his reach and it was becoming difficult to breath. He reached desperately for the blade and saw beyond it that the other hound was closing in on Lilly. She still hadn't moved, hadn't run, hadn't fought. She was flexing and tightening her fingers so much that her palms were bleeding where her nails dug into the soft flesh. Blood ran between her fingers and dripped. In that moment, time seemed to slow. The drop of blood glistened bright red as it fell. As it hit the ichor on the ground, Lilly screamed, screamed with more pain, sorrow and anguish than she had the day he saved her in the attack. All of her pain washed out, Kaln felt the air change, become thicker. She held out her bleeding palms as white light shone from them like a blazing torch in a beam of pale flame wrapped around the hound closest to her before it could even react, the beam then washed over the hound that was pinning Kaln down. Nothing happened for a moment but the sound of hissing like burning flesh as the hounds writhed, showing pain for the first time. Where the drop of blood had hit the dark pool, white fire spread from that point, burning away the ichor spreading outwards. When the cleansing ring expanded to where the hounds were, the flame tongue tightened and split them in two, exploding into thick black curls of smoke. The cleansing fire continued to spread outwards, over the group, across the market square, up the walls. Where the flame touched, the ichor was cleansed until all that Kaln could hear over the heavy breathing of his companions was whimpering.

Vodius, now the only one still standing, paced over to Gleb. Kaln turned on his side with a wince to see Gleb covered in his own green blood. "That was..." Gleb paused to swipe the blood dripping from his nostril with the back of his hand. "A good fight!" he sniffled. Vodius reached out a hand to help the goblin to his feet. Gleb took the hand and spat a gob of blood on the floor "Thanks!" It was obvious to all of them that Gleb's wounds were more serious than he would admit. Lilly ran to him and placed a hand on the open wound but before he could wince or flinch away there was a blaze of light that erupted from her hands. Glebs eyes widened and moments later she moved her hand to reveal a clean spot amongst the grime on the Goblin's flesh where a savage wound once bled. Gleb glanced down and with a huge toothy grin hugged her tight. Kaln could hear her muffled giggles and she hugged him back.

She pulled back with tears in her eyes and whispered "So much death, so much ruin...I'm glad you're ok" Gleb was the first thing in all of this that she felt like she had the power to save and the exhilaration was obvious on her face.

"You healed him." Vodius said in tones that hinted he was impressed. "Well done. I've known kings pay handsomely for such skills."
"Celuna guided me." Lilly replied. It almost sounded like a question.
"Seriously, how did you do that?" Kaln said as he joined the others and inspected the goblin.
"I'm not sure, I wanted to help and I touched the wound. I knew it would…" Her words trailed off as she slipped her hand under his leather jacket to the wound on his shoulder and softly guiding her hand down his broad chest she touched the claw wounds. Each wound closed as she touched them with glimmering fingertips.
"It tickles!" Kaln laughed as he grabbed her hand with his and rubbed his chest with the other. His eyes grew wide as he realised he too was healed. Still holding her hand, he realised that he felt whole again, calm. He looked at the wonder in her eyes and said "Thankyou Lilly, you saved me."
She blinked her big blue eyes, smiled up at him and said "Now we're even." She turned away before any tension between the two could build but they both felt it.

"That was some impressive fighting my goblin friend, you have changed my opinion on goblins quite considerably." Vodius said as noncommittally as possible.
Gleb giggled, "That was nothing, you should

have seen-" suddenly he stopped talking and his grin was gone. With a serious and apprehensive expression, he looked at Vodius and whispered "Friend?"
Vodius cleared his throat and said, "Yes, well, I'm not one for friends per se but, you're on the list." as he straightened his robes and gave a small nod of finality to himself.

Kaln patted Gleb on the back. "I've heard tales of mountain barbarians who fought less bravely than you did, Gleb. I'm glad you're on our side and for what it's worth, I consider you a friend." Gleb, obviously trying to play it cool, gave a tiny fist pump at his side. Kaln noticed but didn't mention it as he patted him on the shoulder. "Well done everyone, that was close."

Cornwalk had a whole different kind of eeriness to it now, no life, no buzzing flies or feasting crows and rats, just an empty town. The autumn wind whistled through the broken buildings carrying dead leaves across the now bare market square. The adrenaline wore off and exhaustion and pain washed over the group, they took refuge back in the Mayor's home to recover. Vodius sat back down at the seat by the table where he spent the night, Gleb threw down his backpack and perched on it, legs dangling lazily. Kaln sat on the broken couch and Lilly sat on the floor in front of it, in the sunlight. There was an exhausted quiet in the room for some time, even

Gleb sat quietly watching the dust dancing in the sunlight.

Kaln, hunched forward leaning on his knees holding a hand to his wounded shoulder eventually said "Ok, what the hell just happened?" Vodius was pinching the bridge of his nose with his feet raised up on the table. Like he was talking to a student he said impatiently, "Those were Gore Hounds, minor demons." he sat up and continued "Similar to rats or other scavengers of our plane of existence. They were drawn to the power of the spell which collapsed." He shot Kaln a glance. "The spell, I assume, having limited knowledge of that particular type of magic, was an offering to some demon lord. I imagine, those bodies" he picked his words carefully and avoided looking at Lilly "and your father, was an offering of pain. A type of effigy or lense to focus the energy. The spell was probably keeping him alive, a conduit for the pain in the name of whichever greater demon was on the other side, one could conclude." Lilly's expression went numb and distant as Vodius continued "The first question is, which demon lord? The second being, why?" He stood and paced as he thought, "I suspect the answers will be with the orcs. Although, I am convinced this is not the orc's doing."

Kaln leaned back on the couch absorbing what he had just heard causing him to flinch with the pain of the bite on his shoulder. Lilly stood and began to dress the wound with the same expertise she had in the woods a few nights ago. Vodius continued "Which leads me to my third question. What now?" He looked each of them in the eye as he said "Well, the job offer I have extends to all of you. I plan on doing two things; The first, finding the second stone, the Rehlk Stone of Celuna's wrath. The second, understanding what drives the Orcs from their homes in the mountains. For these tasks I need people who can handle themselves. Each of you seem capable." He gave Gleb a quick look that did not look at home on Vodius' face. "Obviously you will need to be paid and this I can accommodate. 25 gold pieces each now, 25 more once I have the stone."

Kaln scoffed "You think we would want to put ourselves in danger again after what we have been through?" he shook his head "No, not for 25 gold. It doesn't look like you have a fat lot of options.. 100 gold."

Vodius nodded "Very well, I had assumed 50 gold was a substantial amount to you people-"

Kaln interrupted, "100 now, 100 after" he affirmed.

Vodius didn't even blink "Fine but let this be the end of it, 100 each now and 100 once I receive the second stone"

It was obvious Gleb would have taken any offer as he was nodding enthusiastically throughout the whole conversation.

Lilly stood and padded over to the fireplace where a crooked portrait of her father looked down on them. Her expression was still distant as she said "I have to stay and rebuild." Her voice sounded hollow as she straightened her father's portrait and looked to the destroyed house.

"Where do I start?" she said, asking nobody in particular in a lost voice.

Vodius sighed "Lilly, do you think those abilities were given to you by the stone for you to rebuild a dead village? Do you think there is anything worth rebuilding?" he paused and looked her in the eye "Do you not want vengeance for your people…for your father?" His words hung in the air for a small moment. Lilly locked her eyes on him and said firmly "Yes."

Kaln blurted "Wait, hunting bows and skinning knives are one thing but I don't have the ability to summon fire or…" he paused, glancing at Lilly with the subtlest hint of fear on his face "whatever you can do."

Gleb hopped down, grinning up at Kaln and said "Not a problem!" as he started burrowing into his bag. Moments later, after several grunts from the goblin, a flying hairbrush and a handful of flying spoons, Gleb turned to the group grinning. In his shaking hands were a sword and shield. The fact that he struggled to lift them was one of many signs that they were high quality items.

Kaln walked over, obviously impressed. As he inspected the blade and shield he said "Where did you get these, Gleb?"

"Blacksmith." Lilly said flatly and Gleb nodded with pride.

"The smiths here craft their finest sword and shield as an example of their skill for customers, they are not for sale but inspection. I doubt the sword even has an edge?" She continued.

Kaln checked and confirmed "No..." looking at her as Gleb shook his head in agreement. Gleb snatched the blade and shouted "I sharpen!" as he bounced out of the house. Kaln watched the goblin through the window as he ran to what was left of the blacksmith's, giggling and skipping as he went. The sword looked ridiculously oversized in the goblin's wiry arms. Lilly's expression seemed distant again as she said "That's Whisker's smithy, he was a good man and an honest dwarf." She had a small sad smile on her face as she remembered the dwarf.

Kaln assessed the shield; it really was well made. Dwarves have reputations for many things and one of them that was true was their skill with the forge and hammer. He tested the weight of it and it felt reassuringly sturdy.

Kaln and Vodius spent the next few hours picking through the rubble of the other houses looking for food which they could take with them. Lilly stayed in her home. The group converged at the Mayor's house around mid-day, Gleb being the last to join them, mostly covered with chainmail he had found whilst sharpening the blade. He handed them to Kaln with sheer delight as he watched Kaln's expression change from interest to being genuinely impressed with the goblin. With the chainmail that fit, even if slightly tight around the shoulders, a sturdy blade and solid shield, Kaln felt ready to head North, to avenge his people and his father.

Vodius drew a hip bag from his waist and delved into it. Impossibly, he was almost up to his shoulder in the small velvet bag when he paused realising Gleb was stood inches away with his jaw almost to the floor as he watched the elf struggle to find what he was looking for. A couple of moments passed and after the distant clattering and tinkling of metals Vodius said "Ah, here we are." as he withdrew his arm from the small bag. There was a pungent smell of almonds as he drew his hand holding a bulging leather coin purse. He poured out the contents onto the table. There were more than three hundred gold pieces. With a vaguely disinterested expression, he sat down.

"All the gold you need should be there" he waved a hand as he browsed the few books left in the debris that he hadn't already read. A moment later he brandished a finger in the air and with his decision made, he started reading. Gleb snatched a handful of the shiniest coins and seemed content. Kaln gathered the gold pieces for himself and Lilly and passed her share to her. She threw it into her pack without counting it and gazed out of the window. "Thank you." she said distractedly as the light danced in her eyes.

Vodius felt something at his side, he lowered the book and saw Gleb furiously fighting his natural urges to delve into the mysterious bag on the sorcerer's waist. Gleb was losing the battle until his eyes flicked to Vodius'. Partially to convince himself not to, partially to see if Vodius was paying attention. He was. A flash of remorse and sorrow washed over the exaggerated features of the goblin's face. Gleb didn't say anything. He just hung his head in shame, his ears drooping low.

Vodius placed the book on the pile of other books he had lost interest in, leaned forward and whispered to the goblin, who at this point could only see the floor through teary eyes "How about if I pay you for your valuable assistance by making you your own bag like mine?" and gave the goblin a small nudge with his elbow. Gleb's head whipped up with an expression which was a bubbling concoction of desperation, excitement and sheer glee. There was also a high pitched sound similar to that of a kettle at the point of boiling coming from the goblin.

Adjustments to chainmail, clothing, boots and rations were made by the others as Vodius spent the next two hours finding the correct materials and casting the spell to make Gleb his own magical bag. It didn't take long to find the materials needed. Vodius was beginning to think Gleb's 'Swag Bag', as he called it, had no limits of its own as the goblin consistently and accurately produced the correct materials needed for the spell from it.

He would make a brilliant lab assistant. Vodius found himself thinking as he performed the spell.

The first thing Gleb did with the bag once he had it in his possession was to ask Vodious to hold it flat on the ground and open. He then rolled his Swag Bag into it like a giant snowball, tightened the cord and hung it on his belt with a look of absolute blissful contentment, occasionally dipping most of his arm into the tiny bag and giggling maniacally to himself.

As the group gathered their things and prepared to leave Vodius took Lilly to one side and in hushed tones said to her, "Look, I am no mentor but I need to rely on you. I cannot train you but I do know something which might help. You need a focus until you master your abilities, to channel your power. I need you to answer a difficult question Lilly." he took a breath "I need you to describe what goes through your mind when you use your powers."

Lilly flashed him a look of defiance, then her

face hardened as she whispered "My father." She looked down.

"Be more specific girl." Vodius said with authority.

A spark of anger danced on her face like lightning across a storm cloud as she looked up at him. She took a breath and unclenched her bandaged hands.

"Walking with my father in the autumn, through the woods. His curls of grey hair, his soft eyes..." her words faltered and she swallowed. There was a sparkle of white light in the room coming from her hands beneath the bindings. She continued "His sense of humour and his old leather boots."

Vodius was listening intently as the light emanating from the girl grew. "More." he said flatly as if waiting for something.

Her eyes pleaded with him but she continued, wiping a tear from her cheek "I remember him being so proud of his walking staff, it was passed down from his father's father. He said one day I could have it... I used to hide it and he used to pretend he couldn't find it and we would play a childish game like hide and seek before we would walk through the autumn forests... It was a silly game but he entertained me as a child." Her words were shaky as tears streamed down her face.

Vodius shielded his eyes from the light coming from Lilly's hands, which was now too bright to look directly at.

"Ah-ha! Gleb!" He said suddenly. There was a break in the conversation and from the next room a patter of feet approached before Gleb poked his head through the door.
"Ya?"
Gleb's eyes widened and his pupils turned to cat-like slits as he saw the pale light coming from Lilly.
Without looking at the goblin, Vodius said "While you have been pilfering have you found any walking sticks or staves? I need them. Quickly now."
There was a silence as the goblin checked his inventory checklist and padded away. He returned shortly after with the sound of clattering wood and laid a dozen walking sticks, staves and canes on the kitchen table where vodius and Lilly stood.
"Are any of these your fathers?" he could see Lilly's eyes had locked on one long staff, made of red oak with a dark varnish and what he now realised was a carving of Lilly's family crest, embellished with two mares and a sheaf of wheat. A fine staff.
Lilly snatched up the staff and held it close. The light from her fingers streaked up the shaft of the staff crackling. The light then began to fade. Lilly smiled with teary eyes and understood what Vodius was doing.
She whispered "Thank you" to both Gleb and Vodius.

Gleb collected the other staves and canes and scurried away after smiling meekly at Lilly.

"There is no need for thanks. You must anchor your thoughts using the staff, focus your energy and limit what you use. If you don't, you will tear yourself apart." Vodius said as he gave her an assuring look "I need to rely on you" Vodius repeated and turned to join the others.

CHAPTER 9 - THE ROAD

"We need to head North to Crossay, if they haven't yet been attacked we need to warn them" Kaln said as he tightened his belt.

"As you have probably surmised, I am not from these lands. Kaln, you will be best to lead the way." Vodius said.

Kaln nodded "We go through the Black Rock Woods, we keep off the roads. We can practically follow the stream straight to Crossay".

The group set out. Even in the afternoon sunlight, the village felt hollow and empty as they walked through the silent streets. A crippled husk of the once flourishing village, ghosts of memories moved in her shadows. The tension in the air seemed to ease as they left the outskirts of Cornwalk. It was only once they were free of the place did they fully realise the wrongness of it. They paused to take a deep breath and look ahead, banishing the deep thoughts left clouding their minds.

The earthy natural smells, pines and dead leaves underfoot and the sounds of life in the forest made everyone feel more at ease. It was as though nothing happened here, no thick spiritual weight in the air.

As they ventured deeper into the woods Kaln was walking ahead of the group with Gleb, the goblin humming to himself as they walked.

"Were you there when the attack happened?" Kaln asked, holding a heavy branch back for the goblin to pass through a gap between the thick brush.

"Not to begin wiv', I saw smoke n' came to see wut' wus' appenin'. I was gunna' visit Whitebluff from the south mountains where my clan live." Gleb said in a chirpy tone, seemingly enjoying the brisk walk through the forests slipping back into a hum.

"So, you saw who did this? The orcs?" Kaln said, sudden hints of urgency in his voice. His pace had halted.

Gleb stopped and turned, looking confused "Orcs? No? Lots of Orcs died too. Orcs n' oomans' died togeva' against dem' things in cloaks." Gleb said, suddenly being distracted by an acorn by his feet. He grabbed it and dropped it into his bag like a child might drop a pebble down a well and

started making a note of his latest treasure.
Kaln snapped "Wait. What? The orcs killed everyone in Cornwalk then went North, didn't they?" just as the others caught up.
Gleb looked strained as he scratched his head and sat down on a small rock.
"When I came to Cornwalk, the orcs had killed a lot o' men with weapons." a look of contemplation appeared on the goblin's face "looked like they were goin' to leave when the cloaks came and started killin' orcs an' humans an' dwarves. They all fought against the cloaks but they lost. I fink' some orcs got away an' when they finished killin' people the cloaks went North. I waited until it wus' over and took the stuff they didn't need any more." Smiling at Kaln, Gleb nodded and hopped to his feet.
"It's getting dark. Should we make camp?"
Vodius said "I knew it, orcs are savages but I hear they have some semblance of honour."
Lilly spat "Thats not fucking honour, they deserved what they got."
Gleb said merrily "Orcs bastards yep, but even their children are good figh'ers, they put up a good fight with the rest."
Everyone stared at the happy little goblin.
Lilly said in a serious tone that made the smile on Gleb's face vanish.
"Gleb, were there orc women and children fighting alongside the humans and dwarves against the cloaked people?"

The forest seemed to stand still as they waited for an answer. "Yep!" Gleb said as his smile returned.

Kaln paced as he thought aloud.

"It makes sense... The orcs would never be welcomed to pass through our lands unhindered... If they were fleeing something they would have to fight their way through so the whole clan could pass... Orcs are stubborn, what would they run from? Who are these 'cloaks'?"

"Power attracts followers. Whoever created the spell and markings in Cornwalk, one would assume. The real question is why are they here and where are they going?" Vodius added scratching his chin.

Kaln looked at his companions, weariness was heavy on their faces.

"You're right Gleb, the light is waning and we need to set up camp before the predators begin to prowl the night. Here is as good of a spot as any. Vodius and Lilly, set up the tents. Gleb, is it safe to assume you can start a fire?" Kaln couldn't help but return the fiendish grin Gleb gave him.

"I will bring fresh water." Kaln said as he collected the group's water skins.

Kaln returned after nightfall with full water skins, a few rabbits and a pocket full of mushrooms. He was pleased to find the camp was set up and the fire was blazing, perhaps a little larger than was needed but it was keeping the goblin quiet. He also knew it would keep predators away. The elf looked comfortable, sprawled out on a bed roll pawing through a book. Lilly was picking herbs behind the tents and Gleb was bathing in the glorious majesty of the roaring fire he had created, occasionally throwing logs into the flames and marvelling at the embers as they swirled into the night sky. With the ingredients the group had gathered and the edible food they had scavenged in Cornwalk, they managed to make a hearty stew.

They sat around the fire, which had calmed somewhat since Gleb stopped throwing anything flammable he could get his hands on, onto it. They ate in silence, there was a strange tension in the air Kaln didn't understand.

Eventually Lilly rolled her eyes and said frustratedly "Gleb, just apologise".

Gleb didn't look up, he didn't speak, he just prodded at his stew.

"Gleb!" Lilly snapped as she nudged him with her foot.

He sighed, lowered his bowl and looked at Vodius.

"Sorry." his words dripped with all the stubbornness of an orc.

Vodius didn't respond, he just looked at the flames. Lilly shot the goblin a vicious glare and gleb said, with less contempt "Vodius, am' sorry I burnt ya' book… and am' sorry I laughed while I was doing it".

Gleb gave Lilly a pleading look as Vodius yielded, "It is in the past. Don't let it happen again." Gleb looked relieved as he sighed "Phew! Oh an' sorry for burning ya' slippers too."

"You did what?!" Vodius shouted as he plunged an arm into his magical pouch. The others burst into laughter as an impressive repertoire of elven profanities rang out in the crisp night air.

CHAPTER 10 - A BRISK NIGHT

Kaln woke in the early hours of the next morning and in the low light noticed his breath swirling lazily in the air before his face. The temperature had dropped drastically throughout the night. He got to his feet and his body reminded him of each and every wound he had collected over the last few days with new found enthusiasm. He groaned.
It was dark and the only light was from the dying fire outside his tent. He could sense, even as he laced up his boots, that there was a subtle stillness outside his tent. The sound of silence was torn by the occasional snores of one of his companions in their own tents. He peered out from his tent and found the forest floor covered with a thick layer of fresh snow, large snowflakes still silently drifted to the ground and the light of

the waning fire illuminated the tents, snow and treeline in a sickly yellow hue.

There was a musky, earthy smell in the air that made his nose tingle. Something moved off in the shadows to his right, something large. The crunching sound of snow made his ear flinch and he groped blindly for his sword propped up somewhere in the tent. Turning to look for it didn't feel like an option. A few anxious moments later, he grasped the hilt and slowly drew the blade. The quiet click of the sheath sounded deafening in the silence between the rhythmic snores.

With blade drawn, Kaln circled around his tent to his left and peeked out from his hiding place where the sound was coming from. There, on the fringes of the opening in the forest where the group made their camp, where the dying light struggled to grasp at the trees, was a large creature crouched in the snow. The beast's fur dancing between hues of black, white and the amber of the fire. Its position was only given away by the firelight dancing in its eyes.

Kaln's sword arm fell limply to his side as he mouthed "Shadecat."

Kaln remembered the smell of the fire. He remembered having sore hands and a grin on his face. He was so proud of it. His father had shown him how to make his own fire that day and the two sat gazing into it as darkness surrounded them.

"Tha' dunt' need to be afraid of the dark if tha' can make yer' own light lad. Tha' did well wi' that fire, remember to keep feeding it and it'll give ye light and keep ye warm."

Kaln looked up at his father, "Does nothing scare you pa'?"

His father poked the fire and stared into it, "There's a difference between a child's fear n' a healthy respect for things greater than you, lad."

He leaned back and raised his hands to the dark forest around them. "I've seen almost every creature that call these forests home. I respect each n' every one of em'." He looked back to the fire, "My father told me of a creature, he called her the 'Shadecat'."

His eyes scanned the treeline quickly and he fed the flames with some more wood.

"The reason we kill with purpose, without cruelty or sport, the reason we only take our share n' protect these woods is cus' my father said she," he gestured to the forest around them "can show herself as a spirit. A Shadecat. A beautiful but powerful and wrathful creature if men take more than she can sustain. Aint' never seen her myself, mind. But then, I have spent my life with a healthy respect for these woods."

He smiled at the wide eyed Kaln, "Son you don't need to fear the forest, just like you don't need to fear the dark. Master it, respect it, just like I've taught ye."

The dying fire popped as the last log collapsed in on itself. A plume of embers surged into the sky to meet the falling flakes of snow. Kaln found himself staring into the eyes of Shadecat's, staring back at him. The only thing that had ever scared his father was lazily swaying its tail before him. His instincts told him to drop the sword. It fell almost silently into the thick snow. His breathing was heavy as the cat first crept, then crawled, then crouched and stood before him. Not as a cat but as a woman, her feline features still graced her curves. Time seemed to stand still as she stood a few feet away from him. Her eyes were slits of darkness in the deep green hues of her iris'. She smiled with delicate fangs showing, her eyes lazy as the thick snowflakes danced and pirrowetted down around her naked form. Kaln couldn't help but take in the sight as she closed the distance. She let out a little laugh in response that reminded Kaln of the sound of rushing water, the sound of owls hooting in the night and wind rattling through the branches. There was something very familiar and soothing about it. Kaln was topless, he didn't realise he hadn't bothered to throw anything on until he felt the claw of the Shadecat run down his chest. She took a step closer, pressing herself against him. He could smell rich earth, pine trees and freshwater. It was almost intoxicating as she wrapped her arms around him. He felt the warmth of her body and blushed at the way his own responded. He couldn't move. She pulled him close in an embrace. He could hear a low deep purr as she put her face to his neck. Over her shoulder he watched her tail, still swaying behind her, disturbing the snowflakes on their slow and playful descent to the ground. Her tail rose slowly and he watched as the very tip softly touched his forehead.

A voice rang out in his head.
"Hello, Kaln." he could hear the smile in the softly spoken words.
"Hello?" he probed gingerly. His voice sounded weak even in his own head.
A soothing giggle rang out then stopped suddenly "I am sorry for the death of your father, Kaln."
There was a pause as Kaln felt like he was being assessed "Trust that he is with me, he is where he should be."
There was no doubt in Kaln's mind that she was telling the truth. This was an absolute truth. He felt his waking body shudder in relief and a warm tear fall down his cheek before his attention was drawn back inwards to the soothing voice in his mind.
"You must follow the path set before you, Kaln, do not falter. If you do not, the forest you call home will wither and die. This wake of ruin extends to the settlements within the forests. He

will stop at nothing to find the answers he seeks."
Kaln said desperately "Who?! Who is doing this?"
There was a pause and the Shadecat's voice purred "Go to Crossay, find any survivors. Ask them of Thaldur." The moment froze like one of the dancing snowflakes around them.

She leaned back and looked him in the eye "Will you do this? Will you be my champion, my Warden?"

Kaln stared at her. Mesmerised, he tried to absorb the vision in front of him.

"I-I...yes, yes Shadecat. I will be your warden, this forest is my home."

She laughed a musical laugh of joy as she looked up into the night sky and watched the snowflakes descend upon them. "Shadecat is a name given to me by humans. My true name is Aeathune."

Kaln's legs collapsed under him and he fell to his knees as he realised he was speaking to the goddess of nature, mother nature incarnate.

She looked down on him and purred. With one slender finger under his chin she lifted him to his feet softly. He looked her in the eye and the firelight sparkled in her tears. Then she plunged her fangs into his bare chest.

He felt agonising pain. He felt pain, extacy, pleasure, sadness, rage, power, love, joy and every other emotion and feeling he had ever felt, ten fold. His vision blurred and hazed with the cacophony of sensations assaulting his senses. From one knee, the last thing he saw was Aeathune's voluptuous curves walking away into the night, her tail sweeping left to right with her hips. She didn't look back. As she slinked away she said "Rise, my warden."

As she reached the shadows she crouched back into the shape of a large cat and disappeared into the darkness. A heavy weariness washed over Kaln and he waded through the snow back into his tent, collapsed on his bedroll and plunged into a deep and restful sleep.

CHAPTER 11 - GOOD MORNING

Kaln woke feeling like he had had the best night's sleep he had ever had, he didn't feel sore or bruised. He felt better than he had for a long time. That feeling was compounded by a sound that made him smile deeply as he stretched and dressed. The sound of Lilly's laughter rang out through the camp, sudden and clear enough to disturb the birds in the canopy. She snorted like a startled pig. He could hear Gleb laughing too, obviously finding his own story hilarious. Vodius groaned as the two chortled. Kaln began to dress, as he pulled down his shirt he noticed a dark green wound on his chest, it didn't hurt and it didn't look infected. The wound looked strangely natural, the green was not a sickly pale green but a deep vibrant green like that of moss. He struggled to piece together the night before and work out what was real. His fingers gingerly touched the emerald wound. It felt cold, like stone. Was she real? Did that happen? Kaln was dressed but found himself pausing just to listen to the mirth outside his tent. It felt good to hear them all talking and laughing after so much loss and turmoil. Even Vodius started laughing when Gleb's story came to a crescendo. Gleb described letting all the pigs out as he burned down the barn and rode out into the night with the herd of newly liberated farm animals on the back of a cow singing:

"Rum tum, let em' all go!
Fun! Run! Ridin' a cow!
Watch out Daisy, don't trample the sow!

Farmer Blake, never threaten a goblin!
Gleb take, he's the one who be robbin'!
And he's the one who will leave you with nothin'!"

"Truly eloquent words Gleb, I fear that I will never again hear such delicate and poetic words as yours, to bring tears to my eyes like yours have, ever again." Vodius said in mock horror as he and the others wiped away the tears of laughter in fits of giggles.

As the laughter died down Gleb said, quite soberly, "It true! They even made me sing it at the town hall when I was on trial!" and after a quiet pause he and the others burst into laughter again.

Kaln emerged from the tent to find that there was no snow. Dead leaves, bear branches and a brisk eastern wind was what he found. He stood dumb founded, staring around until Gleb hopped up looking a little hurt and passed him his sword back. There was nothing but a rusted hilt.
"I dunno' what ya did to 'er... found it around back of ya' tent Kaln, coulda' jus' said if ya didn't want it..." looking slightly confused he passed the rusted blade hilt to Kaln then scurried back to the food cooking over the fire that had been given new life since last Kaln saw it last.

Kaln looked down at what was left of the blade in his hands in amazement, turning it over as it crumbled to dust. *How had this happened? Was last night real?* He found his fingers touching the cool stone of the wound under his shirt as he pondered the impossible. *Unarmed, again.* He thought glumly.
Shaking his head, looked up from the blade, still confused.
"I'm sorry Gleb... I must have misplaced it..." Kaln called out to the goblin in a failing voice. Gleb didn't hear, he was now singing with gusto in a baritone voice into the soup he was

stirring. "Watch out Daisy, don't traaaaample the sooooooooowah!"

"Was there snow when you woke this morning?" Kaln said as he warmed his hands by the fire.
"Hah! No, I haven't seen snow for years, not since my studies at Keep Mordune and most certainly not last-night." Vodius said as he served himself a bowl of soup.

Lilly drained the contents of her bowl and clapped her lips.
"I don't think I've ever slept so well in my entire life." she said with contentment as she began one of her top to toe stretches finishing with a lazy smile and pleased groan.
"I'll second that, who thought that camping in the woods like ruffians would give such a satisfying sleep? Perhaps the clean air does the body good." Vodius pondered out loud between delicate blows to cool his soup.
"I always sleep well." Gleb announced as he plonked himself down on the floor like a teddy-bear and started eating.

The group ate well and gathered their things ready to move north. Kaln couldn't help but keep checking the spot he last saw the cat. Other than a disturbance of dead leaves, there was nothing to give away that his experience the night before was real and not a dream, nothing except the blade and the scar.

"Has anyone heard the name, Thaldur?" Kaln found himself asking the group as they were finishing packing their things. Lilly and Gleb shook their heads but Vodius stared at him, his jaw tensing. They all felt the sudden tension in the air as Vodius gave Kaln a stern look.
"I have heard the man's name, I've heard of his deeds and these I have heard from the people left in his wake but not in these lands." He closed his belt pouch and straightened his back.
"Where did you hear that name, Kaln?"
Kaln shifted his weight awkwardly as his mind scurried for an answer that didn't involve speaking to a spirit of the forest. Vodius sensed this and stepped closer to him.
"If we are to trust each other, there can be no lies. Speak your mind."
Kaln glanced at the others who were now listening. There was no use lying. Kaln told them his experience from the night before, saving only certain details to himself.

The group listened in silence with only Vodius pushing for specifics occasionally. When Kaln was finished, Vodius made a *-hmph-* noise and lowered his eyebrows.
"Well, that explains the rusted blade. This spirit of yours obviously has other intentions.

As Vodius said the words, a blast of sensations hit Kaln's mind and body. He was pulled outwards and upwards. Through the trees, streams and mountains to look down across all of the forest. He could sense every cave, every creature and falling leaf within his forest. His mind's eye was pulled to a cave deep underground, he could feel there was a power within that cave, like none he had ever sensed. He knew he needed to go there.

He came back to his senses on one knee surrounded by his friends. Lilly was on her knees in front of him, lifting his face to hers
"Kaln, are you ok?!"
Kaln could distantly feel Gleb's worried finger in his ribs as he locked eyes with Lilly and gave her a melancholy smile.
"I'm fine" he took a slow breath and squeezed her hand as they stood. He could feel in his bones every inch of these forests but where Crossay sat in his mind's eye, was only a sickly black blind spot which followed the path taken by the attackers of Cornwalk. He knew Crossay was lost.

Kaln forced a smile and looked each of the group in the eye. He knew they needed to go to Crossay. Regardless of what he told them. They needed this.
"I… I need to go somewhere, alone. I need you to go to Crossay and I will meet you on the road there. I know you will want to come with me but Crossay needs you now. Please, trust me on this. I will meet you before you get there."

Lilly went to speak but Kaln locked eyes with her and gave her the same look he gave her the day of the attack on Cornwalk. That look that reassured and delivered confidence in Lilly when she needed it. He was her rock as she was his. They both knew that without words. Lilly gave him a short nod and forced a smile. Before the others could say anything she clapped her hands and said "Right, let's get moving! You better meet us Kaln." This time her smile was more playful as she turned to gather her things. Kaln explained the best route to get to Crossay to the group. A way he wasn't aware of until he applied his mind to the task, it stunned him as much as it stunned the others with the level of detail he could describe to them.

Kaln grabbed his shield and nodded to the others and started running. As soon as the sound of the wind in his ears drowned out the sound of his friends packing their things, Kaln felt desperately alone again. Although he was scared like he hadn't been in days he knew he was doing the right thing. As he ran he knew each stone, root and patch of earth to give him sure footing. He knew when to stride, when to leap and when to swing from an overhead branch. As each bound passed, they seemed to get less and less, fewer and fewer until he was practically flying. The pace was impossible, if it not for the fact that he knew exactly where to place each foot he would have reeled out of control. The faster he ran, the lighter he felt. It felt freeing, like the forest was encouraging him to go faster and harder. Like the footing was in the perfect position for him to push harder. He bounded through the forest at speeds which were not humanly possible. It didn't scare him. Eventually the rush of the freedom he felt subsided enough for him to sense his companions and the route they had taken. They were following his directions and heading to Crossay at a fraction of the speed he was. He could make it to the place of power and to Crossay by the time they got there. He grinned as he pushed harder and focused on his destination.

CHAPTER 12 - A TEST OF STRENGTH

The forest was a blur of blacks, reds, oranges and the occasional greens as Kaln bounded through the trees. It wouldn't be long now, the light was waning but his confidence in his footing was no less. He was almost there, he knew he was. Although he knew where it was. He did not know what was at the destination, like a missing memory, there was a blind spot at the place where he needed to go. Different to the sickly streak left in the wake of the forces pushing north. This blind spot did not feel tainted but hidden. Secret.

He dropped into a valley and climbed one of the cliff faces with an ease that surprised him. The footholds and sure grips in the stone wall were obvious to him. Once he had reached the top, he looked down, a drop of twenty feet.

My instincts have gotten me this far, he thought and threw himself off into the base of the valley with only the briefest hesitation. It was a drop that he knew he could leap into. As he hit the ground, it crumbled. Decayed vines covered in earth and dust collapsed, Kaln fell through the earth into the fringes of his knowledge.

He held the shield in front of him and braced as much as he could. As he broke through the earth he plunged into a fast flowing underground river that dragged him flailing deeper underground. A sobering reminder of how small and delicate he is to the forces of nature. The rapids swelled and crashed, throwing him around in the darkness. Kaln gasped for air and desperately tried to orient himself in the darkness as rapid water over smooth stones dragged him deeper into the darkness. His heart pounded as the cold water of the rapids flushed the exhilaration from the freedom he felt above ground, from his lungs. He was smashed and battered as he desperately tried to curl into a ball and protect himself with his shield. The waters were unrelenting; they curled, twisted and suddenly stopped. Kaln had a moment of the sensation of almost flying again before his stomach sank and he started to plummet. He opened his eyes and saw a distant column of pale light as he fell, the rushing sound of the waterfall behind him and the clouds of vapour below him. Another moment and he hit the water praying it was deep enough that his skull wouldn't be smashed on a jagged rock beneath the surface.

He woke in the gravel on the shore of an island which dominated the center of the cave. The waterfall pooled, then ran either side of an island and further into the ground. There was pale moonlight washing over the huge tree in the center of the cave from a hole in the top of the cave. In that moment he knew this was not just any tree, this was the Pale Rua Tree. The mother tree. Her branches were one with the cave walls as they grew into them, now he could feel that each branch was its own powerful tree above ground. He picked himself up, gasping at the pain wracking his body from his journey down here.

As he looked around he saw there were bones littered around and deep looming cracks between the speckled shadows of the canopy of the Rua Tree on the cave walls. At the Tree's base was something protruding from its roots that stood out, a glimmer of pale red light. The canopy shifted as the rushing waters disturbed the air and a beam of pale moonlight rested on the thing at the base of the tree making the glimmering red light brighter. Kaln rolled his shoulders and looked at his shield, he was shocked to find it was still in one piece.

Dwarves really know how to make a shield, he thought as he began to walk closer to the light.

The crunching of the gravel under foot and the sound of the falling water echoing in the cave sounded deafening as Kaln approached the pile of bones closest to him. He knelt. These were elven bones, others human. He tightened his grip on the sturdy dwarven shield as he looked to the base of the tree. Suddenly, from the darkness a roar louder than the waterfall bellowed behind him. He felt the cave shudder as something bore down on him. He turned in time to see a bear fifteen foot tall with gleaming emerald green eyes, yellow teeth and pale grey hair similar to that of the moonlight dancing on the walls. It was already on top of him and swung a huge paw with glistening black claws at his head. Kaln didn't feel anything, weightless, darkness and the sound of falling water gone. The silence crept away leaving the sound of falling water once again, quiet at first then growing louder. More senses returned, he knew he was laid face down in the gravel and his head was throbbing in pain. He blinked and opened his eyes, something felt strange as the moonlit world around him swirled with colours of red. White hot agony washed over his face and his vision began to focus. Nausea washed over him and he grimaced with pain. The ground was shaking, shaking like before...The bear. He leapt to his feet and almost collapsed as the world spun more, he braced himself with his hands on his knees and looked down to see the pool of blood he had been laid in. The world stopped spinning just in time for him to see his eyeball peering up at him from the scarlet pool. Survival instinct got to his nervous system before panic or fear. Kaln raised his shield over his head as the charging bull hit it. Again he felt weightless, this time he was conscious as he flew through the air. He felt himself hit the gravel with a slide and the loud hiss of thousands of tiny stones flying in his wake. He felt the shield and his arm shatter under the force of the blow. He cradled the deep dull throb in his arm as he lifted himself to one knee and looked up to see the bear, not just any bear but Ursol the Bear Lord barreling down upon him once more. Time seemed to slow as adrenaline pumped through Kaln's veins. He noticed the tree almost seemed to be watching beyond Ursol's form, which was closing in on him. He couldn't outrun him, he couldn't survive another hit like that. He looked down to see the stone sparkling from his wrist and with few options, he prepared to punch his fist up as hard as he could. He was going to give the beast a fight on his way out, he might even be able to split the bear's lip. His fist hit the huge bear's jaw. The blow sent the beast reeling over backwards with a hiss of gravel sprayed into the air and water surrounding the island. As the creature hit the ground with a heavy thump Kaln realised he was screaming, no, roaring. A sound that almost did not sound his own. Ursol didn't move.

Around Kaln's feet amongst the gravel were shards of his shield, blood, bear teeth and ancient bones. These were the last things Kaln saw before he blacked out.

Kaln came-to, he did not open his eyes. He tried to push through the pain enough to listen to his surroundings and let his body scream as it shook with agony. The adrenaline had left and could no longer keep the pain at bay as his screams echoed in the cave, waiting for the bear to awaken and finish what it started. Part of his mind pushed through to pain in hopes of sensing his friends were ok. Nothing. They were not there. How long had he been out? Maybe they were already there, already at Crossay. He had to move, he had to try. His eye flickered open and the moonlight from above the canopy of the mother tree dappled the ground still. He tried to lift his head, he could feel that one side of his face was sticky as his head pounded and the world swirled. His vision settled enough to see a large hand push his head back down. A man's face appeared in his sight above him. He had a split lip. The man gave a lazy half smirk showing a couple of broken teeth and stood. He was impossibly huge with thick grey hair covering the chest and arms of his naked body. He put a meaty finger to his split lip and walked out of Kaln's sight into the shadows. Darkness washed over him like a wave, he had no strength to fight it.

When he came around again he saw a very different sight. His head was resting on Aeathune's knees as she knelt. She was just as naked and beautiful as the first time he saw her. She smiled down at him and brushed his hair back. He could feel his hair was stuck in the blood on his face as he tried to focus. "I will tend to your wounds Warden Grey... as best I can." she whispered softly. He fought to lift his head, to talk. She gently pushed his head back down, stroked his head and shushed him. He didn't fight it, he didn't have the strength.

"Tha's done me proud son. Keep going lad." the comforting familiar voice of his father echoed from the dancing specks of light above "Yer on the right path". He felt a warm tear trickle down the side of his face as he gave in once more to exhaustion and let darkness engulf him.

CHAPTER 13 - DID HE SAY LEFT AT THE CREEK?

The group packed their things and looked north to the route Kaln suggested they follow. A vaguely concerned look wrinkled Vodius' delicate features as he watched Kaln disappear into the forest. They started walking, Vodius was deep in thought as he paced, face down with his hands behind his back.

Gleb was quizzing Lilly on the largest rat she had ever eaten, he took great pleasure in describing his own experiences slaying and eating rats. Apparently, Whitebluff's sewers had some of the largest he had ever seen, or tasted. Lilly had the manners and patience to let Gleb finish advising her on which herbs and spices most eloquently enhanced the flavour of the rat. Once he was done, he paused for a moment, licking his lips as fonder times passed his mind's eye.

Lilly took the opportunity to ask Vodius what was bothering him. Though he was often disinterested in what was going on around them, Lilly noticed something was bothering him. Like an old arcanist lost in thought, Vodius realised he wasn't alone with a very uncivilised grunt, followed shortly by a flash of realisation on his face and clearing his throat. Straightening his back and raising one perfectly shaped elven eyebrow, suddenly looking like a head teacher catching students up to no good.

"Apologies Lilly, I was seven stars away in thought. Can I help you?"

"I just wondered what was on your mind." She suppressed a grin.

"Well... I can't help but wonder if I have paid a man who has quite literally ran out on our verbal contract and fled with a pocket of my gold." He pondered aloud, seeming more disheartened and disappointed in himself than angry at Kaln.

Lilly placed a hand on his arm. Causing him to stop and look at her, an involuntary flash of disgust and shock on his face. Followed by a flicker of shame, obviously not used to being touched. Lilly's hand recoiled in response to his reaction.

Vodius held her arm softly "My sincerest apologies again Lilly, you startled me is all."

Lilly flashed a smile, put a hand on his and said

"Don't worry, I just wanted to tell you that your faith in Kaln is well placed. He is a trustworthy man and he will return as he said. Look, his directions have been true to his word. We are making progress to Crossay."
"Yes, yes, you're probably right. If there's one thing I know of you country bum-" he corrected himself "country folk, it's that you are generally pretty honest people."

The group travelled for two days following Kalns directions as they went, they were astoundingly accurate. Right down to where there were large stones, particularly large trees and even large puddles which could be used as waypoints if you were looking for them. Their days generally consisted of Gleb setting traps at night for meat; he was incredibly adept at catching rodents. Lilly collected firewood and mushrooms her father had taught her were edible. Vodius had decided after the first night that physical labour really wasn't for him and worked on an enchantment that could pitch the tents for him. He was subsequently given the task of cooking by Lilly. He didn't mind this, it was basically alchemy on a more fundamental level. It also helped that Gleb seemed to have every herb imaginable in his swag bag and was eager to share his cooking knowledge and the herbs. Spirits were generally kept pretty high by Gleb's inane stories of daring swashbuckling and cunning thievery.

Hearty meals and making progress to waypoint after waypoint on their journey also helped but as time went on and there was no sign of Kaln or when their route took them on the main road, no sign of travellers, the tension began to grow. Each night seemed longer and colder, and food became more scarce with each passing day.

On the third day of travel, their surroundings in the forest changed. The first thing they noticed was that there were no bird calls, there were no sounds of small animals scampering out of sight or the croaks of toads. As they journeyed further North, they noticed a second thing, that all the trees were either dead or dying, the forest floor was covered in dead pines, the bark of the great trees was blackened and brittle. Conversation became less as each contemplated what may be ahead of them.

At the end of the third day of travel, the group emerged from the treeline of dead pine trees which flanked either side of the main road to Crossay. The only sounds they heard was the occasional dead branch giving up its grip, the crackling of dried pines under foot and their own laboured breathing. They all stopped and took a breath after climbing up the bank to the main road. The sun was setting, but it was beautiful even in these morbid surroundings, especially after being in dark and decrepit forests with little sunlight for the last day of their journey.

Another hour's journey North-West on the main road, they saw no other travellers, no tradesmen or guards on the road. The building tension had grown now to the point it was almost unbearable but at least they were in the open air now, away from the claustrophobic forests of the dead and dying. Eventually they turned a corner to see the wooden battlements of Crossay at the top of the hill as the fading sun set behind it. Feeling the desperate need to break the tension, Lilly said "She used to be a trade outpost you know." Nodding to the walls at the top of the valley.

"Perfect position on the crossroad between Whitebluff, Mul'gur and the smaller villages in the South" she paused for a beat but snapped herself out of it before the thought took hold.

"That's why it's called Crossay, an abbreviation of 'The Cross Ways', so pah told me, anyway." She forced a smile and continued.

"She never used to have those walls but with so much money flowing through what was becoming a city, it was decided battlements should be built to deter bandit raids. All of these things together made the city sprout up like a weed as people flocked here to trade. I remember hearing they were building the battlements when I was a wee lass. I remember pa brought me to see them on my birthday." A thick silence hung in the air.

CHAPTER 14 - THOSE WHO WAIT

They looked up to the towering walls on the horizon, the city was surrounded by dense forest. No torches could be seen on the battlements, and with the last of the light fading they ran to the city. They found themselves in the pitch black some way off from the walls of Crossay. They paused and listened. From beyond the walls they could hear wails of pain and screaming in terror. Lilly began to run again followed by Vodius, they didn't get far before Lilly felt a wiry hand on her stomach, she flinched and swung her staff wildly in the dark. She didn't hit anything. Gleb's voice, sounding uncharacteristically serious, said "Wait, you no move. Stay very still and very quiet. I will be back". Lilly tried to grab where she thought the goblin was.

"Gleb! We must help them!" He wasn't there. Some distance off to where Lilly estimated was the treeline she heard Glebs whisper again "Just watch." Neither her nor vodius saw or heard anything as they stood anxiously in the gloomy darkness.

Gleb, like all goblins, had incredible vision in the dark as many of their kind spent their entire life underground. As the group had paused to catch their breath in the last light, he had seen something the others could not.

After telling the others to wait and moving towards the city through the dead trees, he drew a pair of metal claws that strapped onto his hands, a similar pair strapped to his boots. An invention of his own design, he was eager to test them.

In silence he tightened the leather straps and began to climb the tallest tree he could find, careful not to knock any of the dead branches as he ascended. The wind began to pick up and looking around, Gleb decided he was as high as he could climb. From there he threw himself to the next tree, a flicker of a shadow in the darkness. Onto the next tree and another and another. He could see over the Southern battlements of Crossay now. He could see the flames, the carnage and slaughter but that wasn't what he was here for.

He looked down to his friends still on the road behind him, he could see Lilly arguing with Vodius. It was obvious from their body language that Vodius was trying to convince her to wait. Gleb found a sturdy branch and began rummaging through his swag bag. With his tongue outstretched to aid his blind search through his bottomless swag bag, Gleb paused seeing a human run out of the ruined gates of Crossay into the forest below where he sat, trying to flee the onslaught. He didn't make it far before a group of figures previously stood silent and still amongst the trees grabbed him and began tearing him to pieces. The screams of the man rang out down the valley louder than the others behind the wall for an uncomfortable amount of time.

Gleb continued his search and drew two vials, one with a mushroom Lilly had strictly forbidden him from eating or burning. The other contained a clear liquid that smelled acrid and made his eyes water, Although that smell seemed preferable to the sickly sweet putrid smell coming from below. Vodius had told him this was an acid and some of the things it was capable of, even some of the chemical reactions it could cause. This had piqued Gleb's interest and he couldn't wait to try one out. He drew the mushroom from the first vial, he held it in between his fingers and paused staring at

the tiny blue mushroom. It was hopeless, he couldn't help himself, he licked the mushroom and dropped it into the liquid in the second vial. Tasting the thing probably wouldn't have even crossed his mind if Lilly hadn't made it into an irresistible forbidden fruit.
An uneventful moment passed, he was more than a little disappointed when nothing happened. Below there was the distant sound of tearing flesh that prompted him back to action. He replaced the cork and shook the vial lightly before letting it drop down through the branches below. He listened and watched. The glass vial made little *-tink- -tonk-* noises as it bounced through the branches below. It began to emit a blue-green light, dull at first but growing brighter as it bounced off the head of one of the figures standing staring into the dark. The creature didn't seem to notice as the light grew more and more, illuminating what Gleb and his companions could now see were hundreds, no, thousands of figures standing in the treeline surrounding the city.

Gleb was quite happy with himself, his plan worked and he hadn't got caught. He turned to begin his return to the others and his world spun. Fluorescent stars exploded in his eyes and his skin began to tingle. He leaned back against what he thought was the tree trunk to watch what these mushrooms could do. The trunk wasn't there. He did manage to get a glimpse of it disappearing between the beautiful coalescing fireworks, the heavily armoured goat that flew by and lots of branches as he plummeted down. Still falling, he heard a giggle, a familiar giggle. It made him giggle, which made him giggle. Thousands of giggles and they were all his. He bounced from branch to branch. The final branch stopped his fall, his body wrapped around it, knocking the wind from him. He watched as the decrepit tree began to topple from the sudden collapse of so many of its branches.

Gleb decided his new wings were wonderfully convenient and sprinted to the end of the branch as the tree collapsed behind him. He lept, it was only a short flight to safety and back to his friends who waited on the road. He looked down as he flapped his wings into the night air and saw the aqua light of his concoction washing over the forest floor below swirling and writhing with all the other colours he could see. He tried to flap his wings, instead they exploded into more beautiful stars as he hit the ground with a heavy thump and a roll.

Luckily goblins are hardy and capable of digesting practically anything so it only took a moment for Gleb to start regaining his senses and start running from the collapsing tree which was falling into other brittle dead trees which were also collapsing like dominos. He sprinted back to his companions, the last of the mushroom's effects fizzling away from his vision as sober terror set in.

CHAPTER 15 - CROSSAY

Gleb rarely asked anything of the group so when he scurried off into the darkness, it was on these grounds that Vodius managed to stop Lilly bolting towards Crossay. They did as he asked and stood and waited, and waited in the dark listening to the distant cries. Lilly's patience broke and she started to walk with purpose to the city in pain. Vodius' night vision had settled in by now and although he couldn't see like a goblin in the dark, he could see Lilly's vague shape making a move. He knew they owed it to Gleb to wait like he asked. "Lilly!" he barked in a harsh whisper with such authority that to her own surprise, Lilly stopped. She turned on him, "What?! I will not wait any longer!" Over her head, Vodius could see the aqua light starting to grow in the forest to one side of the entrance to the city. He placed a hand on Lilly's shoulder and turned her so she could see. "Wha-" she murmured before standing silent with the elf watching the forest illuminate, presenting an army of motionless figures. Almost as soon as the two had acknowledged what they were witnessing, the trees around the light began to collapse upon one another. With thunderous cracks and ground shuddering booms.

Somewhere distant and quiet at first, they heard what sounded like Gleb's giggle as the trees crashed down on the waiting figures, crushing them in a cacophony of splintering shards of wood that echoed through the valley. The silent army didn't run in fear, they didn't try to avoid the falling debris or cry for the ones they lost. The survivors simply stood in silence amongst the falling trees as if waiting for a command. The light continued to grow as the dead forest collapsed in on itself. There were thousands of them, their vague shapes could be seen in the sickly blue light amongst the clouds of dust kicked up by the falling ancient trees and what was left of the forest. The dust merged with the smoke from the fires in Crossay and created smog around the City. The giggling got louder and somewhere close by. Suddenly, they heard a heavy thump and the giggling abruptly stopped. The light in the distance continued to grow, illuminating countless more figures, motionless. They heard a screech coming towards them and readied themselves, prepared to fight whatever creature of the darkness befell them. The screeching creature paused when it got to the road, there was some muffled grunting and the sound of metal hitting the cobblestones of the road and the screeching continued. Gleb came tearing out of the darkness, still trying to get the last of the climbing claws off his hand. Lilly slid her staff to her side and knelt. Gleb doubled over in front of them, his screeching had finally stopped in favour of gasping down gulps of air. "Undead!" he blurted.

The distant pale blue light illuminating the clouds started to flicker and fade, Gleb's harrowed expression was the last thing the others saw before the inky darkness engulfed them all. "What do we do now?" Vodius asked in a surprisingly calm voice. Lilly couldn't think through the panic. *Why was there an army of undead? Where was Kaln? Were they too late?* She closed her eyes tight in search of clarity, it didn't help. As she tried to calm her breathing she felt a hand on her shoulder.

Vodius' calm voice once again called out in the dark. "After some contemplation it would appear we have two choices." he paused, taking a deep breath.

"The first, we retreat back to the forest and wait

for Kaln. Second, we do what we came here to do and go into Crossay to warn them or help them if we can. It's quite preferable to do either of those things than to linger here any longer."

Gleb was rummaging in his swag bag for something but between grunts of lifting heavy unseen treasures out of the way, he said "Parts of the city are on fire. Maybe too late." He shrugged his shoulders and continued searching.

They had come this way to help, Kaln could be in the city... besides, what was there to go back to if they ran?

"We go into Crossay." Lilly said and opened her eyes to see Gleb holding a tiny vial on a chain which held beetles that glowed green when he shook it. Gleb covered his mischievous grin with a bandana and pulled down his goggles. "If we going in, you maybe want to cover ya mouth, the smoke very thick from the flames. Follow me!" Gleb chirped as he put the chain over his head, slung the beetle vial over his shoulder and started for the city. All that could be seen were the tiny green glows of the beetles being tossed around as he ran. Vodius held a handkerchief to his mouth and Lilly pulled up her scarf and the two followed the tiny bobbing lights into the black night towards the city.

CHAPTER 16 - A SHELTER IN THE STORM

Lilly's eyes stung and she struggled to keep focus on the green lights swirling away in the smoke of the fallen cursed trees surrounding the city of Crossay. Tears streaked down her face as the acrid smoke bit at her eyes. She gulped deep breaths of air that burned her throat and lungs. She focused on her surroundings and could hear the goblin and the elf near-by in the dark doing the same. Their footsteps echoed out on the stone road.

We just need to get to the gate of the city, it's higher up above the treeline and the smoke.

She thought as she tried to suppress the feeling of panic overcoming her. She gave in to the pain and blinked, her eyes felt warm and soothed for a fleeting blissful moment. When she opened them again, she couldn't see the lights. She rubbed her tearfilled eyes and tried to find her bearings. She couldn't see anything now. Only darkness. She thrust out her hands hoping to find something, anything to anchor herself to. Nothing. The only senses that hadn't abandoned her was the pain in her eyes and lungs and the distant sound of the cries from the city. She groped in what she thought was the direction of the city, her heart beginning to pound as blind panic set in. A hand grabbed hers and jerked her to the left, pulling her along. Suddenly she could see the blurry green lights through the tears that streaked down her face again. She did not blink again until they broke the magic smoke.

Standing in the darkness by the side of the shattered wooden gate was Vodius looking into the city, he glanced over his shoulder long enough to nod at Gleb upon his return. He could only be seen by distant firelight dancing on his harrowed features as he looked beyond the walls. Gleb doubled over, pulling the bandana from his face to catch his breath beside Lilly.
"Thanks for coming back, Gleb. I'm going to be honest, I got in a bit of a panic out there."
Gleb lifted his goggles and winked at her with a smile.

Vodius stopped watching through the broken

gateway and turned to the others, his face was sober,

"I can't make sense of what's happening in the city, there is so little light. All of the street lights are out. Even with that distant fire, this place is like a rat's warren. The place is bathed in shadow. Honestly, even assuming the place wasn't under some sort of siege, I have no idea how you people live ontop of eachother like this."

Lilly ran to his side and peered in, she could see no more than him, dark dense alleyways and winding walk ways of varying shapes and sizes twisted out of sight between the crooked buildings. Occasionally shadows moved between the tall twisted and warped buildings. Doors slamming and heavy furniture being moved could be heard through thin walls as the three picked their way slowly through the alleyways, taking Gleb's lead and keeping to the shadows within the shadows. They came to an opening where one of the cart roads crossed the walkways, it was bathed in firelight and as they waited in the gloom they could taste the timber smoke. Silently they waited and listened, trying to gauge what was happening. As they did, a dozen or so families, men, women and children walked passed with arms full of trinkets and jewellery. Their faces looked panicked but they walked with purpose. Lilly went to call out to them but gleb placed a hand on her mouth stopping her. He lowered his hand into a pointed finger. Following several paces behind the family were robed figures. They held lanterns on poles which made the shadows dance around their shrouded faces. Hinting at hideous possibilities. There was something about their gait that was off, their limbs seemed slightly too long, their spines too hunched.

"Cloaked ones…" Gleb whispered as his eyes glistened in the light of the lanterns. They waited for a clearing and darted from the safety of shadows to the alleyway across the road into the open embrace of the darkness of another warped back alley.

Vodius whispered, "How does one even see the sky in a place like this?" as they scurried down the damp cobble stones. Lilly looked back to see his silhouette looking skyward between the leaning buildings. "Cheaper to build up than extend the walls out I suppose." She replied.

"Evidently humans don't possess the craftsmanship required for buildings as tall as this, look they are practically leaning upon one another like drunken louts." Vodius said, sounding both amazed and disgusted at the same time.

Gleb had halted them at another crossroad, this one was not as busy but as they listened they could hear the sounds of dogs barking, muffled arguments and what sounded like metal pots being thrown on a pile somewhere close. He glanced at the others and darted across the opening. A few more tight alleyways that had the smell of "Piss and disappointment.", as Vodius pointed out, and Gleb slid to a stop. They were at an opening to the courtyard of the temple of Celuna. Although they were at the rear of the building they could still see the grandeur of her sculpture that made up most of the temple. This was one of the few buildings in the city that was not crowded by over-built houses.

They could see a huge crowd of people at the front of the temple, surrounded by more cloaked figures. Looking over both them and the pile of offerings was a figure on horseback, he watched silently. Occasionally, more would come in from the roads leading here. They would walk over to a huge pile of trinkets, drop theirs on top with loud clangs and crashes that echoed around the courtyard. Afterwards they would be directed to join the others in the crowd. Behind the temple, a couple of children no more than twelve years old were hiding out of sight, too scared to risk the open space between the temple and the alley ways. Quietly Lilly, Gleb and Vodius watched and as they did Vodius whispered "You see that? Above the pile of trinkets?" They looked and roughly three feet above the pile were dancing lights in different shades of purple, pink and blue.

"'T'is it?" Gleb whispered, his eyes gleaming.

"Well, you see, when large quantities of

magically bound items are placed in close proximity to one another, as you see here, you get an effect quite similar to the Aurorus lights at the peak of the world." Vodius explained, seeming to forget they were hiding until Lilly shot him a look.

He jerked a nod of recognition, stepped back into the shadows and whispered, "Ah yes, apologies. One could safely assume every item on that pile has at least some incantation on it, small or large."

He scratched his jaw and thought aloud, "But why would they be collecting magical items?"

Celuna guide me, what do we do? There are so many of them.

Lilly thought as she watched more villagers herded to the group like cattle. She looked from the others with her, to the scared children that had managed to slip away from the growing crowd of people and cloaked ones.

Where is Kaln? What do I do?

Suddenly a glimmer of light caught her attention. High up above, the clouds had broken and for an instant the moonlight danced on the stained glass windows of the temple, specifically an image of Celuna taking those in need into her embrace and granting them protection from the depiction of a great storm on the horizon. The clouds rolled back to a brooding darkness again and Lilly decided aloud, "With the next offering, we make a run for the rear of the temple."

"Too much light." Gleb said flatly as he pointed to the lantern they would need to pass under to get to the rear of the temple. His ears made soft flapping noises as he shook his head.

"Not a problem, give me a moment." Vodius said with easing confidence.

The group waited a minute or two until the next offering was made, the crashing sounds of hollow metal echoed around the courtyard. Gleb turned to see an expression of concentration on Vodius' face. His elven eyes were closed in the shadows, suddenly, beneath his flickering eyelids was a glowing orange light that ceased as quickly as it began. It stopped along with the dying echoes of crashing metals and as Gleb turned back around to view the courtyard, the lantern's flame had been extinguished. Only tiny wisps of smoke could be seen escaping the glass casing.

"Our path is both clear and shrouded in darkness." Vodius said triumphantly, gesturing ahead of them.

Neither the figure on horseback or the cloaked ones seemed to notice the death of the light nor did they notice the three shadows darting to the rear of the temple in its absence.

They slid to a stop in the alcove at the back of the temple, the children with tear-filled eyes looked up at them in search of answers. Lilly gestured to pause for a moment to see if they had been discovered. Moments passed with no sound.

The young girl pulled on Lilly's cloak and blurted "Please help, mummy told us to hide and we did and now we can't find her and we're scared and-" Lilly knelt down and looked at the two children.

"I don't know where your mummy is, but we are going to get you somewhere safe." She glanced at Gleb and nodded to the rear door to the temple. He was already rummaging through his swag bag and pulled out a bundle which he rolled out, it contained meticulously secured delicate instruments, which he used to start picking the lock on the small door. Lilly had just enough time to give the small girl and her brother an affirming look before there was a subtle click and a victorious giggle from Gleb. He had just rolled up the slender pieces of metal in their case when his ears pricked up and he glanced at the door as Lilly reached for the handle. It opened with a heavy clunk and beyond the doorway were two middle aged men carrying a pew towards the door. They froze as Lilly and the others looked back at them. They were terrified. Lilly ushered the children inside first, then her comrades. She gave one last glance to the winding alleyways dotting the edge of the courtyard and closed the door behind her.

She turned to find the children hugging one of the two men.

"Uncle Jole, praise Celuna!" the girl sobbed.

The man looked worried but embraced them.

After a long embrace he looked up at the group. Lilly grabbed the pew and gestured to Gleb to get the other end and began moving it into position to bolster the door.

"Keep those children safe and bring me the key for this door." Lilly ordered.

The man said something quietly to the children, they nodded and moved down the hallway. He stood and threw Lilly the key.

"The rest of us are down 'ere." he said in a hollow and defeated voice. Then he turned to follow the children with his comrade.

Vodius gracefully stepped aside and began casually inspecting the tapestries on the walls while Lilly and Gleb locked and braced the door with the huge wooden pew.

They followed the two men down the hallway. The smell of torchfire, wood varnish and dusty tapestries filled their nostrils as they followed the men. Eventually they were led into the main hall of the temple. It consisted of a high ceiling stretching up beyond where the torchlight could reach. A raised plinth where the Elder Listener would give her sermons with a dias carved in marble in the shape of Celuna on one knee facing the congregation. Below this were usually row upon row of pews, these had instead been dragged down the multiple sets of stairs leading down to the three entrances into the main hall to barricade them closed. There were men, women and children moving more pews into position, all of them seemed to be commoners with the exception of the Listeners. All of their faces were desperate and scared.

None of them looked more haunted than what Lilly assumed from her outfit was the Elder Listener. She knelt in front of the dias, looking into the sculptured eyes of the goddess Celuna. The Elder Listener sobbed almost uncontrollably between desperate prayers as she rocked back and forth. Above the three great wooden doors were stained glass windows made up of every shade of blue. Between the windows were slots in the stone work that even from here, Lilly could see, were engraved with intricate magical engravings.

Lilly was a follower of Celuna ever since the first time her father let her stay up late so that he could show her the moon and tell her Celuna's story. It was one of the reasons she wanted her father to bring her to Crossay when she was a child. She had marvelled at the grandeur of the temple when she was a child as she did now. She knew the architecture and magical engravings were designed so that The Listeners of Celuna could hear the plights of the people outside the temple and attempt to help them. This was the path for the Listeners and as such, believers would come to the courtyard outside the temple to pray and denounce their sins to Celuna and her Listeners. They didn't need to shout or scream for the Listeners to hear them. The magic in the stonework picked up their voices and carried it to the Listeners.

What this meant now was that everyone in the hall could hear the scared whispers, prayers and terrified sobs of the villages crowded in the courtyard. The pain was almost unbearable especially when Lilly felt so powerless. Her attention was drawn back to the Elder Listener rocking back and forth before Celuna's caring visage. The Listener was an incredibly old woman with dark eyes and a lifetime of pain shown plainly on her features. The cracks in her old wrinkled skin accentuated by the streaks of tears.

A spark of anger flared in Lilly as she lurched the Elder Listener to her feet and looked into her glassy eyes.

"What are you doing?! These people-"

she snapped a hand in the direction of the sixty or so towns folk and Listeners desperately trying to block the doors

"look to you for guidance, to be reassured... And what do you do?! You sit here and sob like a child-"

Lilly saw the children from earlier helping to carry more heavy things to the doors.

"No, worse than that, at least they are trying to do something!"

She hadn't meant to, but her impatience in the

situation had left her screaming at the Listener. Everyone in the temple stopped and stared at Lilly holding the Elder Listener by the collar of her robes. Lilly let the Listener drop back to her knees and a silence filled the great hall.

The silence was broken gradually by the sobbing of the old woman growing louder and louder until eventually she fell silent again. Then her weathered voice pierced the silence.

"We deserve it, we deserve everything that man brings upon us."

Sounds of confusion were coming from the group of people who had stopped building the barricade.

Lilly glanced at Gleb and Vodius but only received confused looks in return. She turned back to the Listener on her knees, now two other listeners were helping her to one of the few pews not used in the blockade. Lilly followed as everybody waited and watched.

Vodius was the only one to notice Gleb take his leave and start making his way up into the rafters, climbing one of the tapestries which flanked the walls of the huge temple, obviously already bored with the intricacies of human interaction.

The old Listener looked at the crowd of scared townsfolk with a flash of pity then looked up at Lilly. Her voice came again, more resolute this time.

"My name is Alasa and I was only a small child

the last time I saw that man."

She paused, as if building courage, then corrected herself .

"The last time I saw Thaldur."

Lilly knelt in front of her but before she could say anything, Alasa continued.

"A plague washed the life from the crops, cattle, water and eventually the people of Crossay when I was a little. At the time it was barely more than a village and so, so many people died…"

Her words trailed away and came back hollow, weaker.

"I lost my mother, father and brother to the plague." Her glassy eyes saw horrors no others could as she cast her thoughts back to a lifetime ago.

"The things people do in desperate times…Horrific things."

The group of townsfolk were all standing around in a crescent shape around the dias and the pew where Alasa sat.

She took a breath and with one more glance at the people stood around her, she said in a hollow voice

"You must understand, when there is no food, no hope and no answers people do desperate things, things they would never normally do if their lives and the lives of the ones they love were not in danger.

Before this city became the city she is today,

some 70 years ago, it was barely more than a village getting its footing on the world. A plague hit and it hit hard. It almost wiped what was a blossoming town off the map.
People turned to doctors for answers. They could not help, though they tried. After months of little food and increasing numbers falling to the sickness, all of them succumbed to the plague with the exception of one. A young man named Dr. Thaldur Rosencroft.
What was left of the starving, sick and dying village all turned to him for answers. Bless him..."

She took another moment of self reflection before continuing.

"He tried everything. He travelled out of the village to get help, food and other possible cures. All the while more died of the plague and starvation. Eventually he got so desperate he tried magic."

She looked around the room at the much younger faces and continued.

"Now, you must understand, this was a time where magic was not commonplace, especially not in our little village. A time and place when magic was something to be feared and distrusted as most things are that are misunderstood.
He was desperate to save this village and all the

people relying on him... Like I said, when people get scared and desperate they will do things you cannot even imagine but most of those need not be detailed for this tale.

Those who were left, yes I was a child but I was there, banded together and went to his home on the outskirts of town one night. It didn't take much for someone to get the crowd worked up. Not then.

We didn't thank him for risking his life for us or for comforting the dying in their final moments. No.

We turned on him for not giving us a cure. For trying magic out of his own desperacy after all other options failed.

Somehow, to the masses, everything was his fault. They wanted him dead, perhaps they thought the magic he was using was the cause. I heard some say he had created the plague with his magic so that he could practice further on the dying. Merely justification for what we did.

This wasn't true, he had a gentle soul... But I didn't stop them, I didn't tell them they were wrong. I just watched it happen."

She wiped a tear from her cheek with a shaky gnarled hand.

"The mob barred his doors and windows and burnt down his house with him, his wife and infant daughter inside." She continued.

The tension in the air of the temple was thick.

"After that, everything got worse, we were all left feeling hollow, not righteous. For the most part, it was just the same but without the doctor holding your hair while you threw up blood or bringing you what little food was in the village or even just checking in on you. What was left of the community was devoured by its own guilt. People either locked themselves away and died alone or turned on eachother. It didn't take long to turn to utter mayhem...carnage. Killing the doctor and his family was only one of the horrific acts that happened in those dark times. Only more occured in the days after his death. Thievery, plundering, murder... Even cannibalism."

She looked up at the tapestries hanging on the temple walls.
"I gave my life to Celuna after that day." She said more to the building than the people crowded around her.

"Prey tell, how is he out there rounding up people as you sit here telling your tale dear bard?" There was a deep bitterness in Vodius' voice like Lilly had never heard, she could see from the anger in his face that he had his own personal experiences with people ostracising magic wielders. She didn't interject.

Alasa didn't look at the elf, she stared down and nodded.

"I locked my doors and windows and awaited the fate I deserved. I wept and I listened to the sounds of a community turning on one another. After the scorched building finally stopped burning, I finally stopped hearing the phantom screams of their baby or the smell of burning flesh."

She took a breath and tried again, avoiding the dark rabbit hole yearning to be explored in the recesses of her memory.

"Days after, in the still of the night, we heard his cries. A sound I cannot describe to you. An agony so pure... Those who could stand, came out onto the street to look as he kicked through the charred door covered in ash and soot holding the corpse of his daughter. A tiny black figure that he cradled so desperately. The rage had gone from the mob, extinguished like the flames at the Rosencroft home. But Dr.Rosencroft's rage had only just been ignited and it was as pure as his agony. You could feel it as he cast his eyes over every doorway, every villager.
He didn't say a word. He bundled up the corpse of his wife and daughter and rode out of the village leaving us to our own fates.
You see, we later found out that he had procured the means to a teleportation device whilst in

discussion with arcane academics and would use this to consult with doctors, wizards and priests. To bring us food. It meant he could search further a field for potential remedies. He spoke to anyone he could, far and wide. To try and help us. The people who burned his wife and child alive…"

She buried her face in her hands and sobbed again, nobody came to her side. They just stared at her in silence. Eventually she gathered her composure and continued.

"Things only got worse from then but eventually the plague ran its course, though the village would never be the same again. I am the last from that time, the last who can tell this story. I had prayed to Celuna that Thaldur would be with his family and at peace."

She extended her arm and her wrinkled finger pointed out to the courtyard.
"Yet, that man sits atop his horse looking not a day older than the last day I saw him as a child. He still has the same hollow expression on his face but his eyes betray his rage. I can feel it."

Lilly looked at the figure on the horseback. She couldn't make out any details from here but something told her that Alasa was telling the truth.

CHAPTER 17 - PICKING UP THE PIECES

Kaln could feel soft blades of grass on his fingertips and the back of his neck. He could smell the warm spring air and hear birds chirping between the flecks of light coming through the tree canopy above him. He laid there peacefully witnessing nature's beauty for a moment, until a slender form leaned forward blocking out the shifting spots of sunlight. He didn't panic, he only felt peace as Aeathune's face appeared in his vision, only then did he feel her shape against him. She purred as she spoke, a purr that made his chest shake deep inside.

"Time to wake up, Warden." She purred as the dream began to slip away.

"I have done all I can for you though I could not save your eye." Kaln felt the cat-like tail wind itself up his leg and along his inner thigh. He tensed and she gave him a wicked smile with her delicate fangs showing. Her lazy eyes never moved from his.

She purred again, "Wake up warden. I have another gift for you".

As she said this he felt the temperature drop, the warm spring breeze turned into a cool damp draft. The speck of sunlight turned to dancing moonlight broken up by the Rua Tree's canopy. The soft grass was replaced with sharp stones in his hands and the chirps of the birds were drowned out by the falling waters.

He laid there for a long moment, staring at the moonlight dancing on the ceiling of the cave between the branches of the mother tree. He slowly brought a hand up to his face. Gingerly, he felt his cheek, the tacky blood was gone. He braced himself as his fingers probed towards his wounded eye. There was nothing there. His stomach sank as he let his hand drop back into the cool stones.

What would pah do?

Kaln thought, distracting himself before panic struck.

"Don't look at what tha's lost but what tha' kept and what tha's gained lad."

He convinced himself he could hear the words,

because it helped.

Kaln felt something in his hand that didn't feel like loose stone. He sat up slowly expecting his head to spin and pound in pain, but it didn't. He used his arm to help himself up and flinched expecting his shattered arm to scream in pain, but it didn't. He raised his hand to see what he was holding, it was the fang of Ursol amongst the pieces of gravel. The tooth was as long as his finger and incredibly sharp. He wrapped a leather binding around it and wore it around his neck. It was a victory only he could understand. It was a trophy he had earned. He lost an eye but he won the fight and the favour of Aeathune. Placing the tooth around his neck subtly changed something within him, he felt it deep in his soul, though he could not explain what the change was.

Kaln sat, amazed he wasn't in blinding pain. He looked down at his shattered arm, which now looked perfectly fine, with the exception of what looked like an acorn embedded in the skin of his fore-arm. He turned his hand over and twisted his wrist. No pain. He picked at the acorn for a moment before common sense told him it was probably best to leave the gift Arathune had given him in his arm.

He blew out a deep breath and stood. His balance was fine and he could see perfectly well. He rolled his shoulders and neck and turned to the

Rua Tree, he was much closer now. Only ten feet away. He could see what was causing the silver moonlight to shatter into a pale red light. He knew what he was looking at, his extra sense made that clear to him. He walked closer and knelt to inspect the marvel as his heart started to pound.

Amongst the white roots of The Mother Tree was a vicious looking crystal shard jutting out of the earth at a steep angle to a single point with a ragged edge. The crystal was translucent and as he looked deep into its depths, he could see shimmers of magical light dancing between the roots within it. The crystal itself was a wonder on its own but coming out of the ground at an opposite angle was a thick root of the Rua tree. It looked like the roots of the Rua tree had lanced out and pierced the mystifying stone. The pale white root was solid, straight and about the width of a wood axe handle.

The root met the crystal about half way up its length, creating an angular archway that came to Kaln's waist. Hundreds of tendril-like roots of varying thicknesses and lengths seemed to have burst from the root into, through and around the crystal. The two were fused.

He knew what he was expected to do. He grabbed the root at its base with both hands and pulled.

The root broke cleanly from the earth with a solid snap. Kaln strained, his muscles flexed as they reached their limit but the crystal didn't give. He held his grip and suddenly he felt the fang hanging from his neck begin to vibrate. At that moment he was bombarded with images of his battle with the bear lord Ursol, the mighty bear's fearsome roar blended with his own, he didnt know which was his and he liked it.

Bellowing, he heaved once more and the crystal broke cleanly in a loose crescent shape with a deafening crack. Kaln stepped back from the tree to look at his prize as the sundering of the crystal continued to echo around the cave around him. Kaln held in his hands an axe like no other.

The broken crystal edge was as sharp as any blade Kaln had honed, the opposite side to the blade was a savage spike and the haft of the axe was smooth and sturdy. A solid weapon that would put even dwarven craft to shame. Where the root had snapped under the earth, there was a slight angle at the end of it, useful for momentum Kaln knew from chopping trees in the forest.

He felt the weight of it as he swung it. It was perfectly balanced. He also realised he had been given a more subtle gift to supplement the last from Aeathune as the axe felt like an extension of his arm. He knew how it would behave when he swung it and he knew how to swing it as a weapon, not a tool.

This is it, he thought, *a weapon I can use to stop whatever darkness has crashed over this land like*

a breaking wave. He flourished the axe and a wave of exhilaration and confidence, for the first time, washed over him. There was only one thing missing from this perfect weapon, a name.
"Emmental." Kaln said aloud.

He raised the axe to his shoulder, tiny pale white vines lashed out from the axe and wrapped around him. He released his grip on Emmental and the vines tightened around his chest and shoulder, leaving the axe comfortably across his back.
Suddenly, he felt a low rumbling in his chest. Then he heard it. He steadied his footing as the tiny stones began to skitter and dance by his feet. He turned to face the great tree and saw that her branches were parting, twisting and groaning like the hull of an old ship. As the branches curled out of the way, they revealed a moonlit staircase to the stars and the moon beyond. Starlight washed into the cave from a single hole at the very top of the tree's reach. Kaln began to climb. He made his way up through the branches and as he did, he found pools where each of the huge branches connected to the tree. The pools reflected the light from above and shimmered like liquid silver.
It felt like days since he had eaten or drank anything. He paused to kneel and drink from one of the pools knowing beyond doubt that it would be safe. The liquid was cool and soothing to his

dry throat. He drank again, his thirst, hunger and exhaustion washed from his joints and muscles. The ripples in the pool calmed back to a mirror-like surface. In it, Kaln saw his face. It made him stop. How it had changed, weary though it was he could see his features had physically changed, his stubble had grown to a beard, he was covered in dirt and blood but that wasn't what made him pause. One of his eyes was now just an empty gaping socket, his other eye had changed too. His pupil had changed from that of a normal, human eye to a slit like that of Aeathune's cat-like eyes. He paused to fashion a makeshift eye patch using some leather strapping cut from his pack. As he took another look in the pool and positioned the patch, his mouth gaped open as anyone's mouth who is trying to manoeuvre the features of the face in a mirror does. In doing so he was struck with another change, though it was subtle he could see his fangs were longer than before. These were not like Aeathune's, which were needle-like points, his looked more canine. He knew his change was complete and that these were the last gifts to be given to him as Aeathune's Warden. What they meant, he knew would take more time to understand. He continued his climb into the moonlight, to the surface and to find his friends.

CHAPTER 18 - A WOUNDED SOUL

Lilly, like everyone else who had heard Alasa's story, stared out into the courtyard of the temple with a numbed expression. Now that she looked, she could see a second pile beyond the crowd of townsfolk and offerings. Corpses. Specifically, corpses of the guards who should have been at the destroyed gates, should have been protecting the city. The fleshy mound made her stomach turn as it brought back memories of Cornwalk. Her heart started to pound and she started breathing heavily, somewhere behind her there were sobbing sounds. She didn't care who or why. She was numb to everything except the single point of dull pain anchored to her heart that pulled her down a dark hole. Deeper and deeper she fell. She doubled over and grasped her knees as her

surroundings spiralled.
Not again...

Further she fell and harder she breathed as her world closed in around her. She barely noticed the soft footsteps nexts to her until a delicate hand adorned with more than a couple of expensive looking rings grabbed her hand and squeezed tightly. She squeezed back on the life line and looked up to see Vodius trying his best not to look uncomfortable as he tried to help her. The gesture was enough and she wiped the first tear from her eye before it had time to fall and snorted a desperate laugh that snapped her out of it. Before Vodius could move she grabbed a hold of him and hugged him tight. He stood there stiffly and gingerly patted her back.

"Thank you Vodius." She whispered into his chest. Then released her hug and turned back to the courtyard. She didn't look him in the eye but she heard him say from behind her, "Channel it, girl. Don't you dare give it power over you."

She forced herself to look again out to the courtyard. The enchantments were picking up every sound. The whimpers of children in the crowd, some asking for their parents, others just sobbing. The sounds of parents asking if others had seen their children in the crowd and people who had recognised loved ones in the pile of dead guards weeping. There was a louder, much clearer voice shouted with shaky confidence to the man on the horse.

"We have done as you asked, please, take your plunder and leave us!"

Thaldur dismounted from his horse and held out a tiny silver box that he withdrew from within his dark robes. He seemed to pause to inspect the delicate item in a moment of eerie silence until his attention was drawn back to the crowd. Then said in a voice that was cold and calculated,
"Yes. Yes you have done as I asked. We will soon be on our way and you can go back to living your lives." Even from here, the sound of it made Lilly's skin writhe.

Thaldur stepped over to the pile of magical trinkets and oddities that had been offered, raised the small metallic box and began to utter the magical words of a spell. As he did, the glow above the magical items seemed to thicken into a dense cloud above him that began to swirl and grew larger and larger until it was almost thirty feet wide. Even standing in the temple Lilly could smell almonds as the magical energies were being torn and wrangled. The courtyard was washed in swirling lights as the crowd huddled together in fear. Thaldur's words rang out clearly, though they didn't make sense to anyone who did not speak the ancient language he was using.
Vodius stepped forward to be beside Lilly. "It

would appear he is searching for the Rehlk Stones." He said in a curious voice.

The voice from before called out from the terrified crowd "Please! You have what you want! Think of the women and children, they have done nothing! Leave us in peace!"

Thaldur's chanting stopped suddenly. The swirling light stopped in a tight ball above him that was jerking and twitching like it was trying to escape. The temperature of the temple and the courtyard seemed to drop a few degrees as Thaldur turned to the crowd. In a voice so cold it was as a blade of ice, he said, "No, they don't deserve to be caught up in the folly of men." he paused and the silence grew thick and heavy.
"They *are* innocent," his voice was acidic and bitter.
"You would be astounded at what *innocent* people are capable of..." He hung on the word like it tasted foul in his mouth

In one violent action he dragged the thrashing magical mass above the cowering crowd and barked a dark and ancient word into the night sky driving the magical force down. The spell crashed down on hundreds of them like a liquid wave of black fire. It washed over them all. They did not burn but their agony seemed worse. There was no smoke or heat and yet they screamed and writhed as their life essence was drained. There was only silence as the last of them fell to the floor. Their bodies were not burned cinders, they were kissed by the darkest of magic. Now there were two piles of corpses.

Thaldur held up the small silver box and an essence much harder to see was drawn into it from the crowd. Like a fine pale mist driven by a strong wind. Only silence and bodies remained. Lilly and Vodius, along with those standing around them, stood in stunned horror as Vodius whispered the word, "Necromancy."

The pulling sensation at Lilly's heart twanged as she realised there was nothing she could do against such a force. They had come all this way and for what? To watch mass murder? To stand here scared? What can she do? What *is* within her power?

She noticed her hands and jaw were aching, hurting enough to snap her out of her own thoughts. They were both clenched so tight that she had to flex her fingers and roll her jaw.
"Where is Gleb?" She asked Vodius, sudden determination in her voice.

His eyebrow twitched slightly higher than normal, as it often did when he was offended.
"I do hope you haven't mistaken me for his keeper." He continued to look out to the courtyard like he was watching a horse show.

Lilly looked around for the goblin but couldn't see him. Frustrated, Lilly pushed her way past Vodius and others in the crowd to Alasa. She hadn't moved, hadn't watched what had happened. She just knelt staring at the floor. Lilly crouched down in front of her. Her voice commanded a response. "Does this city have a warning system for other cities? Runners? Fires? River message? Heaven forbid, magic?" the last was tainted with bitter sarcasm.

Alasa nodded and looked up at Lilly. "There is a stockpile of dried wood and oil containers at the peak of the highest building in Crossay. These act as a warning signal to Whitebluff and Mul'gur when lit."

Lilly paused a beat and snapped "Well?"
Alasa gave her a sad smile and said, "It is at the top of this temple but even with warning, it will not help them."

Lilly suppressed a snarl of disgust as she said "How do we get-". Suddenly there was a distant, hollow and metallic sound ringing out. The longer the crashing sound went on, the louder it got and the closer it seemed to be. Silence washed over the people hiding in the temple as the source of the awful sound showed itself. An empty metal barrel bounced down into the rafters up above then eventually smashed into

the pile of pews blocking the doors with a mighty crash. It was only when the echoing of the cacophony stopped that a second, more familiar noise was heard. Everybody watched as Gleb giggled all the way down from the rafters, down the canopy and padded over to Lilly giggling the entire time. Wisps of smoke swirled from his ears and the top of his head and embers still glowed on his shoulders. His sharp pointy teeth looked white in contrast to the scorch marks on his face as he stood grinning. He was obviously immensely proud of something he had done.
"Wots up?" he asked innocently.

"Where have you been?" Lilly couldn't help but soften her expression at the goblin's cheeky grin.

"Went for look around. Found some good burny bits." He tried to play off his excitement with a nonchalant shrug of his shoulders, though his eyes glistened like those of a child that has a secret to tell.

Lilly glanced up, she could see deep within the darkness of the rafters some distant amber light flickering "Did you-"

"Yep!" Gleb giggled, "Big fire!" his hands flailed in the air briefly to show just how big the fire was. Then he plonked himself down and fished out a mouldy sandwich from his pouch, dusted it off and began eating it. He paused only to pat out some of the embers which were beginning to take hold on his cloak.

"Well that saves you a job, doesn't it?" Vodius said, shaking his head while smirking.

Lilly stood and dragged Alasa to the front of the crowd to look out to the courtyard, the robed figures and Thaldur were all looking at the temple and its roof. They had moved the smaller pile of guard corpses onto the larger pile and now Thaldur was standing outside of the doors to the temple.
He had drawn back the hood of his black robes. Now Lilly could see the robes were covered in intricate silver symbols and shapes that she did not understand, though some made her feel uneasy just looking at them. His head was now exposed, revealing a bald head and face that was covered in intricate scars. The scars resembled to the shapes and symbols similar to those on his robes as flecks of starlight that peered between the clouds made them shimmer like silver. He was an attractive man, not the monster Lilly had expected, with delicate and angular features. What stood out most were his dark, ancient looking eyes, as cold as his voice. They reminded her of the eyes of a shark she had once seen caught off the coast. His gaze washed over the building and locked onto Alasa. He stared for a long moment. Lilly, still holding Alasa, felt her tremble and collapse under his gaze. Then, he

turned to speak to the robed figures. "Once the spell is complete and you have gathered as many as you can, join me at Whitebluff."

The voice was frigid and biting but not angry, if anything, it sounded frustrated and a little impatient.

They watched as the man walked over to his horse and mounted it. He gave one more glance around the courtyard, withdrew the tiny magical trinket and barked another dark word that didn't sound like it could have come from a human. A pale swirl of light plunged from the box into the pile of corpses making it pulsate and writhe like there was a great beast beneath it. Then he turned his horse towards the northern gate and disappeared into the night, leaving a handful of robed figures standing around the corpse pile.

They chanted more evil words as the mass of bodies pulsated and writhed, each time becoming more intense. With each throb the breaking of bones, tearing of clothes and flesh could be heard. The sound of sloshing fluids and deep lifeless groans as air was squeezed from crushed lungs resonated through the buildings.

Lilly's mind's eye flashed back to her father atop the pile in Cornwalk. It showed him writhing in pain atop this pile. She stood there lost, trying to force herself to breath. The listener in a crumpled pile at her feet.

Not again...
Her hands began to glow with a pale light and searing pain coursed through her hands and up her arms, she dropped her father's staff and curled her hands up in agony as she fell to dismay. All she could see was pale light. All she could smell was almonds. All she could feel was burning pitch in her veins. But what she could hear was Vodius' voice, masterful in a way she hadn't heard before, in a way she didn't think the placid elf was capable of.

"Don't you dare give it power over you girl! The power is yours to command." He shouted at her through the haze of her crushing emotions. There was a hint of fear in his voice she noticed.

Suddenly she was incontrol enough to follow the teachings Vodius had given her when they had time alone on their journey. Techniques to channel the emotion and power into a place in her mind where she could control it. She went there, she went to the apple grove with her father and she was a child again. All around her was an ambient pale light but this time it wasn't overwhelming, it wasn't all consuming. She didn't feel like she would implode. She would stay with her father until she felt ready to peer through the pale light, but not just yet. She did miss her father so much.

Vodius looked down at Lilly's prone form in the foetal position wrapped around her father's staff.

The light was dancing up and down the staff now. She seemed to be controlling it. *Clever girl.* He thought and looked up at the stunned and scared townsfolk staring at him.

"If you intend on making it through tonight, I suggest you continue to barricade those doors and give her a wide berth while you work." he said as he covered her with her cloak.

"Oh, and you may want to tend to the elder listener." He gestured a dismissive wave in the direction of Alasa's form and paced over to Gleb. He passed him a list scribbled on a piece of paper. "Gleb, I require an assistant who can aid me whilst I attempt a new spell. Can I count-" The goblin stood beaming up at Vodius, wiping the remnants of the sandwich from his face with the back of his hand.

"Very well. Pay close attention" Vodius continued, passing him a small pouch.

He stepped into the center of the room, Gleb following, looking wide eyed into the pouch.

Vodius took a moment and with a quiet utterance of an arcane word, the dust and dirt from the immediate area was blown away with a warm blast of almond scented air. The crowd had burst into action at Vodius' comment, giving him space and a clean area to begin his work.

Two of the younger listeners hurried over to Alasa as activity surged in the people taking refuge in the temple. There was a busied moment until a sudden scream of woe rang out at the top of the stairs leading to the temple.

"Shes dead, Alasa is dead!" one of the listeners cried out kneeling by her form.

"...Cold to the touch already" She said in a quieter tone, not meant for anyone listening.

The other listener covered Alasa with a blanket. Many of the townsfolk were struck hard by this and began to weep and pray to Celuna.

Vodius didn't even pause whilst drawing out a complex arcane symbol on the floor around his feet but he glanced up from his spellwork in time to see them cover Alasa's face, he noticed she had a peaceful expression on her face.

How can she be cold already? Vodius thought as he pondered over the stare Thaldur had given her.

Surely not, surely it was just the fright?

His brow furrowed. He pressed on with his work and for the next ten minutes the temple was a hive of activity. People were moving the remaining pews to block the doors. The listeners were moving Alasa's body to one of the rear rooms. Gleb followed instructions from Vodius, drawing further runes on the stone tiles around those which Vodius had drawn and burning small amounts of mundane, rare and wondrous components at key locations on the runes drawn on the ground. Meanwhile Vodius had spent his time drawing arcane symbols in the air, one either side of the long front wall of the temple then a third in the center. His hand gestures seemed to drag the outer symbols which glimmered softly, bearly visible with a blue light at either end of the wall to the larger symbol that hovered in front of him. Once the symbols were drawn, Vodius uttered a final arcane phrase, with this the spell was complete. A web-like net, between the two anchor points and the central symbol could be seen momentarily covering the entire wall until, like the runes, they faded from sight. Leaving a fading crackling sound and the scent of the arcane. The townsfolk gasped at the grandeur of the spell. Vodius turned to praise Gleb on the part he played in completing the spell but realised the goblin was keenly watching something outside.

Gleb pointed beyond the windows, magical wards and listening spells and said one word.

"Orc."

CHAPTER 19 - A GLORIOUS DEATH

Kruul was sprinting as fast as his legs could carry his muscular mass through the shadows of the alleyway. His keen senses could hear the rats scurrying from his path as he gained speed down the dark, dank walkways between the warped looming buildings. He was in shadow but he could see the wretched cloaked ones standing around the pile of human corpses at the edge of the courtyard illuminated by the street lanterns. The alley twisted the sounds of their dark chants into hollow echos that would have staggered a less determined mind. His heart pounded in anticipation of the battle to come, he felt a grin creep across his face.

Cleanse the filth.

He drew both his axes. The worn leather bindings, crow feathers and curved blades reminded him of his tribe and his purpose here. The feel and weight of his father's axes reassured him, letting him know that his ancestors were with him in this. He threw them with a precision only a battle hardened warrior could, at the backs of the two closest to him. Before the axes had even found their inevitable target he lurched from the shadows through the air howling at a third. He landed with his weight on his shoulder where it was perfectly placed to carry the third robed figure to a skull-crushing death as it was dashed against the wall absorbing his weight and momentum. All three of his targets were slain within a second of the assault beginning. Their bodies lay broken and spasming in impossible ways.

Two more.

He pushed off the jerking figure as its twitching corpse slid down the blood soaked wall. There was resistance as he pushed off the dead creature. There was a suction where its head used to be, strands of unnatural viscera attached to his blood soaked arm. The smell of the creature's rancid blood only pushed him deeper into a battle rage. He jerked his arm away and the alien tendrils gave up their grip on him. The snapping sounds were satisfying.

The others were moving to confront him now,

they screeched empty cries like the haunting screams of a wounded animal. He jumped into a roll and recovered one of his axes from the spine of one of the other dead cloaked ones with a satisfying crack and stood to throw it directly at the cowled face of one of the last standing foes. The axe left his hand, he knew the creature was already dead.

One more.

Before he could pull back his extended arm from the axe throw and begin his assault on the fifth, a tentacle lashed around his extended arm and bit deep into his flesh. He had time to watch the axe sail through the air and imbed deeply into the shadowy hood of his fourth victim. Its charging, shambling form was brutally jerked off of its feet.

The tentacle yanked him to face the last. With one of its arms now a pustule covered tentacle, the other was a wretched twisted arm that looked more like a claw. The skin was black and decrepit, there was little flesh on its wiry arm. Its fingers were curled and tipped with vicious pale claws. It spat and hissed magical dark curses at him. Flecks of angry purple light began to gather in the clawed hand.

Got to move quickly.

Kruul grabbed the scaly tentacle with both hands and bit down hard as he twisted the flesh. His orcish fangs slashed through the fleshy arm and slime that tasted of putrid fish filled his

mouth as the tentacle writhed up his forearm. It stunned the monster enough for Kruul to pull on the torn tentacle and jerk the creature closer. It stumbled forward trying to keep its footing and Kruul grabbed the head of the thing with both hands and squeezed with all his might. His huge muscles flexed as the creature sputtered a muffled cry. Its feeble arm, clawing at his battle scarred arms weakly, not even able to break the orc's skin. Putrid blood poured from Kruul's mouth as he bellowed a victorious roar over the sound of the skull breaking in his hands. It fell limply to his feet, only the ruined tentacle still thrashing around.
Breathing heavily, Kruul grimaced and spat on the corpse of the cloaked one.
Disappointing.

Kruul tore the other part of the tentacle from his arm and wrapped his forearm in a bandage made from the robes of one of the dead. The nearby corpse pile was still writhing and pulsing and the bodies now seemed to be mangled and twisted. He didn't understand the darkness of what he was looking at but he had become numb to it. He placed his foot on the back of one of the creatures and yanked his axe free. He noted how frail the ribs were as they cracked under his weight. He then pulled the axe from the face of the other creature. As he pulled on the axe, the cowl fell back, revealing what looked like a beak with a bulbous skull and bulging eyes. It was only for an instant before the body of the creature dispersed into a thick oily smoke that seemed to seep out of the cloak and linger there. He stepped back unsure of what was happening, he noticed all five of the creatures were also now swirling pools of smoke. He stepped away and watched as they coalesced and were sucked in by the pulsing writhing mass of bodies.

Fire.
He thought, looking at the street lanterns flickering uneasily around the courtyard. Before he could reach the closest he noticed townsfolk watching him from the gaps in their window shutters. No. Not him, the pile. The hair on his neck stood on end and he tensed and turned to see the spell holding the twisted pile of corpses come to its finale.

The monstrosity was as wide as two carts, it was thirty feet long and reared up almost as tall as some of the buildings. Hundreds of human arms and legs jutting out from its bulging flanks. All of them scrambled wildly to move the mass. At the tip of its tail was a bulbous mass of heads, most of them were flayed, a barely identifiable cluster of deep reds and bone white. Some still had enough skin intact to identify tormented faces, black ichor pouring from their empty eye sockets as it swayed lazily. All of them clustered around a wiry black tendril. There were human spines protruding through the torn human skin which covered the back of the monster like a quill boar. Kruul could see the stretched forlorn features on the faces that made up the skin of the creature. On its chest, embedded within the warped and twisted flesh, were the breastplates of the fallen guardsmen. Fifty or so plates covered the mass of beating hearts that could be seen throbbing beneath them. It turned to look at him. On the upper part of the mass were hundreds of eyes, some bulging, some hanging on exposed nerves and some sleepy looking slits barely able to open between the folds of skin and flesh. They spotted the head of the creature like angry pustules, each bloodshot eye blinking and searching independently in an un-easing display. Its mouth was a quivering black hole lined with a swirling whirlpool of human teeth, it drooled in anticipation, thick dark slime pouring out of it. It bellowed a cry so deep and sorrowful it could only be felt, not heard. Kruul's chest rattled at the void of sound that trembled the loose stones around his boots. The metallic smell of blood and mutilated flesh mixed with the sickly sweet smell of almonds and dark magic hung thickly in the air. He was no stranger to gore and violence but the monster turned his stomach as he stepped uneasily away. His resolve was shaken for the first time since he was a child. He staggered, looking up at the spawn of black magic.

The thing reared back its head like a viper ready to strike, Kruul recognized the body language and threw himself to one side as the monster struck at him. His warrior instincts kicked in, breaking him from his terror. The violence of its lunge carried it most of the length of the courtyard; it slid hard and side-long into the temple as it tried and failed to correct its direction. Statues and pillars fell under its form. Kruul looked up at the huge building, though it was not the same as what his people used to represent Celuna; he recognised the imagery.
The finesse of an enraged bull.
He winced as he watched the creature barrel into the temple, unable to control its mass and momentum. Huge chunks of the front wall collapsed and as he stood, preparing to run from the falling building, he saw glimmers of pale blue light as the creature tore itself from the ruin to find him. The building still stood.
It lashed and wriggled, human arms and legs grasping and clawing to find purchase in the debris. Finally it righted itself and hundreds of eyes snapped to him. All that could be heard in the blistering moment of silence was the creaking of leather gloves against the bindings on his axes as Kruul prepared. With more fury than before the monster snaked towards him with incredible speed, blazes of sparks flew high into the air where the guardsmen breastplates

were dragged across the cobblestones on the creature's chest. The sound of screeching metal on stone and a small army charging came down upon the orc. He waited and watched, ready to avoid the viper strike, but it didn't happen. Instead the thing threw its mass to one side, coming to a sudden stop and throwing Kruul off. He realised too late that it had thrown all of its momentum into the skullclub on the end of its tail. He sailed through the air, his chest washed with a deep and dull pain, weightless and gasping for air. He didn't find it, instead he felt a fresh pain break over his back as he crashed into a pile of crates just inside an alleyway. He found his breath as he threw pieces of wood off him and got to his feet. Already he could feel tremors in the ground as the monster charged to gain its prize. He spat blood and looked out on the courtyard to see the evil coming straight for him.

Not in the open.

He hooked the hand axes on his waist and ran as fast as he could into the darkness of the alleyway. It was only as he started to gain momentum did he hear the large mass behind him crash into wooden crates, planks and outhouses. They splintered and caved under its weight. He pushed on, leaping over gateways and dipping under clotheslines. Anything to slow the thing down, to give him time to plan. It was right behind him, he could feel the deep bellow of the thing

on his back and the scratching of nails on stone as they grasped at the floor and walls of the alleyway. Up ahead a street lamp illuminated a tight corner. He pressed on, throwing his weight up towards the wall, took a pace or two up the wall and across to the other wall and leapt onto the roof of a shanty hut built onto the back of a building. Kruul threw himself as far as he could knowing the monster was turning the corner right behind him. He rolled to a stand and turned to see the flesh worm crash into the corner, unable to match his agility or manoeuvre properly in the tight alley. It crashed hard and the wall it hit gave way, exposing a couple hiding in their home. They barely had time to scream as the worm plucked them from their bedroom and swallowed them like a swan. Kruul watched their thrashing mass go down the gullet of the beast and their screams were silenced. It turned to him again, somehow the creatures mangled inhuman features managed to read "Where were we?" as it started to move towards Kruul. He started to run again and from the corner of his eye he saw a small human child peer out from behind a rotten pile of crates as he passed.
Run fool.
He ran a few more paces but could not hear footsteps behind him, his instincts told him to keep running, his mind agreed but his feet slowed to turn and help. He drew his axes and saw the child frozen in fear as the maw of the

worm plunged down on her. Kruul grimaced and ran at the monster, it swallowed the child mercilessly as it had with the others and charged at Kruul with an inaudible roar. As the worm lunged at the orc with its bloodied gaping mouth, Kruul threw himself flat on the ground, under the monster. He dragged both axes down every inch of the monster that he passed. Sparks of metal on metal were all he could see at first, then vibrant red and pink as the axes tore down the flank of the worm. His heart pounded hard, he held on tight to the axes as they gained purchase in the flesh. He slid to stop in a tangle of twisted legs and arms grasping and kicking blindly at him. The creature was too big to turn around between the buildings, Kruul realised as he hacked his way out of the thicket of limbs. The club at the end of its tail slammed from wall to wall causing stones to fall and upper floors to sag. He knew he couldn't get past it easily but he could climb on the creature's back.

He lept up and darted between the spine spears jutting from its back. Its flesh under his feet was moving and stretching. He glanced down to see the eyeless harrowed face of an elderly woman as he hacked his way through the spines. The monster bucked and writhed like a wild mustang as he climbed. Eventually he reached the top of its head. The buildings on either side of them were beginning to collapse from the monster's thrashing.

Kruul raised both his axes and started to hack down with all of his might. Hacking into the faces of men, women and children. He roared as he swung his axes, as he felt the spray of blood up his bare chest, as he felt chunks of flesh rain down around him. He roared.
Suddenly the worm bucked almost upright and twisted in the air. Kruul managed to throw himself on top of the debris caused by the flailing tail as the thing came down to face him. The buildings were collapsing now. He ran back towards the courtyard. He felt only a moment's grace before he heard it break through the stone, lintels and rubble. Light spilled out of the ruined buildings to illuminate the blood pouring down its face. Kruul was getting tired, his lungs burned as he gulped deep breaths of air.
This had indeed been a glorious battle.
He saw another alleyway, hidden by shadow the first time he ran down here, he slid to turn just in time. It was more cluttered with detritus and refuse than the other alleyways but he knew fighting in the open was certain doom. Another corner. A dead end.
Other than its three walls, its only defining feature was its pungent reek of piss. Kruul grimaced and turned with his axes drawn. He listened to the worm as it clawed and smashed its way to him.
This is it.
It exploded around the corner, its eyes searching

for him. He wasn't hiding. It reared up ready to crush the orc into a piss soaked grimy dead end. Just as it reached the peak of its height a figure appeared from the rooftop above it. In the figure's hands was a huge axe, its wicked blade glimmered red, more like a gem than metal. The figure threw itself from the shadows of the rooftops down the chest of the monster with a war cry that sounded more like a bear than a man. The axe dug deep and sliced through the breast plates on the chest of the worm like they were made of wicker. The mass of beating hearts were exposed and the man with the red axe was knelt as the base of the worm. Kruul wasted no time. He ran and leapt off the back of his newfound ally and drove his hand axes into the cluster of beating hearts. He too used his axes to slow his fall as he sliced open the monster's hearts. He landed on his feet but didn't even have time to take in his surroundings before the man with the red axe threw them both to the corner of the alley way. The death of the monster was as hideous as its birth. It screeched and lashed uncontrollably as bones cracked and snapped. Skin tore and blood flowed filling the alleyway until there was nothing but a huge pile of mangled bodies and a thick oily smoke disbursing into the night air. And the two warriors.

CHAPTER 20 - THE ENEMY OF MY ENEMY

Kaln was on his feet first. He looked down on the orc, who was still catching his breath and gathering his senses after the battle. Part of him wanted to grab Emmental and cleave him in two. A wiser part of him knew he didn't have all the facts and to blame the orcs for everything that had happened was foolhardy. Only when he held out a hand to help the orc to his feet did he realise the brutish looking orc already had his hands on his axes, probably thinking similar thoughts. There was a quiet moment as each assessed the other. Kaln broke the stillness with a nod to his hand which had remained outstretched to the orc. The orc's meaty paw grabbed Kaln's hand and almost pulled him off his feet as he stood to look down on him. Kaln stepped back to look up at the warrior.

He was head and shoulders taller than Kaln. His heavy shoulders were meaty and broad, he was barrel chested and every visible inch of his skin was covered in toned muscle beneath deep black and red tribal tattoos and pale green and white battle scars. A race bred for battle. He had a short, dark grey strip of hair down the middle of his head, at the back this trailed into a long cluster of braids adorned with beads and feathers from some unknown fantastical bright red and white bird. He wore the pelt of a monstrous grey wolf as a cloak, the head of which rested on one of his shoulders, its yellow teeth glistening in a vicious defiant grin. Thick hide breeches and heavy set boots, obviously designed for the harshest terrain, covered his lower half. He wore a dark leather belt that seated the hooks which held both of his hand axes either side of his waist. The axes looked savage, harsh and well used as they dangled, seated at his hips. His strong jawline was covered in a thick, short and dark beard. The grizzly dark facial hair of the orc emphasised his huge lower fangs which jutted up from his lower lip. There was wisdom in the pale blue eyes that assessed Kaln for a moment before speaking.

"My name, 'es Kruul." In a gruff voice that rolled the common tongue with a thick mountain tribe accent. Even so, the way he said it sounded stunted, like he was not used to introducing himself this way.

Kaln returned the favour with a nod "My name is Kaln Grey. You fought well. Why are you-"

Shutter doors creaked open above and along the upper levels of the walls flanking them. A young man, pale with fear poked his head out into the gloom and peered down at the two. In a quiet, almost questioning tone at first he shouted down "Roku...Roku..Roku" more shutters opened, more silhouettes looked down on them, joining in the chant "Roku! Roku!"

Kruul reached for his axes, his body language had changed to that of a cornered beast. Kaln held out a hand in a gesture of placation. "They mean you no harm, it is a gesture of thanks."

Kaln stepped back, giving the orc space.

"Roku, means 'teh thank?" Kruul asked, looking confused "They owe me 'nae thanks. I will leave." He turned to climb the mound of corpses and down the alleyway towards the Northern entrance to the city.

Kaln let him pass and once they were beyond the corpses and rubble, walked beside him. There was no conversation for some time as Kaln found himself surprised how little the great pile of corpses had affected him. Or the way it had been twisted by dark magic. Was he numb to it? Did he not care anymore? Was it adrenaline or another subtle gift from Aeathune? If it was, could you call it a gift?

As they walked, more and more shutters and doors opened in the dim light and the calls of "Roku!" could be heard. Kaln almost had to shout over the cheering and occasional whistling as they walked towards the welcoming lantern light and open air of the courtyard of the Temple Celuna.

"Roku is a dwarven term for 'family', although since the dwarves, elves and humans came to these harsh lands, we use it as a more general term for solidarity and unity. Kind of like 'We're in this together'" Kaln explained.

Kruul paced determinedly on through the shadows and debris.

Kaln continued, "Look, I need to ask you about Cornwalk...", he watched the orc's body language, looking for a tell.

Kruul turned up his lip in a sneer and grunted, that was all. He kept his eyes on the windows and openings above.

This nonchalance kicked up the embers of a fire of rage in Kaln and he grabbed the orcs' shoulder just as they emerged into the courtyard. Kruul turned on him with such speed and ferocity Kaln staggered back. Kruul pushed on, his formidable size towering over Kaln as he backed into a wall on the outer circle of the courtyard.

"Ask yer questions, Kaln but dun'nae be offended if ye be given a straight 'n truthful answer." He growled in a low grumble.

Kaln never was a fan of bullies, especially bullies

that were bigger than him. He pushed off the wall, straightened his back and pushed his face into the face of the orc.

"Don't mistake my pleasantries and welcoming demeanour for fear, Kruul." Kaln spat the words. "Answer my question in truth and you are free to leave." Kaln found himself growling back at the orc as the two stood inches apart. Kaln saw a flicker of something skim across the orc's face for an instant and then was gone again. Respect?

Kruul relaxed and with a nod said "Aye, that's fair. One question, make it snappy. Least I can do fer yer help back there."

He put his hands on his hips and looked around the courtyard waiting for the human's question. Distant sounds of cheering, whooping and chanting "Roku!" coming from around the courtyard and alleyways began to die down.

"What happened in Cornwalk?" Kaln said as neutrally as possible. His fists were clenched.

"That Dark One ye call 'Thaldur' snaked his way from the cracks of the mountains my clan called home. We were given 'nae choice but to fight him or flee. The only way our entire clan could get away meant going through yer village o' Cornwalk."

His eyes flicked to Kaln's clenched fist and he continued, unfazed.

"We approached the people in the village with our weapons sheathed. We waved and hoped maybe we could pass unharmed. We were 'nae enemies nor allies, after all. Unfortunately, even with children, the sick and elderly in tow, they saw orcs and assumed it was a raid." He shook his head.

"They came at us with weapons drawn, moor' out of fear than fury I 'thenk. It was 'nae my intent for any 'teh die but we could'nae turn and run and we could'nae talk to ye humans, so we were forced to cut our way through."

He sighed, a long drawn out painful sigh of frustration and anger.

"I lost many that day, too many. As we fought, Thaldur's forces fell upon the village. You humans at least had the sense teh at least fight with us against these monstrosities." He gestured to the crumpled cloaks on the floor.

"But they were 'nae warriors and there was 'nae victory for us that day. I took the survivors 'o my clan and fled. We were hounded day 'an night until almost all 'o my people were lost. I was their leader, Their Clan Lord and I failed them."

A look of shame washed over his harsh features.

"They demanded Rum'zoka 'an now, here I am, hunting down Thaldur as they cling 'teh life 'oot there in the forests. Once the largest and mightiest of all the mountain clans, now The Pale Tusks are 'lettle 'moor than a desperate tribe with nae Lord." He shrugged and started to turn away.

"Rum'zoka?" Kaln said blankly, still putting the pieces together.

"Clan tradition, enforced upon a leader who has failed them. Either I contest the remaining Banner Lords in mortal combat until I am slain or there is none left to stand against me and I regain my position as Chieftain... Or, as I have chosen, banishment from the clan." Kruul explained as he began to walk away.

"Wait. I believe you." Kaln said to the orc's back.

"I dun'nae care if ye believe me." He continued to walk.

"I was there that day too." Kaln said coldly. The words seemed to hang in the air. Kruul stopped walking.
"I lost everything that day too. But I found a handful of people who want to put a stop to Thaldur, like you do. For the same reasons you do. You might think you're alone in this and if that's what you want, I will leave you to your own death, but you could do much more by our side."

Kruul's response was snatched away as his and Kaln's attention was drawn to the hurried footsteps echoing across the courtyard, coming from the temple. They turned to see Lilly and Gleb running towards them in the low mist that had formed since nightfall. Kaln knew it was them the second he saw their small shapes. Gleb's floppy ears and excited giggling gave them away instantly. Kaln raised a hand to greet them and managed "These are my frien-" before Lilly bolted past him at a full sprint. He started to shout to her but was struck in his gut by Gleb, whose legs flailed from Kaln's waist as he spun to stop Lilly's assault on the orc.

She screeched with Kaln's tiny dagger, Cheddar glinting as she threw herself through the air at Kruul. Kruul caught her by the wrists and used her momentum to spin them both around and pin her to the ground with his massive weight. She struggled, writhed and screamed in frustration.

"Fucking orc bastard! She shouted and spat at the orc. Kruul roared in Lilly's face, his huge jaw and fangs looking more like a predator that could have engulfed her head. Though not as intimidating as the orc, she screamed back with just as much fury.

Kaln ran over to the struggle as quickly as he could with his new excitable belt.

"Stop! Both of you!"

Lilly shot Kaln a look of rage.

"These bastards raided my village, killed our friends…My father!" Her hands started to glow illuminating the mist in which she and Kruul were laid in.

"These orc scum tried to rape me!" she screamed. Pale light washed through the low mists. The two were engulfed in a pool of pale golden light that danced through the mists like lightning through tempered storm clouds.

Before Kaln could do or say anything, Kruul dragged Lilly to her feet, the sound of the tiny blade clattering to the floor as the light faded.

"Us orcs, are all the same, aye? So 'yer sayin' it's safe to make the same assumptions about all humans? All goblins?" Kruul shook her to stop her wriggling. She fell silent at his words.

"My clan did 'nae raid yer village, if we had ye'd all be dead. We tried to escape the dark one but 'you humans' attacked us. Yer people fought with us in the end but it 'were too late."

He loosened his grip on her wrists and she fell on her feet, looking up at him defiantly.

"I will 'nae mourn the ones you lost, nor apologise for what you experienced. Me and my people lost as much as you."

Lilly was stunned, processing what she heard.

"Liar! I saw it!" she shouted desperately.

Kaln put a hand on her but she shrugged it off. He said in a calming voice "What did we see that day, Lilly? Gleb's story lines up with Kruul's."

Gleb stopped hugging Kaln, plopped to the ground nodding at Lilly.

Kaln waved a lazy hand to Kruul

"That's his name by the way. Kruul."

Kruul, pacing away the adrenaline paused to nod his head at Lilly.

"And he did just save this city from many more deaths." Kaln said thoughtfully.

"Lilly, given the circumstances, you did

incredibly well not to incinerate yourself and our big green fellow here. Well done indeed!" Vodius was suddenly stood by Kaln, inspecting him like a piece of artwork. Everyone jumped. Gleb screamed.

"What the devil happened to you Kaln? You're a changed man I can sense it, also you appear to have lost an eye… But what you have gained seems much more intriguing…"

Lilly snapped out of her thoughts and for the first time looked at Kaln's face without the red mist.

"Your eye!" she whispered as she ran to him and held his face.

He smirked, flashing a pointed fang.

"Better to have two, I guess, but I traded it for a few other things. I'll explain later." He looked pointedly at Kruul.

"These are the others. Are you with us or not?"

Kruul wiped a big paw across his jaw and stopped to look at each of the group.

"I've two conditions." He grunted

"Name them." Kaln said.

Kruul gave a toothy grin.

"First off, I'd like to say how your words have wounded me deeply. I may not look it, but I am a sensitive soul, A delicate flower." The words dripped with sarcasm.

"I think an apology is in order. Secondly and most importantly, I get your axe if you fall."

He fired a playful grin at Kaln who shrugged his shoulders with a smirk. "If I die, I won't need it anyway." Kaln replied. He felt the vines tighten ever so slightly.

Lilly scratched her neck, she was fierce but not too proud to apologise. After a long moment and in a quiet voice, she said flatly "I'm sorry I tried to kill you. I-"

Kruul patted her on the arm playfully, the grin still spread on his face.

"Nae bother lassy, I've seen bears fight with less aggression than you threw at me. Ye don't have teh explain 'yerself and dun'nae expect it of me. We've all done things to be here we wished we did 'nae have to do. As long as our enemy is 'teh same. Just make sure ye point that fury at 'thes Thaldur."

Lilly's body language screamed impotent frustration and anger and light fluttered in the mist around her clenched fists.

Kalns voice was flat as he said "We killed an orc, infact, we killed the orc that tried to rape Lilly. I would do it again if I had to."

Kruul's eyebrows raised at Kaln's honesty and he said "Well, if an orc, or any other tried to do that to me or my chieftess, I'd have done the same."

Kruul seemed to assess the tension in the group and after a sigh said, "Look, either you take what our people did 'teh each other personally, which would make us enemies."

He shrugged his bulky shoulders and continued.

"Or we work together 'teh stop 'thes Thaldur who caused, and is still causing, all thes' mayhem.

Your choice but let 'thes be the end of it either way."
His voice commanded attention and respect. It was obvious, at least at some point in the past, that he was a clan lord or chieftain as he claimed. Before it could become a discussion, Kaln said "We need all the help we can get, especially with your skills. Roku." With an absolute finality.
Gleb nodded enthusiastically "Yep Yep!"
Vodius nodded his head to nobody in particular. "You know, I've never seen an orc in combat until today. Truly an impressive specimen…" he tapped a finger on the tip of his chin until suddenly he seemed to be aware of the others around him.
"Ah yes, I presume you will want a cut." and held out a pouch of gold.
Kruul swatted the pouch of coins from the elf's hand. The pouch didn't hit the ground, Vodius flicked his finger towards himself and the pouch, levitating inches from the ground, moved nimbly to his waist without a sound. Vodius seemed unfazed by Kruul's obvious frustration. "Very well, suit yourself." Vodius said through his nose as he began to inspect Kaln's axe with distracted interest.
"Roku." Lilly said stubbornly, looking at the big orc.

The group made their way back into the warm embrace of Celuna's temple. As they passed the large pillars of the temple they saw groups of people that had gathered at the entrance, they were already organising a militia to man the gates and send riders out for aid. As Kruul passed them their frenzied planning stopped. There was a silence that took the crowd, causing the group to stop and look upon Kruul's broad back. Kruul, who kept climbing the stairs of the temple, showed indifference in his gait.

"Kruul." Kaln's voice broke the silence. The big orc turned to see the crowd of people kneeling before him, all except Kaln and the others who were looking at the crowd.

They began to chant "Roku, Roku, Roku."

Kaln nodded to the orc as his own sign of thanks and even Lilly seemed to look at Kruul slightly less harshly. Kruul turned to the kneeling mass and waved a dismissive hand "Ye dun'nae owe me any tha- roku. Tend to yer gates and bury yer dead, I'll be gone by morn."

Kaln stepped up and turned to the people. "He's got a point, man your gates and send riders in the morning to Whitebluff for aid."

Vodius spoke up next, "I believe it pertinent that nobody goes to Whitebluff, under any circumstances. Don't worry Kaln, we will update you shortly."

Now he too turned to the crowd "If you send for aid, I would suggest sending riders out to Mul'gur."

He pointed high up above them to the pyre burning atop the temple "The beacon has been lit, hopefully, they will expect your rider's arrival and send aid. Now we must be on our way." He ushered the group inside the temple. They could hear the cityfolk had taken heed from their warnings as they arranged for riders to go West to Mul'gur.

The remainder of the evening was spent in Celuna's temple. In one of the smaller rooms in the back, the group gathered by the fireplace as they spoke. Gleb started with a somewhat over-embellished reenactment of what he saw Kruul do to the monstrosity in the courtyard and some more which was almost definitely made up. Kaln filled in the blanks from what he could see from the rooftops. Kruul didn't engage, he was sharpening his axes in the corner of the room. Only the slightest glimmer of a smirk on his face. Lilly told Kaln, Kruul and Gleb Alasa's tale and how they had heard Thaldur say he was going North to Whitebluff. Gleb wasn't paying attention and was, instead, throwing tomes from the temple into the fire.

Kaln told the others his tale, Gleb listened to every detail like a child listening to a village elder telling the deeds of ancient heroes. Vodius was taking notes and asking for specifics throughout the story. Kruul stood behind the others who were seated and listened to every word intently.

Kaln noticed a look in his eye, it was what he'd seen before. Respect.

They prepared themselves for the journey to come and ate what food the listeners could spare. Through the night, they could hear the townsfolk of Crossay rebuilding their wounded city. After everything they had been through, they didn't give in to despair. They picked themselves up and rebuilt. None of the group could tell if it was because it was the first safe place they had rested in a long time, maybe it was being in the temple or maybe the sound of the people's spirit refusing to be broken by the darkness. Whatever it was, they all slept well.

CHAPTER 21 - AN UNEXPECTED PATH

Kaln awoke to a sound he hadn't realised he had missed for the last few days alone until that very moment, laughter. In addition to Vodius' quiet laugh and Lilly's snorting, there was a new laugh. A raspy, boisterous and infectious laugh. Kaln opened his eyes to see Gleb holding what looked like a huge fang in both hands as he finished off his story, dramatically illuminated by the firelight.

"So I put it in my pack and I ran!"

Kruul bellowed a hearty laugh that took him some time to recover from, each time it sounded as though he had control over it, he burst out laughing. His laugh was so infectious it set the others off laughing again too. The moment of levity was indulged by all. Kaln found himself laughing along too as he stood to join the others. He sat across from the big orc who wiped a tear from his eye and passed Kaln a bowl of stew, shaking his head with a big grin on his face.

Kruul said "All 'thes time Domkur, Lord of the Black Tooth tribe was telling other clan lords he lost one of his fangs in a fight with a troll!"

There was just enough time for Kruul to replay Gleb's story in his mind before he broke into laughter again.

Gleb was on his back still clutching the fang, his legs kicking in the air as he giggled uncontrollably.

Kruul took a breath, "Ye know, by the laws of the Black Tooth tribe, you could have claimed rights to be their chieftain."

Glebs giggling stopped. He sat bolt upright and looked at Kruul with a serious expression on his face. The two stared at each other for half a beat and broke out into renewed laughter punctuated with the occasional pig snort from Lilly laughing and holding her stomach.

It felt good to be around his friends again and he could tell from the energy in the room they felt the same. Kaln hadn't asked how long the orc had been alone but he was sure Kruul was happy for the company. The morning was light hearted and jovial as they ate and spoke of anything except the night before. It felt good to allow themselves a temporary reprieve from the horrors they had to face. It was over too quickly and they found themselves standing on the stairs of Celuna's Temple looking out over the courtyard. It was like looking out over an ant colony, a hive of activity as the people of Crossay rebuilt and fortified her defences. There was a warm breeze that took the chill out of the air and even the sun shone down on the city.

"Today will be a better day." Kaln said to himself.

"Aye, let's hope so, lad." Kruul agreed.

Kaln didn't mind being called 'lad', it somehow reminded him of his father and although Kruul was in no way a father figure to him, he did carry a wisdom that Kaln admired. He tightened his belt and felt the weight of the stone at his wrist. He had become used to it being there and didn't even notice it, until now. Now it felt alien again. Like it didn't belong to him anymore. He knew what to do.

"Vodius," Kaln said as he turned to him "I think my time with the stone is at an end." he held the stone in the palm of his rough hand, the bindings had untied and the sunlight reflected at just the right angle from the stained glass windows of the temple to illuminate the stone in his hand with a deep blue light that swirled and danced within the Rhelk stone like the swelling waters of a rising tide. Vodius' eyes darted from Kaln's to his hand.

"Are you sure?" his long fingers gingerly touching the stone. The bindings lashed around his wrist as it had Kaln's.

"I am now." Kaln replied with a smile that carried a hint of sadness. He had never felt truly alone with the stone in his possession but he knew he had fulfilled its needs by finding the Rua Tree.

Vodius held up a slender hand to the sunlight and admired the stone as the binding tightened.

Kruul said absently "I'm not gonnae' to lie to ye, Vodius. Right until this very moment I thought ye were a vampire." as he brushed past the group to help one of the townsfolk turn over a cart that had shed its load outside the temple. The human looked terrified for a moment, then realised the orc was helping and his expression changed to shame. Kruul turned the cart over with little more than a grunt of effort.

The old man said, stumbling back with a gasp "Thank ye kind sir! 'an thank ye for what ye did last night. Roku."

Finally realising who the orc was.

Kruul grunted "Roku." and turned to rejoin the others.

While this was happening, Vodius hadn't taken his eyes off the stone dangling from his wrist. It shimmered in the midday light breaking the light into bright colours that splashed across his face as he admired its beauty. Vodius' eyes were momentarily vacant, lost in an abyss of lurid colours as his eyes reflected that of the splintered sunlight that dappled his face.

The spell broke leaving Vodius with a desperate and weary expression suddenly drawn upon his face. Like an old memory had risen from the ashes.

"No, no, no, no, no." Vodius frantically patted the pockets of his robes. A flash of fleeting relief flickered across his face as he withdrew a small leather book, its cover was weathered and worn. He flicked through its pages with a frenzied pace.

Lilly stepped closer to him, "Vodius, what's wrong?"

Vodius glanced at her then to Gleb. "Lilly, a moment please. Gleb, the tome you took two nights prior, I need it back, now." His voice was calm and measured but his body language told of frustration.

Gleb padded over, smiled calmly up at him and said, "Which one?"

Vodius pinched his brow. "Arcanus Chronomasium." He sighed.

Gleb held up a knobbly finger with a flash of recognition and delved into his pouch with both arms, his tongue sticking out for extra precision as he combed through his stockpile.

"Ah! Here you go!" Gleb chirped as he passed Vodius the heavy tomb with a cheeky wink.

Vodius snatched the book and flicked through it. Lilly asked again with rising confusion and

frustration, "Vodius! What are you doing?!"
Vodius continued to look at the tome, its very pages crackled with magic as they turned.
"Ah ha!" He blurted, holding up a hand to placate another moment as the index finger of his other hand combed the page. Suddenly he poked at the page. At his fingertip was an illegible arcane symbol which swirled with different shades of purple.
He started to mutter as he read. "No, no time." he shook his head "No time."
Lilly grabbed him by the shoulders and shouted "Vodius! Explain yourself!" there was panic in her voice.
Vodius was shaking his head "I'm truly sorry Lilly, there is no time. Please everyone, with me."
He hurried through the temple back to the small room, he cleared the rug from the floor and started drawing symbols on the stone floor. He was uttering magical incantations as he did so.
The runes he drew were complete, the air popped and fizzed with energy and the sweet smell of magic was pungent.
Vodius looked to the group, "If my calculations are correct, I think it best that If I do not return within two days, go on without me."
For the first time since they met him, the elf looked humble as he said, "I have never met a more trustworthy, brave, perfectly infallible group of individuals. It has been an honour to meet each of you and I wish you the very best of

luck." There was sadness in his eyes as he smiled. He uttered a final magical word and what looked like a six foot tall mirror appeared in front of him. It was roughly the shape of a flame of a candle and like a candle flame, it danced and twitched, never truly still. The reflection was not of any known world and shrouded in darkness. The room filled with a darkness that drained the illumination of the fire in the hearth to a tiny flicker. Vodius gave the others one more smile and stepped through the portal with a determined grimace. Before any of them could respond or intervene, he appeared to step straight through to the other side and stood before the fireplace. The portal closed like a flame extinguished and thick oily ropes of smoke coiled to the ceiling and crawled outwards until they disbursed. As the last wisps faded, the fire regained its hold on the light once more, illuminating the elf's face. His features were the same but his hair was beginning to grey, his clothes were different and worn, one of his cheeks was spotted with old healed scars. His eyes had changed too, now they reminded Kaln of his father's eyes, weary pools of knowledge.

He looked at the others for a moment and gasped as if his breath was taken away. He staggered back and steadied himself on the fireplace which seemed to shock him as much as seeing the others. He whispered to himself, "Such incredible light." as he stared down into the flames with tears in his eyes.

"Vodius? Are you ok?" Lilly said quietly, glancing at the others.

Vodius' head snapped up to her, "My name! I haven't heard that name in so many years…" His eyes scanned the room. "You waited for me? I told you to leave if I did not return."

Kaln stepped closer to Vodius and stood behind Lilly. "You were gone less than a moment Vodius?"

Vodius began to laugh "Then my calculations were indeed incorrect! Fantastic news!"

He pointed to Kruul "You there, when did we first meet?"

Kruul arched an eyebrow and gave the others a confused glance. "You there," he mimicked "we met last night."

"Brilliant!" Vodius said as he took in the sight of his friends like it was the first time in many years.

Lilly paced over to the door, closed it and turned to Vodius "We're not leaving this room" she paused, "through this door or any other until you explain what just happened."

It was not a suggestion.

Vodius was nodding but was still distracted, taking in his surroundings and the group with a heartfelt smile.

"Vodius!" Lilly snapped.

Kaln put a hand on her arm. "Just give him a moment Lilly."

She gave Kaln a minute nod but didn't take her eyes off Vodius.

He seemed to be thinking, casting his mind to a time long ago, until eventually he nodded, tapping his finger on his pursed lips.

"First of all, I believe I owe you all an apology and to that end; You have my deepest apologies, truly." His hands were clasped together and he gave a small bow of sincerity.

Lilly snapped again "I don't want an apology, Vodius. I want an explanation."

Vodius nodded in agreement and took a deep breath.

"Yes, yes quite right. For me to explain myself effectively I must first give you a brief description of my past. Long before we met, before I travelled to this land when I was still the understudy of my old mentor, Vul."

Vodius paused, assessing if the entire story was required.

He shook his head "Time is still of the essence, so I will make this short. My mentor was banished for studying the means and ways to travel to different planar existances. Well, not the travelling exactly but more specifically attempting to contact the beings which resided within these different realms. Needless to say I am a quick learner and had learnt enough by the time he was gone to know where to start looking for the same answers he desired. Such knowledge was dangerous and until…" he paused again "Today, I had never had reason to test my theories. To be perfectly frank, I had all but forgotten about the methods I had learnt. That is until the stone bound itself to me."

He held it up and it danced silently in the firelight dangling from his wrist. He then began to pace back and forth in front of the fireplace as he continued to speak.

"I have been developing a theory since we met. One piece of the puzzle I could not place was the gore hounds in Cornwalk. Obviously not the orcs doing."

Kruul shrugged.

Vodius continued, "Nor were they even Thaldor's doing. We have all seen he would much prefer twisting and binding the dead to his will. Then there is the second piece of the puzzle which eludes me. Why does Thaldur keep moving? Why does he not see his spell through to completion, both here and Cornwalk?"

Vodius stopped and took another breath, looking at Lilly.

"I travelled to a realm beyond the darkness of the night. I plunged into the black abyss to speak to the one known as, The Wielder of Shattered Time. An old god, Koh'Thuun. As with all ancient gods, a pact must be made for power or knowledge. I traded ten years of my life for information on Thaldur. Koh'Thuun had me bound as his scholar, his emissary and his assassin for ten years in his realm, and others.

True to his name, and his word, time was frozen here while I earned the information we needed. The answer to the puzzle? Thaldur is being hunted by another god. He made a pact with a demon god, a desperate attempt to return his daughter and wife to his side. I was told he was offered their return for the souls of ten thousand. I believe his goals are twofold. First, to gather the ten thousand souls and in the process, an army. Second, to acquire both of the Rehlk stones. Either of these two things could be used to return his family to him. Something has gone awry with the pact between him and the demon god, now the god and his minions hunt him."

Lilly was stunned. Gleb sat on Kruul's shoulder, who was leaning against the wall, both listening to the tale.

Kaln stepped closer to Vodius, he could see now that the elf indeed looked older, and said "You gave ten years of your life for that information? Are you mad?"

Vodius scoffed and said "I'll have you know elves live far longer than humans and no, I'm quite sane. That was not the only information I gleaned. Thaldur is an intelligent and meticulous man. A Desperate man. He will have a plan, I've heard of wizards binding their soul to an item of power, an effigy and if they were to be slain they would be reborn of this spell bound to the effergy. Unless the effigy is destroyed. Now, if my limited knowledge on this particular subject has illuminated this possibility, his most certainly will have. What I'm telling you is that even if we find and slay him, he will return. Unless we do not find him at all, we find his effigy."

An evil grin spread across the elf's face.

Gleb screeched a roar of excitement, caught up in Vodius' charisma. It made Kruul jump and the goblin was promptly demoted first to the wall, then the floor.

Lilly's concern was evident as she said "So we leave Whitebluff to its fate? Is that what you are suggesting?"

Vodius' expression softened as he replied, "Even now we are already too late to help Whitebluff, Lilly."

"It's true." Kaln said "I...I can sense the land and I can feel that Thaldur's siege on Whitebluff will begin before we can lend them our aid."

Vodius pointed a finger at Kaln, nodding and continued, "Our choices, as I see it, are as follows. We travel North to Whitebluff in time to see the great white walls fall like the crashing waves of the Pale Sea beyond and Thaldur's numbers swell. Or, using the insight I have gained, we go South."

"South?" Everyone interrupted.

"South." Vodius confirmed before continuing, "Think about it, Thaldur came from the South, from the mountains. Where his fortress waits for his return. His effigy will be there. I'm sure of it."

Kruul grimaced as he said "So ye suggest we go the opposite direction to the man we hunt? What say the rest of ye?" looking at his companions.

Lilly had stepped closer and was inspecting the changes to Vodius. She reached up on the tips of her toes, her fingers brushed against his scarred cheek.

She muttered more to herself than anyone else, "I trust him."

"Aye, I trust him." Kaln said.

Kruul shook his head, muttered something in his native tongue and ended with, "but sure, why not!" In the common language.

Kaln nodded to the elf, "We do as Vodius suggests. Gather any supplies we may need from the market and meet at the South gate in an hour."

CHAPTER 22 - BLOOD IN THE SNOW

Denno stood looking down on the farmer and the farmer's son with a cold indifferent leer as thick snowflakes tumbled slowly around them. He had beady, sunken eyes and a nose that had been smashed more than once. Strands of thin greasy hair clung on to his balding scalp and he reeked of leather, sweat, booze and blade oils. He wasn't a particularly powerfully built man but many men who were, answered to him. There was something chilling and inhuman about him. He gave the two a cold calculating appraisal. His eyes were like a shark's, assessing its prey. Predatory and haunting.

The silence was broken when the farmer blurted

"Please, don't do this. I beg you!" clasping his hands in a desperate plea.

Denno enjoyed this part but his expression changed only subtly to show them a flicker of irritation. Then after a moment's pause, he threw down two daggers. One blade landed with a dull thud that was muted by the fresh snow at the knees of the farmer. The other knife landed blade down almost silently into the snow at the knees of the farmer's son. The two looked up at him, stunned confusion slowly draining away from their faces and being replaced by chilling realisation.

Beyond this, Denno didn't acknowledge them until his gang had finished handing over money to one of his men with excitable chatter. There were enough men to surround not only him and the two poor bastards at his feet, but the farmer's wife and two daughters too. The family were surrounded by figures between the trees, a few torches making their shadows dance between the thick snowflakes like demons in the forest. One of Denno's men stood with a blade to the neck of the farmer's wife. She wept silently, too scared to move, she clenched the hand of her daughter. Her eldest daughter was close to her fifteenth birthday, and her younger sister gripped her hand. The three women stood petrified as the men arranged their bets. They were exhausted, filthy and terrified. Their tears made streaks through the dirt on their faces.

Denno got the nod from the man collecting the money and looked down at the two men as they shivered in the cold as silence fell over them. All attention was on the two men.

It was obvious this wasn't the first time he had given this speech as he walked around the two men on their knees.

"Right chaps, each of you 'as got a knife. Last of you standin' gets to live. Simple."

Father and son looked at each other in horror.

The farmer shook his head and started to plead "You don't have to do this, please!"

Denno continued as though expecting the pleads for mercy, "If one of ya does not kill the otha', my men will have your wife, then your daughter and the other daughter."

The farmer bowed his head to the ground and sobbed "Please…"

Denno continued, "Now, I'd rather not do that on acount'a they're werf' more as virgins. So, when ya ready."

He took a step back to give the two men space.

"Oh, same applies if you kill 'yerself." Denno added with a courteous nod "That wouldn't be any fun now, would it?"

He waved a hand and a yelp came from the farmer's wife urging them to action.

The farmer's son whispered "I can't." As he cried, looking at his father.

The farmer looked to his wife and daughters

and his tears glistened in the torch light as he shouted "I love you all so much!" he turned his gaze to his son, the two were a couple of paces apart knelt in the quickly thickening snow. The only sound was the flames of the torches in the cool night air. In a voice laced with pride he pointed to his heart and said "Right 'ere son, make it quick won't you? It's cold out ere, your ma' an' sisters will catch a sickness."

He gave a hollow smile and added "I forgive you son, this ain't your doin' and don't you ever think it is."

He closed his eyes, one finger pointing to his heart, a final lesson for his son.

A long moment passed, and another.

Denno sighed as he said "For good or bad, I'm a man of my word. Bring the wife 'ere, I'm goin' first." and began loosening his belt.

The farmer's son screeched and drove the knife deep into his father's chest. He released the blade and grabbed him as he fell back. The farmer could feel his son's warm tears on his face as he took his last breaths. With a feeble hand he managed to hold his son's face one last time. Then he was gone.

Denno stepped forward "Hah! I knew the lad would win! Pay up and the rest of you keep yer' mitts off them, they won't sell for a decent price if they're covered in bruises." His voice showed the first sign of emotion, excitement as he started counting his winnings.

The thugs exchanged money as the wife and daughters wailed uncontrollably.

The farmer's son had his head against his father's as he said silent thanks, apologies and farewells to the most important man in his life. He turned and through bleary tear filled eyes, he saw his third and youngest sister who was watching from the shadows of the treeline sprint into the darkness of forest unnoticed. The snow around him turned red.

CHAPTER 23 - THE ROAD SOUTH

Kaln waited with Vodius where the south gate once stood. Now there were only shattered remains of the gate, along with a dozen youths and a couple of older men in ill-fitting armour. None of them were fighters, most had never even seen a fight. They fussed at their straps and bindings and complained amongst themselves at the weight of the breast plates they wore, a distraction from their anxiety.

Vodius was basking the midday sun as it glinted off the helms of the nearby guards. It wasn't particularly warm but the sun's rays took the edge off the chill of the imminent winter.

Distantly, he said "You know Kaln, I haven't seen so much light in so very long. You don't realise how much you can miss a thing as abundant as light."

He turned his hand over and admired its shadow on the floor.

"I have existed in the shadows for too long, I feared it would take something from my very essence. Like a bird released from a cage having forgotten how to fly." He continued as he created a bird shape in the shadows of his hands on the floor.

He gave a sigh of joy as he looked down the valley of dead trees.

Kaln watched him with a small smile as he said "I don't know what you went through in there but for what it's worth, it's good to have you with us."

Vodius looked at him with his cool smirk, nodded and said "I must admit, I never dreamed I would long for the day I could return to-" he glanced up at the battlements as two of the militia guards were in competition to see who could spit the furthest. "-This."

Kaln scoffed and rolled his shoulders as he looked down the barren road. There were only shades of grey as far as the eye could see, above, a cool blue cloudless sky perched on the bleak horizon.

"What use is the light if all you can see is death?" Kaln said bitterly, assessing the damage that had been done to his forest.

"Why, to see our companions of course!" Vodius said with a chuckle as he turned Kaln to see the others emerging from the city with thick winter cloaks that were stacked so high that all that could be seen of Gleb was a shambling pile of furs and the shine of his new boots. Kruul and Lilly were walking beside him with bundles under their arms. Kruul was giving occasional adjustments to Glebs blind wandering by lifting him by his head and pointing him in the correct direction. Gleb's muffled nattering could be heard from beneath the cloaks as their conversation came to a close.

Kaln looked at Vodius for a long moment as the elf chuckled at Gleb, in some ways he felt like he was talking to a different person. In others, he was entirely the same.

Gleb's fingers wriggled as he stood amongst the group swaying.

His muffled voices said "Soooo, can you all take your cloaks now?!"

Gleb spent the first couple of hours of the journey south telling the group how he combed the market stalls for the best boots he could find. Then he explained how he traded a handful of shinies that Vodius had given them for his new boots. Then he told everyone how he stole the shinies back, in case he needed them for trading later.

"He wasn't using em anyway." Gleb said with a

shrug as the others laughed.

Vodius rolled his eyes and began saying, "Those are coins and -" Vodius shook his head as he realised the futility of trying to explain to Gleb how trade in civilised society worked.

Kaln welcomed the idle chatter, it distracted from the rows of dead trees that flanked the road. From the sea of lifeless grey that grasped at the distant mountains. From the wake of Thaldur's path.

Each with new thicker cloaks and clothing ready for the winter Kaln had said would be upon the land within the next day or so, the group travelled down the South Road. Usually a road patrolled by guards from Crossay, like all the main roads out of the city. Now it was barren, no guards or travellers. Kaln had decided to follow the road back south instead of the route he had shown the others. It meant another day of travel but knew if the winter snow came it would be an easier journey on the road than through the forests.

On the morning of the third day of travel, the group had packed up their campsite after rising to a particularly chilly dawn and climbed the steep bank back onto the main road. It was a dark and glib morning, the sky was a grey-yellow colour, the clouds full and brooding.

"Looks like snow." Kaln said as he started walking south with Gleb beside him, he could hear the goblin's ears flapping as he nodded in agreement.

"Kaln, can you tell me how to hunt?" Gleb said whimsically as he padded alongside him, thumbs through his pack straps.

Kaln smiled. The Goblin had an insatiable appetite for learning new things and listened intently as Kaln told him what he knew, making notes and asking questions as they walked.

Kruul was in front a few paces watching the horizon and listening to the two chatting as they walked.

Lilly and Vodius were at the back of the group as they travelled. "Lilly," Vodius said "I think it is time you had this back. I just wanted to thank you for entrusting it to me." He held out the stone on its leather bindings and smiled at her.

She took the stone and tied the bindings around her neck. "You're welcome Vodius, I do trust you and you have given so much of yourself to help all of us." She looked up at the greying elf.

He smiled down at her, "I gained a little more than just knowledge for my deeds." and winked. Changing the subject, he continued, "I've taken the liberty of imbuing the bindings on the stone with a spell shroud. It will mean Thaldur, or anyone else searching for the stone will not be able to track it using magical means."

Lilly looked down holding out the gem and realised the stone she grew up with had changed, the veins and patterns inside the stone had changed, slightly different angles and hues glimmered inside it. Although touching the stone, she knew it was hers. The stone had been on its own journey. She could now see the runes inlayed into the leather bindings. "Thankyou." She said as she admired its beauty.

They stopped to eat at midday. Kaln sat on the roadside as he and the others ate. He listened to the conversations and tried to push his new sense out into the path ahead of them. It was difficult, like peering through fog or hearing a whisper through a crowded bar wherever Thaldur had travelled, left a mark on the land that affected his senses and killed the forest. He could sense something ahead but couldn't work out what. Something was there, waiting. The harder he focused on who or what it was, the harder it was to sense. Eventually, he gave in and joined in the conversation which was on the topic of a drinking game which Gleb called "The Battered Clam".

They continued on their journey south and as the sun started to set, the clouds shed their burden and thick snowflakes began to fall. Kaln's mind continued to probe at what he was sensing but like a splinter he couldn't gain purchase on or a word that danced on the tip of the tongue, he couldn't grasp the details. The group setup camp for the night. They talked, bickered and joked and as they ate but Kaln found himself distracted, it was all he could think about. He took himself away from the noise to think. He sat on the furthest reaches of the campfire's light, looking south as it's amber glow illuminated the dancing snowflakes behind him. Finally, a breakthrough! In the fog of his mind, he sensed two things. Not just the thing that was waiting but something coming towards them. He stared out into the darkness between the trees. Whatever it was, was right there, he could feel it. He let his eyes adjust to the darkness and watched. He saw a face looking back at him. He jumped to his feet with a start, snatching his axe from his back, he shouted to the others as he sprinted into the darkness. He charged to the tree expecting to see the figure running away but behind the tree he saw that the face belonged to a little girl, barely ten years old. She was filthy, cold, half starved and terrified as she screamed at Kaln looming over her, Emmental in hand.

"Who are you?" Kaln managed before torchlight and the crunching footsteps of his friends in the snow were behind him.

Gleb thrust what looked like a long metal pipe at the girl viciously. Lilly Shouted at him, "Gleb, put that thing down!" as she stood between the girl and the goblin and crouched.

"You're Farmer Gimmock's daughter, aren't you?" Lilly's nose scrunched as she tried to remember the Gimmock family's first names.

The terrified girl's eyes darted from one of the

looming figures to the other and locked on Kruul as he peered over Kaln's shoulder. She started to scramble away feebly in the snow. She didn't have the energy.

Kruul shook his head "Despite what ye might have heard of orcs, lassy, I've nae' interest in killing a wee girl scared half 'oot her mind in the middle of the woods."

After scanning the edge of the darkness, he grunted, shrugged his shoulders and started making his way back to the camp fire with Gleb in tow. They seemed to be discussing the metal pipe Gleb was brandishing with bristling pride.

"Rosey!" Lilly blurted, clicking her fingers triumphantly.

The girl jumped at the outburst and a flicker of hope illuminated her face.

"Ye-yes, that's me. Do you know my father?" she whispered, flinching at her own words like they were physically painful. She bit her lip to stop it from shaking from the cold and curled tighter into a ball.

"Yes, I do." Lilly gave a soft smile as she reached out a hand to the girl.

"I am Mayor Cooper's daughter" her own words hurt but she hid it in her smile.

"Let's get you by the fire and get you some food in your belly. Then you can tell us where you came from and get you back to your family." Lilly said, giving an encouraging nod to the girl.

She held Lilly's hand and they took her to the

warmth of the fire. Kruul distractedly passed the girl a bowl of stew as he said to Gleb "So 'av ye got a name for her then?"

"Yep! Thunderbastard!" Gleb said proudly as he flipped the device over in his hands.

Rosey hesitantly took the bowl, keeping her eyes on the orc for a moment, then devoured the stew like she hadn't eaten in days.

The group watched as the girl ate, guzzling the hot stew and stuffing the bread into her mouth. Lilly sat by her side and put a hand on her back. Rosey flinched but continued eating.

Lilly said as softly as she could "Where are your parents, Rosey?"

Rosey told them how she and her family ran when the orcs came to Cornwalk, they ran into the forest as far as they could run, how her father carried her so that she could keep up. How they got lost and almost starved until they were found by a man named Denno and all of his men. They scared her, so she hid and watched. That's what her father told her to do if she saw someone or something that scared her. Then she told them what the man named Denno made her father and her brother do to each other. Denno didn't know she was there. After that, she ran and ran until she saw a campfire and here she was.

The group looked to each other, pale with the horror of the girl's story.

Kaln stood "Fucking Slavers... Everyone get some

rest, we leave in a few hours to find these bastards." He turned and climbed into his tent. Kaln was not just shocked but visibly angry and disgusted. It was understandable but none of the group had seen him like this before.

Lilly was holding the girl, who was sobbing, having relived the experience telling her tale. "You can stay in my tent with me. We will get you back to your family."

Some time after the others had climbed into their tents, Kruul passed Kaln's tent and whispered "Ye awake lad?"

"Yeah, what's wrong?" Kaln's voice replied sharply.

"Just wanted to check that ye were okay, that's all." Kruul said.

There was a long pause and in a softer voice, Kaln replied "It's old history I didn't think would be brought up. I don't want to talk about it."

"Aye. Okay. Well, g'night lad." Kruul turned his back to the tent.

"Thankyou." Kaln said. Kruul smiled softly to himself and climbed into his tent.

Lilly was the only one who didn't fall straight to sleep, instead she played with Rosey's hair while she slept and thought about how much she missed her own father.

Hours later, Lilly and Rosey emerged from their tent to find the others stood talking. Kaln was shaking his head. There was an anger in his otherwise placid demeanour that Lilly had never noticed before. She thought the way Kaln was acting before was frustration or shock from hearing Rosey's story but it was obvious something was getting to him.
"I know their kind, I've dealt with them in the past. I have a plan but it involves springing their trap. We won't even see them if they think it's a fair fight. I'm also pretty sure I know exactly where they are." He said.

"I fockin' hate Slavers. Let's go!" Kruul said bitterly. He grimaced and spat.

"The rest of you in?" Kaln glanced at each of them, each of them giving him their nod. Gleb just seemed eager to test his new invention. He looked at Lilly, and she too nodded without hesitation. It was the right thing to do. After all, if they wouldn't try and help this family, what were they even trying to achieve?
"Great, I'll fill you in on the details of the plan while we travel." he continued and began packing his things.

CHAPTER 24 - FINDING THE LOST

A hunched man wrapped in furs and cloaks hobbled along the snow covered path leading down into the raveen. His staggered steps revealed to any watching that he was leaning heavily on his walking staff. At its top swung a small lantern. As he got closer to the base of the raveen he glanced up at its two flanking walls, the tops of which could barely be seen in the thick snow and strong winds. They were at least thirty foot tall on either side and made of rough brittle red stone. The path ahead narrowed to just wide enough for a horse and cart. Snow had collected at the base of the two cliff walls where the wind had carried it.

He hobbled on.

Now he was between the two stone faces that grimaced down at him. The shadows from the lantern were haunting as it swung in the wind to the rhythm of his awkward gait.

A man stepped out in front of the traveller and gave an exaggerated bow. The hunched man stood still, only the lantern continued to move, splashing the man's features across his face momentarily. A man with a broken nose, balding with long oily strands of hair stuck to his scalp and cold empty eyes smiled at him as he strode towards him with long legs that were almost insect-like in their movements.

"Cold night for travelin', 'specially alone, my friend. Though, it's your lucky night. 'Ya see, the guards don't protect these roads anymore. Summink' tah do 'wiv an attack on Crossay so we 'ear. These roads are now under our protection. O'course, for our protection, there is a tax. That being five gold pieces."
It was a speech that was well rehearsed and it was obvious it had been given to more than one unfortunate soul.

The cowled man uttered something that the wind snatched up.

"You wot?" The lanky man snapped with his

hand outstretched. He dipped his head to peer under the traveller's cowl.
"You might have only got one eye but surely you can see there 'aint really an option 'ere. I was'n askin', I was tellin'." He spread his arms and gestured to the dozens of men that had emerged from the shadows to encircle the lone wanderer. Each of them wore scars and tattoos and stared at the traveller with hungry eyes, their hands on the hilts of their blades.

The cowled man waved for the man with eyes that shone like the eyes of a spider's in the lantern's light, to come closer.
He obliged and said with a gap toothed sneer "Don't make me ask you again." and pulled out a long thin pocket blade that had obviously seen a lot of use.

The cowled man said just loud enough for Spidereyes to hear "Do you have a runner, a messenger amongst your men?"

Spidereyes barked a laugh and scanned the crowd "Smiley! Come 'ere! This one wants to pay me an extra five gold for your running services."

A scruffy looking young man who could not have been twenty years old ran up. He had a scar that followed the corners of his lips almost to his ears and bright blue eyes that glimmered in the lantern light. He had a vicious grin on his face, like he knew how this ended.

Spidereyes gestured to the young man like he was a steak that had been ordered. "Now, ten gold, an' no more pissing about or I'll cut your fackin' eyelids off." He paused, "Lid." He corrected, "I'll cut your fucking eyelid off." He said, laughing nastily.

The cowled man glanced around at the dozens of men and nodded. Then he straightened his back, in fact he stood up so straight that he was taller than Spidereyes and Smiley, he uncurled his broad shoulders and turned his walking staff right over and slung the pale red crystalline axe head over his shoulder. The lantern fell to the floor, splashing pale orange light across the ground and illuminating the scarred face of Kaln, fury on his face as thick snowflakes danced in the wind and light around them.

There was a moment of stunned silence as everyone in the bottle neck of the raveen watched the old man turn into Kaln. Kaln took advantage of the shock and tore his hand through the air in an upward motion towards Smiley, "You stay there and watch, Smiley." he said in a dangerous tone. Thick roots and wiry vines with savage thorns lashed out of the ground and twisted around the small man with horrific speed. The rich smell of earth and sweet smell of magic was thick in the cool air.

His muted screams could be heard from within the cocoon of vines and roots that tightened around him leaving only his nose and eyes uncovered. Thin trickles of blood ran between the tightening bindings and he was wrapped in place.

Spidereyes fell back and skittered on his arse, pointing at Kaln in horror.
He screamed "Kill this wanker!"
He disappeared into a wave of knees and boots as his men closed in on Kaln.
There were so many more than Kaln expected but it was too late now. Time seemed too slow to Kaln as he watched them charge at him, bulging eyes and vicious grins as they shouted.
Some distant part of him thought *Why aren't I scared?* He tightened his grip on Emmental. *The terrified boy I was a week ago is gone?* He bent his knees ready to pounce. *Have I changed so much that I am ready to fight these animals?* He picked his first target. *No, I'm not scared,* he thought. In truth, something inside of him was excited for this battle. Something bestial. A wicked grin crept across his face.

A huge bald man with a superb beard brought down a monstrous club on Kaln as he pushed the first attackers back with a swift arc of his axe. It was instinct that made him raise his arm to try and protect himself. The acorn that was embedded in Kaln's forearm exploded into thick dense brambles in the circular shape of a shield, as quickly as it formed the shape, it petrified into stone, catching the brunt of the blow. Stone chips and shards of the bramble shield exploded into the air. The weapon was too heavy for the bearded man to recover quickly and Kaln brought his axe down on his shoulder. Emmental did not stop cleaving until it reached his solar plexus. He hit the ground heavily and the men surrounding realised they were fighting a man who knew how to use a weapon, not their usual prey. Kaln had a moment to admire this gift from Aeathune as he swept his axe, keeping the attackers at bay. He shouted up into the darkness of the windy cliff tops above, "Now!"

Gleb kicked a hefty barrel down into the far side of the natural choke point with a strained grunt. It tumbled down above the men furthest from the melee who were rushing in to do Spidereyes' bidding.
Gleb screamed "Thunderbastard!" as he pulled the metal pipe-like object over his shoulder and pulled the trigger. A flash of light that illuminated the snow around him followed by a cracking sound and a red hot ball of metal ripped through the air on a trail of sparks, plunging into the barrel. The barrel exploded just before it hit the ground with a deep boom and a shockwave that washed out over the crowd of men. Shards of metal, wood and bone impaled dozens of

men. Others were knocked to the ground as chunks of redstone peeled from the cliff walls and plummeted down onto them. Gleb cranked the handle on the side of the device and aimed at Spidereyes who was trying to push a body off him. He pulled the trigger again. Another crack and red hot ball of metal ripped through the air, through the snow and through Spidereyes' knee and blotted the snow with more blood. He screamed, wriggled, squirmed and clutched his leg, but he had stopped trying to flee and was instead trying to hold his leg together. Gleb slung Thunderbastard back over his shoulder, drew his sword in one hand and clutched the rope in the other. He ran and threw himself off the cliff edge letting out a shrill battle cry.

Kaln looked up to see the barrel drop and explode, just as Gleb said it would. He crouched and raised his shield as chunks of flesh splashed down around him. He was prepared and recovered faster than his attackers, he swung the axe in a wide arc in front of him. The strike disembowelled two stunned thugs and destroyed the kneecap of a third attacker. The others recovered and began to swarm him, it was everything he could do to keep his footing. Then he felt a flash of white hot pain in his thigh from behind. Then his shoulder. He roared in pain and spun to cleave the men who wounded him. One of them lost an arm, the other caught the spiked back of the axehead in his face and went down in a bloody mass, clutching his face. Kaln's breaths were heavy and ragged. His legs refused to hold him up, his arm refused to lift his axe. He heard a second crack from up above and heard Gleb's roar join his own. Suddenly a blazing pain in his chest erupted. He couldn't take in air. His vision began to swim and the thugs surrounded him. More pain, more distant now as he drunkenly swung his axe catching one careless thug across the throat. The smell of blood was thick in the night air. If this is how it ends for me, so be it. *I'm coming father and I bring many of them with me*, he thought and spat blood.

"Wait for the boom." Lilly repeated to herself and the others as they watched Kaln walk down into the bottleneck wrapped in old cloaks, the lantern swaying in the night. They watched him talking to the man they hunted.
"Wait for the boom." she repeated quietly.
They watched the thugs encircling him, there were so many. *What was he thinking?* She thought.
"This'll be fun." Kruul said, she could hear the grin in his words.
"They appear to be surrounding him. There are so many of them." Vodius said, concern laced his words.
"Wait for the boom." Lilly repeated, ignoring them. She clenched her fists, trying not to think

about the oppressive sensation of the magic Vodius had cast on them to make them invisible. It made the hair on the back of her neck stand on end and the inside of her mouth taste like metal. The man shouted another from the gathering crowd who ran over. She watched the man become entombed in place by hundreds of vines and all hell break loose.

"Wait for the boom!" She told everyone.

Suddenly from the far side of the raveen, atop one of the cliff walls, the silhouette of Gleb could be seen in a flash of light and an instant later there was a crack followed by a ground shaking boom from within the raveen.

"There's the boom!" she shouted and all three of them broke into a sprint down the road Kaln had taken, behind the thugs. Vodius' spell had now broken and they were visible to anyone who may have looked behind them in the fray.

She was running to Kaln. *I have to get to him,* she thought as she fought to keep her eyes locked on his form in the chaos.

Suddenly a thug from the forest beside them appeared in front of her but before she could even slow her pace, a huge Kruul shaped mass tackled him back into the shadows. Behind her, she could hear Kruul shouting his terrifying, deep and rumbling battle cry as he hacked at the man with his axes. The battle cry made her feel empowered. The killing machine of an orc was with her, her ally. She pushed harder, gulping down deep breaths of cold air, she was close now but there were so many of them. Some of the thugs turned to see them coming down the hill behind them and began to charge at her.

She slid to a stop in the snow and the tip of her staff exploded into a point made of blistering blue-white light. There were a handful of men charging towards her, beyond them she could see Kaln being overwhelmed. She prepared to fight. *None shall force me to abandon him!* She thought and readied herself. One of the men lunged at her but she jumped back and used the length of her spear to her advantage thrusting it through his heart with a savage hissing sound as it was plunged into his chest. The others began to surround her like wolves. She kept them at bay with her spear but they spread out so they were on all sides.

Just as they were about to overwhelm her, a ring of dark purple flames erupted around her and washed outwards like molten waves of purple lava. The snow hissed violently against the liquid flame and all of the men surrounding her were consumed with terrifying speed. They screamed, thrashed and rolled in the snow trying to put out the flames but they only intensified. Lilly glanced up the road to see Vodius with his hands in front of him wreathed in the same purple flames and wisps of dark oily smoke illuminated from his eyes that were glowing the same colour as the flames. He relaxed, the flames that danced in his eyes and the palms of his hands ceased into curls of thick smoke. The burned thugs stopped moving. He looked at Lilly and nodded as the form of another thug's body was thrown past him with a sickening crunch. Kruul's war cry got louder as he ran to join her charge. She could feel his heavy thumping footsteps as he ran past her. The air itself seemed to tremble at his bellowing roar. There was little light but she could make out the manic grin on Kruul's face as he dived into the wall of flesh and blade before him. His rumbling howl was awesome. She could see Kaln now, he was crouched low and covered in blood.

Kruul leapt into the fray with the fervour for battle that only his people held. He liked to believe he was not brutal and savage, but by the gods of Kor he did enjoy battle. Eyes bulging and huge teeth bared he crashed into a crowd of thugs with a sickening crunch as the head of the man he landed on gave way to his crushing momentum. The others skittered back like roaches, all except one. A troll, taller and wider even than Kruul, the monstrous creature swatted thugs aside to get to him. Kruul pointed his axe at the Troll as the two sized each other up, circling in the small space that had been given to them in the melee. "My name is Kruul Skull Crusher, Chieftain of the Pale Tusks." The circle widened as Kruul's title obviously had an impact. He grinned nastily at the troll who gave no heed to his words and instead charged at him with a huge branch it was using as a club. The troll tried to shoulder barge into Kruul but he stepped aside at the last moment. Using the club and his momentum, the troll swung the branch catching Kruul as he tried to find his footing. A dull thud followed shortly after by the sound of Kruul hitting the ground. He did not move. The troll let out a dullard's laugh as he approached Kruul's prone form and said "My name is Nook and I don't give a fuck who you are!" He raised the club to finish the job and swung.

Gleb used his momentum to swing into the crowd, he slashed the throats and faces of the thugs at the back of the fight as he swung in. Then, when he reached the pinnacle of his swing, he leapt into the crowd and started hacking at the backs of knees of anyone who got in his way. He was hacking his way towards where he saw Kaln last. He spotted him, crouched low and covered in blood. For a moment, between the legs and blades of the melee, Gleb thought he saw a wounded bear. A wounded animal can be a dangerous foe.

The troll hit only the ground, splintering his club as Kruul rolled to the side with surprising speed, leapt to his feet and hacked at the troll's bulging gut with one of his axes. Nook stared at Kruul stunned and then with a flash of anger grabbed

Kruul by the throat, lifting him off the ground and choking him. There were warm wet flops of fluid pouring out of the troll but he seemed more intent in choking the life out of the orc. Kruul hacked at the arms of the troll with his axes but the flesh on its arms was too thick to cut through. His vision was beginning to swim as the huge troll squeezed the life out of him. His head pounded and throbbed as his body fought to keep him alive. He dropped both his axes and kicked the troll's gut as hard as he could. There was more viscera sloshing out of Nook and he loosened his grip in pain, but only for a moment. It was enough for Kruul to grab the troll's head in both hands. They locked eyes and muscles flexed and blunged. There was no sound from either of them save heavy breathing and grunting as they stared at each other in the deadly embrace. Finally, Kruul croaked "This is how I got my name." There was a final flex of muscles and a dull crunch. The troll's knees buckled and he hit the ground lifeless. His head crushed and bowels poured out over the snow.

Kaln released the shield from his arm instinctively as he slung it at the face of an attacker with a dull crunch that dropped the man. He forced his body to submit to his will as he staggered to his feet with his axe in both hands and roared. Like in the cave, his roar did not sound entirely his own and though most of his body was numb and weary, he felt the beartooth around his neck rumble as he bellowed his last battle cry.

As his roar washed out over the battle, others joined him. One was by his side, a high pitched screech. The other was beyond the mass of bodies, a deep bellow that could only have been Kruul. He took in as much air as his lungs would allow and nodded to Gleb to let him know they were going to die together in battle. The goblin nodded back without fear or hesitation.

Then a pale blue light washed over them both. It was violent and blazing. The magic was so intense it should have incinerated them but only the thugs closest to them felt the blazing light's wrath. Kaln watched as Gleb's wounds closed. He felt his lungs begin to work again, his vision and strength return. He felt Lilly's comforting touch along with something unfathomable as the magic blazed through his flesh. At that same moment he had visions flash into his mind, of Aeathune, of Ursol The Bear Lord and of his father.

His vision changed, it was now focused on the threats around him, nothing else. His muscles swelled and he felt his body change, his jaw and teeth becoming a weapon. He looked down at his hands, now hair covered paws tipped with savage black claws. He could feel his muscles tighten like coiled springs ready to explode. He realised he was now looking down on many of the thugs. They were looking back up at him with absolute terror in their eyes. He felt invincible. Distantly he felt Gleb scurry up his back and giggle maniacally before screaming "ThunderBastard!" and a crack went off somewhere on his shoulder followed by a cluster of thugs being knocked off their feet. Kaln could hear the hearts of the men closest pounding, he could smell their sweat, their blood and their fear. He let Emmental fall to his feet. The great axe didn't hit the ground, vines lashed out and it wrapped itself to Kaln's back, as he knew it would. He let out the beast, the part of him that let him stand his ground against so many. The part of him that scared away his fear. The part of him that wanted vengeance for his mother. The Great Bear that was now Kaln ran down and viciously destroyed what was left of the thugs with the help of Gleb on his back and the others coming to join them. It was a massacre.

In the middle of the valley filled with the dead and dying, the group stood before Smiley. He hadn't moved, like a scarecrow tending to its field of flesh. Kruul had one meaty hand on the shoulder of Spidereyes who was whimpering on his knees beside him. After the battle had ended Kaln changed back to his human self, a process that felt as natural as blinking.

With a subtle gesture from Kaln the vines and roots unravelled slowly exposing the ruined flesh of Smiley. He slumped to his knees and screamed in pain, the sound of it echoing into the night. Kaln grabbed his ruined bloodsoaked coat and hauled him to his feet, pulling him close to his face.

"I've a use for you. You're to go to any other raiders, Slavers or bandits that I know you know reside in these forests. You're to tell them what you saw today."

Smiley looked down at Spidereyes. Kaln slapped him. Hard.

"Don't look at him. Look at me."

Smiley nodded desperately and locked terrified eyes with Kaln.

Kaln continued. "You're to tell them that I am the warden of these forests and I will hunt them down and slay them like rabid dogs if they do not leave. My name is Kaln Grey and this," he hefted the axe up into eyeshot for Smiley to see, "is Emmental. Remember me."

In a different tone entirely and without looking at them, Kaln said to the others, "I'll go fetch her." and walked through the corpses, back the way he came.

A silence fell over the group in response to the intensity of what just happened. It was broken by Kruul saying "Well, that was cheesy." All but Spidereyes laughed at the bad joke. Even the

nervous Smiley laughed and said, "I know! Who names their weapon after a chee-" The rest of the words didn't leave his mouth as Kruul punched him straight in the jaw, knocking him to the ground and scattering his teeth.
"I dunnae' recall sayin' ye could speak?" Kruul said with disdain.
Lilly put a hand on Kruul to calm him and said to Smiley "You won't come to any more harm if you do as you are asked." Lilly glanced at the vague shape of the now approaching Kaln, helped Smiley to his feat and healed the wounds on the young man's face with a flash of pale blue light and added, "Kaln is a man of his word." She watched Smiley's response to make sure the message had got through to him before turning away from him.

Kaln appeared out of the gloom, picking his way through the corpses with Rosey on his shoulders. She had a blindfold over her eyes and they were playing some sort of guessing game.
"Is it...A Donkey!?" Rosey giggled at her own guess, blissfully unaware of her surroundings.
"Nope! Close though!" Kaln said in a playful tone and continued walking. He nodded to Kruul who dragged the pair of thugs with them as they left the valley of corpses.

Kaln walked ahead, chatting away to Rosey. Lilly spoke to Smiley who was keeping his eyes down. "Show us where that little girl's family is, then

you can leave."
Kruul gave him a shove from behind, Smiley stumbled and looked at him defiantly, only for an instant before thinking better of it. He pointed West, off the road just up ahead. Kruul whistled and Kaln turned to follow their new direction into the forest. It was maybe a further ten minutes walk through the snow laden forest before they saw a campfire between the trees.

Kaln pointed back to the main road and glowered at Smiley. The message was clear and he scrambled into the eerie pale darkness of the snow covered forest, towards the road. Once the Slaver was out of sight Kaln gave a nod to Kruul and Gleb, Both nodded in return and Gleb scurried off into the forest towards the Slaver camp. Kruul dragged Spidereyes away into the forest while the others got closer to the camp. The Slaver didn't have much say in what happened to him next, he was barely conscious from the bloody wound that was left of his knee.

Kruul returned alone some time later, It wasn't long before Gleb returned. "Yep, there were only two of 'em. They were drinkin' lots'a wine."
Gleb uncorked a tiny vial and sniffed it, his eyes dilated and he had to steady himself against a tree. "I doubt they drinkin' now!" he shook his head like a dog with water in its ear to shake off the effects of the concoction and gave them a big toothy smile.

Vodius sighed deeply. "Gleb, what have I told you about sniffing lethal chemicals?"

The two lifeless thugs were slumped over a table by the fire, there were many tents and even a horse and cart with a cover over the cart. Kaln could smell the fear of the family in the cart, the smell was clinging to the cool night air like burning fat. He pulled back the cover to find all four of them huddled together in a cage trying to keep warm. The farmer's son moved quickly to put himself between the cage door and his family, a defiant glimmer in his eyes. The eyes of a man who had lost so much, Kaln recognised. They were terrified. Kaln lifted Rosey up so her nose poked over the edge of the cart and removed the blindfold.

"Mommy!" She squealed.

The family rushed to the cage door, which Gleb was now hanging off of, his tongue sticking out as he adjusted several delicate instruments into the keyhole. It was a matter of moments, to Kaln and Gleb at least, before there was a metallic click and the cage swung open.

CHAPTER 25 - SEPARATE WAYS

It wasn't long before they were out of the cage and warming up by the fire. Gleb had immediately got to work on cleansing the camp site of any valuables and arrived by the fire with a bundle of furs for the Gimmocks. The family were too weak and exhausted to do anything at first but sat in the glowing warmth while Lilly and Kruul handed them bowls of food and covered them with furs and blankets. Once they began eating and feeling their extremities again, their hunger only seemed to increase, like an old habit coming back to someone. They ate furiously between bouts of thanking Kaln and the group. Their hollow eyes began to show signs of life and they even began to smile. The empty smiles on their faces were an improvement, even if it was for the sake of politeness. The boy finished his second bowl and looked to Kaln.

"Names Kally sir, Kally Gimmock, I know ye've heard it a hundred times by now but I mean it when I thank ye for what ye done 'ere." He filled his bowl again.

"You don't have to thank me, these vermin deserve everything they get coming to them."
He measured the farm boy's reaction for a moment. Then he drew Spidereyes' dagger, the same one he had told Kally to kill his father with. The boy's eyes widened in panic as Kaln dropped it in the snow at his feet, just as Denno had days before. There were still flecks of his father's blood on the hilt. Kally picked up the blade and turned it in his hands, watching its silhouette in the fire light through teary eyes.
Kaln stood, breaking the boy's engrossment, "About a mile east of here, this Denno..." he spat the name like it tasted bad, "He is injured and tied to a tree you will pass him on your way to the main road. He is completely harmless. Harmless like your father was to him, like your mother was to his men. Decide his fate, as he felt his right to do to you and your family."

Kaln could feel the eyes of the boy's mother boring into him but she did not speak. He continued to look at the boy who was looking up at him, his eyes searching for answers, for a hint of what he should do next.
"I won't tell you what to do, nor will I judge ye on

your decision. Your sister told me what he did to you. I wish I got the same opportunity you have. You are the man of the family now. Make the decision."

Kaln turned to look at the rest of the Gimmock family now, the sisters were looking at Kaln and his friends like he was a hero of legend, like they all were. It felt strange.

The boy's mother was staring at Kally realising his new burden. Kaln continued, "We must leave and where we go, you cannot follow."
The mother's eyes snapped to Kaln and she blurted, "Wait! You can't leave us!"
Kaln gave her a small, reassuring smile and said, "When you're ready, gather what you need here and head east to the road and follow it North. It should be safe now. Travel by daylight and keep going North until you get to Crossay. Don't stop at Cornwalk, there's nothing left."

Mrs Gimmock obviously didn't want to believe Kaln and looked at Lilly, her eyes pleading for her to say it was a lie and that Cornwalk was fine, that everyone was waiting for their return. Instead, Lilly put a hand on her shoulder and said "If you don't have anywhere to go in Crossay, go to the temple of Celuna and tell them we sent you. They will give you somewhere safe to rest."

Kaln handed Kally a few gold coins. Whatever

the young man's decision was, Kaln could tell he had made it. He nodded to the others who were also standing and started to leave the camp. He glanced back to see Kally slip the dagger into his belt and start preparing the horses.

They travelled South through the thick snow and dense forest for about an hour, conversation was light and the snow was heavy. It was around this time that the travel, lack of sleep, battle and general exhaustion hit them like a sack of potatoes. Their pace slowed, except for Kruul's. He was much more used to the harsh terrain and long travel.

Lilly spoke first, "I need rest."

"Me too." Kaln agreed instantly.

"Thank goodness, Elves are certainly not built for travelling in such disagreeable conditions." Vodius managed to give several falling snowflakes a look of contempt in the gloom as he buried his mouth and nose back into his scarf.

Gleb gave a sigh of relief at the news and plonked down in the snow.

Kruul turned to the group "Aye. Fair enough, I must admit, I wondered when ye would want teh stop."

He rolled his shoulders and neck, "Well, we can either set up camp here, in the dark and in the snow or," he jabbed a meaty thumb over his shoulder, "about another mile that way is The Rocking Horse Shite. Personally, I dunnae' mind which we do but a nice ale, a proper bed and some warm grub would'nae go amiss." A distant pleasant smile crept on his face as he imagined all three.

Kaln could sense on the southernmost fringes of the forest was indeed a building. Further South beyond that, he could not sense the land. This is where the forest ended and the mountains began.

"I'm in. Those do sound nice. An inn, this Rocking Horse Shite?" Kaln asked.

"Of sorts, aye. That an' much more. If two orc tribes were teh meet on neutral ground, this be the place. If humans wanted teh make a friend with an orc, this would be the place. All races, professions and past times are welcome and no violence under its roof is tolerated. Have teh warn ye though, there's some rough shapes that frequent the place. Not just human bandits and Slavers either. If we go there, we keep teh ourselves and dunnae' cause nae' drama. It's the last 'civilised' place before we hit the Greyfang Mountains."

Kaln had never been this far South but trusted in Kruul's judgement. He agreed and so did the others.
"Very well, I am there only to eat and sleep. You have my word. Lead the way Kruul." Kaln said,

gesturing beyond the grinning orc as he helped Gleb back to his feet and started walking.

Another mile as Kruul had said and they saw the massive building by the treeline of the forest. The building was made of stone, wide and squat. Obviously a product of dwarves at some point long ago, additions of wooden buildings attached to the larger stone building created a mishmash of cultural architecture. A figure could be seen leading horses into a second smaller wooden building. Tiny windows poured warm golden light out into the snowy night from all sides of the Rocking Horse Shite.

As they got closer, they could hear the sounds of muffled conversation and even laughter. It was stunning at first to hear joviality. All the more inviting.

They approached the building and realised that although the wooden additions were not dwarven in design or craft, they were well made and solid. As all things had to be to survive this far out in the wild. The sounds of clattering jugs, chairs scraping on a well trodden floor, the smell of roasted boar and ale. A pang of sadness struck Lilly and Kaln, even Kruul. A reminder of what normality used to feel like. It was quickly washed away when the smells and sounds washed over them as a dwarf opened the door, increasing the sounds and smells momentarily. He placed his clenched fists on his hips, took a deep breath of cool night air and belched into the darkness. He didn't see, or didn't care that the group were emerging from the darkness surrounding the inn. He passed them on the stairs leading to the door as he began unclipping his belt. He had decided which bush he was going to use. He barely acknowledged them, a grunt of greetings was all they got out of the distracted dwarf. Kruul returned the grunt and held the door open as the group entered the inn.

Rich amber firelight illuminated the large hall and its thick dark wooden rafters above, making the place feel cosy. There were large wooden benches and tables haphazardly dotted around the room with mugs and plates on them. Almost all of the seats were taken by various races. They were all huddled around talking, swearing, shouting, playing cards, drinking, eating, throwing dice and telling tales. In the gaps between the tables were old threadbear rugs which mostly covered the wooden floor boards. The boards themselves were so worn they had a shine to them, much like the furniture. The sound of conversation was dense and the smells of hoppy ale, heady pipe smoke and rich roast meats filled the air. At the far end of the hall was a large fireplace with a fire blazing, doorways dotted the back wall, windows lined the wall where they had entered and to their immediate left was a long bar made of pale wood.

As Kaln and his friends entered, the room hushed for half a second as they felt the entire room stop and take note of who had walked in. Relief washed over him as they returned to what they were doing before they entered but Kaln's gifted sense of hearing picked up the words 'Emmental' and 'Kaln' from various tables in the room. This didn't bother him. If he had made enemies doing what he did, then so be it. He would be glad of these enemies. He scanned the faces for hostility but nobody made it obvious they were looking at him or approached him. He saw one or two orcs wave a gesture at him but he quickly realised they were acquaintances of Kruul's as the big orc grinned and gave a strange playful gesture in return.

From the crowd appeared a lady, she was stocky and large breasted with messy hair tied up and beaming green eyes. She had a wholesome and welcoming face with a pale green grey tint to her skin. She was wiping her hands on her apron and smiling a toothy grin that showed her bottom fangs. Kaln noticed that the crowd of people parted for her as she hurriedly paced around the room. She shot a scalding but benign look to someone in the crowd that seemed to bring some finality to an unfinished conversation and her expression was back to warm and welcoming by the time she had turned back to the group standing by the door.

She took an exaggerated breath and said "Hello there, I see ya travel with Kruul." She gave the big orc a playful swat with a dish cloth. "Well, aren't ya gonna introduce me to yer friends you great oaf?"

Kruul flinched with a cheeky smile and said "Aye give me chance lass! This is Kaln, Lilly, Vodius and - " Gleb peered over Kruul's shoulder, wide eyed and grinning as Kruul prodded a thumb upwards and said "this is Gleb. You lot, this is Mrs.Murphy. She owns the Rocking Horse Shite with her husband, Mr. Murphy." He pointed a finger at a blonde haired Dwarf behind the bar who was idly chatting to a goblin. The Dwarf gave Kruul a nod of acknowledgement and continued his conversation with the goblin.

Mrs.Murphy gave Kruul a small nod of approval like only a mother could and said "Ya all certainly welcome, what'll it be then?"

Vodius stepped forward and gave a small bow "I would very much like a table by the fire for myself and my companions, four ales and a sherry glass, just the glass, five plates of whatever that divine food is that tantilises the senses and five rooms for the night please. A hot bath in each if possible." He slid three golden coins from a pouch and handed them to her "Will this be sufficient?"

Her eyes bulged and the coins "I'll tuck ye in at night and a little more for that me kind sir!" she giggled.

"That won't be necessary, thank you. Where are we to sit?" Vodius said, oblivious.

The others couldn't help but smirk at each other as Mrs Murphy frowned and gave a slow nod to the elf, patted his cheek and said "Right this way then!"

She led them to the back of the room where there was a table by the fireplace in the corner. "A cosy nook." Kaln idley commented as they settled into their seats.

Mrs.Murphy pulled out a tatty notepad, scribbled something down and said "Righty, ya will be in rooms six, seven, eight, nine and ten. Far end of the hallway." She pointed to a doorway by the bar. "I'll be back with some lovely warm grub for ya in a wee while. By the time ye've eaten I'll have got the girls to sort yer baths." She gave them one last smile and disappeared into the bustling crowd.

After a handful of trips, the table was laden with food and drink, more than they ordered but a fraction of what they paid for. All of them gorged themselves and threw back pints of ale. All except Vodius, who had retrieved an old and expensive looking bottle from his pouch and carefully poured himself a glass. He watched the oily liquid swirl around the delicate glass as if nothing else mattered, as if Gleb's inane chatter wasn't there. As if the crowds of thugs, traders, bounty hunters and bandits watching them, assessing them and chatting amongst themselves weren't there. He raised the glass to his nose and inhaled. His eyes fluttered as his nostrils excused the smells of blade oil, leather, sweat, cheap ale and gravy in favour of the rich smooth smells of his favourite drink. He raised the glass to the firelight and swirled it once more watching the light dance in the liquid and tried to take a mouthful of the ambrosia he had reserved for himself. There was a sudden clang as the delicate glass was almost knocked from his hand. Kruul had mistaken Vodius' quiet moment of appreciation as a gesture of cheers. The big orc was wiping one meaty paw across his grease covered mouth while absent-mindedly selecting from the pile of food what he was going to eat next.

Kruul said, still chewing "Aye, cheers! We've been through quite a lot and I'm sure there's more to come."

Lilly gave a deep smile as she looked at the bottle Mrs. Murphy had just handed her and poured her and Kaln a glass of Black Beck. "To those we've lost and those who remain!"

Gleb let out an excited screech in between frantic mouthfuls.

They all clinked their drinks against the others and shouted "Cheers!"

An hour or so later their hunger was sated and the drink had left them feeling suitably relaxed. That in itself made them feel strange. This was the first real taste of normality since before everything, before mayhem became their normality. There was a need to fill the gaps in conversation. Silence left them feeling like reflection on what they had done to be there could creep up on them or realisation of the gravity of what was happening or thoughts of what was to come suffocated them.

Lilly put her empty flagon down on the table with a hollow wooden clank, slurped the ale from her top lip and said "Kaln, I've - we've backed you all the way with the eh..." She glanced around the room, nobody but her companions seemed to be paying attention to what she was saying.
"With the Slavers? The ones we butchered?" Kaln said, obviously showing no attempt to hush his voice.
Lilly nodded "Well, yes. We did the right thing and I would do it again. You know I trust you. I...I just need to understand why. Not why we did what we did but why it meant so much to you. Don't act like it didn't."
Everyone at the table, except Gleb stopped what they were doing and looked at Kaln. Gleb took the opportunity to take some scraps from the other's plates that obviously were not wanted.
Kaln took a long drink and finished his ale while the others sat in silence waiting. He gave a

satisfied gasp, wiped the back of his sleeve across his mouth and looked at Lilly. There was no anger nor mirth on his expression, just a distant numbness that they could all relate to.

"When I was a small lad, we used to have a house in the woods, by road. I'd watch the traders, soldiers and cattle pass by each day." The expression on Kaln's face softened as he recalled a happier time.

"One day, whilst out hunting, father came across a group of Slavers harassing a family travelling North to Whitebluff. He watched from afar and when he could, he set them free at night while the Slavers were sleeping. From what my father later told me, word got back to 'em. Me, my mother and my father were dragged from our home in the middle of the night." He took a swig of Vodius' liquor.

"Only mercy they showed my mother was a quick death. We had to watch helplessly while she bled out in the rain. I still remember her final moments were not spent weeping or begging. She just looked at me and my father and smiled. Proud that my father did the right thing."

Kaln snatched a tear from his good eye and tried to clear the lump in his throat.

"It was a message sent loud and clear to my father for doing the right thing. After that, we built a new house up on the cliffs and hid the entrance. Father was never the same after that... Neither was I. I spent most of my life believing they were monsters, lurking between the trees in the darkest shadows. I had nightmares almost every night. I was barely old enough to understand what happened but I was old enough to ask questions. Eventually I got the truth out of my father. I've been in that lad's shoes. I wish I was given the same opportunity he was tonight."

Lilly felt the weight of guilt slowly rest itself on her shoulders. "I'm... I'm sorry Kaln." She looked at him, desperately trying to read his features. He looked up from the table and gave her a warm smile but before he could say a word, a fat grimy hand slammed on the table snatching everyone's attention. There stood a slimy blob of a man, he had a goatee which was tied at the end, bulbous eyes, a short ginger ponytail and only a few teeth. He leaned over Kaln with a slight sway. With a quiet voice that only drunk people can produce, the man practically shouted "Nah den! Wonderin' if ya could answer a quest'n for me..." He swayed, staggered and rested his arse on the edge of the table.

"See me n' me friends ere." He pointed a black nailed fat finger at a table a dozen strides away where several other men sat, dressed in a similar manner to the fat man. Bandits or Slavers.

"Well, we were bettin' on ow' yer face got so fucked up." The fat man seemed sincere in the question but the men at his table burst into laughter.

The fat man leaned in further and boozy breath washed over Kaln as he said more quietly "See, I bet ya did it crossin' someone ya shouldn't 'av. Did you learn a lesson that day?"

Kaln looked at him, his wolf fangs bared in a snarl. His fists were clenched tightly, he stood from his seat to tower over the drunken man.

"I did this in a bare knuckle fight with a bear. You really don't want to interrupt me and my friends again." Kaln said in a dangerous, sobering tone.

The fat man flinched at Kaln's words and flustered red. "Dun think ya' can threaten me ya' little shit! Do you know who I am?!" The fat man barked as he stood up right but barely made it to the height of Kaln's chin.

Kaln caught a glimpse of Kruul over the man's shoulder. He was still, watching how this played out over the rim of his flagon. Kaln knew he had given the orc his word, and so he sat back down and without looking at the fat man he said "Please be on your way." in as neutral a tone as he could muster.

This disregard seemed to enrage the fat man even more and he grabbed Kaln's collar but before anything else could happen, Orc tribesmen from one side of Kaln's table and a group of human and dwarf bounty hunters from the other side grabbed the fat man. They dragged him to the door and threw him out into the snow. They saw Mrs Murphy follow them outside but couldn't hear what she said.

Kruul said, with a subtle hint of pride "Well done lad."

Kaln noticed the general bustle of conversation in the inn had barely dipped throughout the whole altercation.

"This place survives for everyone on the understanding that there is no violence. It's an unspoken rule around here. Nothing would get done without this place as neutral ground." Kruul continued as he retrieved stolen parts of his meal from a sullen Gleb.

The orcs and bounty hunters returned shortly after. Dragging in the cool night air, they gave Kaln the briefest of nods and returned to their own discussions.

Mrs Murphy appeared soon after that "Yer rooms and baths are ready, if you are?"

CHAPTER 26 - A WARM BED

Lilly watched the ever so subtly dancing flame of the candle beside her bed as she sat in the copper bath tub by the fire. The herbs that were burning released a thick pale smoke that swirled around the wooden ceiling of the small room. The smoke's effect on Lilly finished what the food, ale and bath oils couldn't. She was in a heavenly stupor. She just let every sense enjoy the pleasure of a hot bath after a hearty meal and a healthy dose of ale. Her eyes felt heavy and her skin tingled with the hot water washing away the grime of travel and soothing her sore muscles. She moved her arm from beneath the water and the falling water sounded almost deafening as it broke the deep silence of the room.

I could stay here forever, she thought distantly

now allowing herself to hear the crackle of the fire and the subtle fizz of the herbs as they burned. If she tried, she could hear the distant conversations of the Inn's food hall. She was the furthest room away, next to hers was Kaln's, then the other's rooms.

She climbed out of the bath and stood in front of the fire naked, enjoying the heat. It felt so good to be clean. The mere prospect of her clothes being cleaned for her excited her. She started to feel human again as she wrapped a towel around herself and sat on the edge of her large bed. A sudden pang of guilt pulled her stomach to the floor.

What right do I have to feel normal? To enjoy food, laughter, ale and a warm bath? The poor folk of Cornwalk will never enjoy these things. She berated herself until a more painful thought entered her consciousness.

If I survive this, I'm alone. What do I have to go back to?

She curled up in a ball on the corner of the bed next to the wall as she delved deeper into her own guilt.

What if I die and change nothing? What if I disappoint Celuna with the gift she has given me? What if I don't tell Kaln how I feel and something happens.

The last thought shocked her, she knew the feelings were there but she had been putting them to one side, they were an indulgence she had not allowed herself. *Does he even feel the same way? This isn't the time for feelings. No, wait… This is exactly the time! I may not get the chance later. There may not be a 'later'!*

Kaln was sitting on his bed in his towel after his bath, fighting with similar internal struggles of guilt and fear when there was a light knock at the door. So light he wasn't sure if it was the wind outside his small window. He stood, tightened the towel around his waist and listened at the door.
He heard a hushed voice "It's now or it could be never."
There was a second knock at the door, this one was more sure.
He opened the door to see Lilly, she too was wrapped in a towel. He noticed the shimmer of light reflecting on the water still on her pale shoulders as the flame of her candle wobbled in the dark corridor, illuminating the apprehension on her face. Stunned he just stared for a moment, a thousand things rushing through his head.
Why was she at my door? Why wasn't she dressed and was she standing with only a towel? Why haven't I invited her in yet? Why was she looking at me that way?
He stepped back, gesturing for her to come inside. "Are you ok? Come in."
She padded past him barefooted leaving damp little prints on the stone floor and sat on his bed

by the fire.

"I'm fine. There's something I want to tell you." She said looking into the low flames of the fire. They reminded her of that first night they stayed at Kaln's home after fleeing Cornwalk. There was something very reassuring about being in the same room as him.

Kaln closed the door and came to sit next to her on the bed facing away from the fire. Lilly watched him approach and reflections of firelight danced on water still on the muscles of his chest and arms, she didn't look away.

There was a silence, not an awkward silence but like the calm before a storm, where unseen energies gathered.

Lilly spoke first "Each day we see danger and each day I feel guilt for thinking this, but one day soon something may happen to me and I would regret not telling you-"

"I love you." Kaln interrupted, his expression steeled and honest as he turned to face her.

"I love you too!" Lilly blurted.

"The mere chance of seeing you and maybe even speaking to you was the only reason I went to the market with my father." Kaln said.

Lilly grinned conspiratorially "Did you not think it a fine coincidence I was there every time you came? That I needed to purchase something as an excuse to speak to you every market day?"

Kaln returned the grin "Every day since the attack on Cornwall, my feelings for you have grown. I should feel fear and anger, instead my thoughts are of you and keeping you safe. I carry a burden of guilt for these thoughts."

Lilly shook her head "Imagine feeling that way and having to watch me fall in battle surrounded by dozens of Slavers! My heart almosted shattered! We must live for us, not those we have lost."

She stood and turned to face Kaln. She let the towel drop to the ground and the firelight illuminated every curve of her magnificent body. His wildest dreams could not compare to the beauty that stood before him.

He stood too, leaving his towel behind and the two turned so that they were both in the firelight. Lilly took in Kaln's form. The scrawny boy was definitely no more and it would seem that her imagination had failed her too.

They embraced and it felt good to their souls, to be held by one that was their everything, their entire world.

Their skin against one another tingled with electric excitement. He could feel her soft warm skin and she could feel the powerful muscles beneath his.

Lilly looked up at Kaln and he kissed her. Passion overcame them as emotions of guilt, sadness, fear and anxiety washed away and they both fell onto the bed. Their hearts were pounding as they let them free to feel. That night, they found out why people called it 'making love'.

CHAPTER 27 - ON THE ROAD AGAIN

Kaln awoke facing Lilly, their legs and arms were tangled in a loose embrace. His arm was around her waist and he could feel the small dimples at her lower back as he lightly stroked her soft skin. He couldn't keep the smile from creeping across his face as he admired her beauty in the morning sunlight. She must have felt his eyes on her because she woke to see a grinning Kaln. She smiled back.
She started to say "Last night was-".
"Exactly what we needed." Kaln finished her sentence and kissed her.
Both of them relaxed, it wasn't a dream, it wasn't booze or a glimmer of normality. It was what they wanted. They both melted into the kiss and

back under covers.

Kruul and Gleb were refreshed and once again gorging themselves on the monstrous pile of sausages, bacon, eggs and bread Mrs.Murphy had prepared for them. It was a flurry of snatching hands, prodding forks and finding space for another sausage to be stashed away.

"Did you sleep well gentlemen? I honestly don't recall the last time I slept quite so soundly." Vodius said, simply a bystander on the assault on the pile of meat.

He made a note in his tiny leatherbound notebook and waited for the feeding frenzy to slow enough for him to select his meal from the pile of food without fear of losing a finger.

"Mmmmmrph phrrmp!" Gleb said enthusiastically as he slowly forced another sausage in between the other sausages already filling his mouth. His jaw was straining so much it made his head shake.

Vodius watched in a disgusted curiosity for a moment, sighed and said "You can both slow down. Nobody is going to take it off you."

Kruul glanced at Gleb conspiratorially and the two looked across the feeding hall at the handful of other groups all eating their own breakfasts, looking for potential threats to their meal. There were less than half the number of people here now, then the night before.

Vodius shook his head and risked grabbing some

bacon "Look, there's more meat than you can possibly eat-". Vodius stopped and held up his hands at the stricken look Gleb and Kruul were now giving him.
"Fine, I believe in you." Vodius said with a chuckle. He then waved Mrs Murphy over and asked her to bring him some tea and a sandwich.

Lilly and Kaln walked down the hallway towards the feeding hall, they were holding hands as Lilly said "I want this to be private for us until we're finished with Thaldur."
She wasn't sure if Kaln would take this the wrong way and gave him time to process what she'd said. It didn't take him long.
"Agreed, I don't want anyone to use this against us. I want last night to be ours." He gave her hand a gentle squeeze, let go and opened the doorway to the hall.

There sat his friends around what could only be described as an empty trough. Kruul and Gleb were groaning and resting their hands on their swollen bellies. Kruul noticed them walking in and let out a strained chuckle as he pointed to Kaln and Lilly. "Told ye. Pay up boys!"
Gleb and Vodius both assessed Lilly and Kaln for a moment, then began counting out gold pieces to hand over to the bloated orc.

"Well. That's that cat out of the bag." Kaln said with a smirk and the two sat down just as Mrs

Murphy scurried past with her hands full of dirty plates. Somehow, with a couple of subtle gestures and silent mouthing of words. She made it clear she was heading right over with breakfast for Kaln and Lilly.

"Honestly, I'm oblivious to these things." Vodius slowly shook his head in disbelief looking at the two as he handed the gold to Kruul.

"You two are clueless, could see it a mile off." Kruul said. He puffed out a long queasy breath "I'm so full I couldn't eat another morsel."
He picked something edible off his shirt and ate it.

One of the orcs from the night before approached the table, his attention was on Kruul.
The orc had grey hair and stubble. His skin was scarred and weathered. His lower fangs were yellowed and worn. He had a wooden leg from the knee down. The old orc approached Kruul as a soldier would approach their general. It was obvious he respected Kruul.
"Ruth'gok, Kruul, Clan Lord" he said.
"Ruth'gok." Kruul replied in a measured voice.
"Those we threw out last night, I heard down the grape vine they're after a wee bit o' vengeance oot' on the roads. Watch yer backs."
The grizzled orc softly tapped a thick knuckle on the table a couple of times, nodded to Kruul and turned to rejoin his group at their table.

Some time later, they stepped out onto the porch of The Rocking Horse Shite. The food hall had filled back up now but Mrs Murphy made time to poke her head out of the door as they left "Best of luck to you. Thanks for staying with us. You're always welcome."

She smiled sweetly and went to close the door but paused, looking at Kaln. "Thank you for not bringing violence to my Inn."

Someone did something behind the door that made Mrs Murphy jump and giggle. The door closed and the sound of the crowd was muted. It seemed so far away now.

The group stood for a quiet moment watching the golden sun rays glimmer and shine on the snow and icicles, the only sounds were the creaking of the inn as it warmed in the morning sun, distant birds chirping and the hum of activity from inside the inn. A thick slab of snow abruptly slid off the porch roof in front of them, breaking the moment's tranquillity.

"Right, I'll lead the way then." Kruul said. He'd learned a long time ago that the prospect of doing something was almost always worse than just doing the damn thing.

Spirits were higher now, not that their task had changed but they had eaten well, bathed, slept well and were wearing clean clothes. They followed Kruul away from the forest's edge, the inn and that flash of fleeting normality.

They walked for a couple of hours before the terrain began to change from level snow-covered ground to an incline with savage rocks jutting out from the ground, the foot of the mountain.

The cold wind whipped through the gnarled spikes of rock and earth. There was no green up here, only shades of greys, browns and deep shadows. Their heightened spirits soon began to wane. The path became twisty and finding solid footing became a rarity as they climbed. Suddenly the brutal winds carried the sound of a cry to them.

They all froze and looked at Kruul. He instinctively crouched low, the others followed his lead. They crept around the next corner, the cries were louder and now, there were more. Kaln's inhumanly keen senses could smell warm human blood. Kruul noticed Kaln's pupil's dilate, then he smelled the blood too. They all heard the sound of chittering and something heavy moving around beyond the next ridge. They also saw the colour drain from Kruul's face.

They froze in fear, looking at each other. Suddenly a streak of blood ran down the stone they were standing next to. They all jerked their heads up to see a face staring down at them from atop the rock. The bulging eyes of the fat man who had tried to provoke Kaln was looking down on them. He tried to mouth something at them but only succeeded in vomiting blood. His shaking hand was outstretched towards them. Suddenly a sound similar to the executioners axe doing its work rang out between the rocks. The life in the fat man's eyes faded and he was roughly jerked back out of sight. The sound of tearing flesh followed.

Kruul seized the opportunity and moved cautiously around the next bend, the others followed. They climbed up several vicious looking rocks to avoid having to follow the path. The entire time ripping flesh and chittering could be heard right next to them, beyond the rocks they hid behind. Eventually Kruul stopped climbing, peered over the edge of the nearby ridge, grimaced and whispered, "Aye, thought so. Corpser. Looks like those boys were planning an ambush."

They all looked down. They saw an opening between the rocks, the rocks and ground were bathed in crimson. In its center was an insect-like creature. It was as tall as the biggest horse Kaln had ever seen and twice as wide. It had mantis claws the size of great swords, under the blood was grey chitin covering its entire form and bulbus black eyes that scanned the carnage. Its abdomen was covered in pike-like spikes that jutted upwards. There were corpses of all manner of creatures in all states of decay piled on its back. The most recent of which were Kaln's would-be assailants. Some of them were still moving feebly as the creature used its tail to add more bodies to the pile. It had a thick tail like a scorpion but instead of a stinger, the end of this creature's tail had a brutal claw that grabbed men, alive or dead and threw them onto the spikes.

"By Celuna, what is that monster?" Lilly let out a horrified gasp and covered her mouth with her hand in disgust.

"Told ye, Corpser." Kruul said, throwing a tiny stone at a nearby wall absentmindedly.

"That, Kruul, is an Acanthas. I've heard tales of them being tamed and ridden into battle..." Vodius said with awe thick in his voice.

"Oh aye? Good luck taming that!" Kruul laughed.

Vodius continued "Did you know they let some of their victims live intentionally? Of course, I use the term 'live' in the loosest sense. You see, those spikes drain nourishment from their victims over-"

"Ok Vodius, we get it." Kaln said grimacing, "Better them than us."

Kruul started making his way further up the mountain and the others began to follow. Lilly's eyes were following Gleb's footing; she was suddenly aware of how vulnerable she would be to the elements and creatures who hunt in these mountains if she were to twist an ankle or fall. She felt a strong hand grab hers from behind. She turned to see Kaln, he stepped to one side and gestured at the view they had missed because of the distraction below. Now she faulted at the new sight. The entire forest could be seen up here. A sea of snow with glimpses of golden leaves breaking through occasionally stretched as far as the eye could see. Right through the middle of the forest was a streak of bleak earth, rot and decay. The decay led from the mountain, down through the forest, through the fields. Kaln's grip tightened slightly when he saw her eyes lingering on the husk of Cornwalk in the distance. She snatched a tear before it could fall and her eyes followed the trail of death and rot back into the forest, North into Crossay and further North towards the pale cliffs of Whitebluff on the horizon. Kaln put an arm around her, she slid her arms around his waist.

He kissed her forehead and said "For all of them."

CHAPTER 28 - ANOTHER RUINED HOME

The mountain granted no respite from the unrelenting harsh wind during their ascent but as their endurance was reaching its limits, they emerged on the lip of a vast plateau on the mountain's side. This place was strange and savage. There were trees, shrubs and even fruit. All of it gnarled and covered with spikes. Every living thing here fought to be alive here. They took some time to rest and eat the food they had brought with them. Kaln could sense the tension in Kruul sitting quietly as the others chatted about what they thought they might find ahead.

"Kruul, a moment?" Kaln said and stepped away from the small fire that the others sat around.

Kruul stood beside Kaln quietly, looking at the twisted treeline.

"Are you ok?" Kaln said.

"Aye lad, have'nae seen home or what's left of it, since we fled all those moons ago." He kicked a pebble that bounced into the thick bramble bushes. "Guess I'm jus' anxious." he turned to return to the others, patting Kaln on the shoulder as he left.

Kaln stayed where he was looking at the thicket of rugged trees ahead of them. He tried to reach out with his new sense to see if the land would lend him it's aid like his forest had. These trees, creatures and its earth just seemed to snarl back at him, Aeathune's influence did not reach these mountains. Not entirely. Faintly he heard the familiar voice of Aeathune, barely carried by the cool mountain winds, whisper "...Help Yassvyr..."

"Yassvyr?" Kaln echoed quietly and waited. He was greeted only with a lonely silence.

He scanned once more for danger and returned to the conversation by the fire.

"Dragon. I bet he's got a dragon if he's so powerful." Gleb said.

He bit down on a sausage that was clearly too hot and quickly began to toss the morsel of food around his mouth as he gasped for cool air, refusing to spit it out.

The others watched until he eventually swallowed, there were tears in his eyes but somehow he seemed proud of his victory over the sausage. Conversation continued as if nothing happened.

"Don't be ridiculous Gleb, have you ever seen a dragon this side of the seas?" Vodius said, waiting for his food to cool.

"Have you ever seen a man appear from a mountain and wreck so much havoc?" Lilly said defiantly "We should be prepared for anything."

"Indeed," Vodius agreed thoughtfully "but we can't possibly be prepared for everything."

"Aye, that's true. Best we can do is stick together... Put that fire out, we've stayed here too long. The scent will bring predators." Kruul said, his eyes never leaving their surroundings.

The others ate their food quickly, their attention was drawn to the ridges and treelines around them, every falling pebble and breaking branch in the wind keeping them on edge.

Another hour's travel and Kruul had not said a word since they stopped to eat. The others soon realised why when they emerged from the trees to look upon the ruins of his tribe's camp. Not the ruined tents and fire pits as Kaln and Lilly had imagined, but stone buildings, much like their own. Ransacked and abandoned, others were burned down. It was harrowing even for the others seeing the ruin of a place which was once home to so many. Kruul stood in silence looking out over the village. His broad shoulders began to convulse and he quietly shook as a tear trickled down his weathered features.

"Roku." Gleb said in a tone that hinted, for the first time, that he understood the gravitas of what he was looking at.

"Roku." The others said in agreement.

Kruul wiped away the tear and took a deep breath. He blinked a couple of times, nodded to himself and with a determined look on his face he said "Aye, Roku. Let's get this bastard where it hurts. Hope you're right Vodius." He led the way.

They walked through the ruined village and the further in they ventured, the more they saw grey lifeless earth, dead plants and small animals like a blight had passed directly through the village. They all knew this is where the scar which ran through the forests started.

They reached the edge of the village and Kaln said "What was her name?"

Kruul gave him a soft smile and said "Thronkah, one of the largest and most respected orc Villages in these mountains."

The village ended, its outskirts led back onto the steep mountain incline, the plateau had ended.

They hadn't ascended far when they saw the gaping opening of a vast cave on the mountain side. Even from this distance they could see it didn't look natural. Their thoughts were confirmed as they got closer. They could see what they now called the 'Bleak Scar' had originated from this cave. They got closer and could hear the wind howling in the huge cave opening. In its depths, the walls of the cave glittered and glistened eerily like the eyes of millions of creatures in the failing daylight.

"Goblins love a good cave but maybe we sleep out here first..." Gleb said, weary eyes staring into the black abyss of the cave mouth.

"The last thing I want to do is sleep out here exposed on the mountain side..." Lilly blurted.

"But somehow I'd prefer that to trying to sleep in there..." she muttered uncomfortably as she tried to drag her eyes away from the dark opening.

"Nae' bother lass, we can take turns to watch through the night. I dunnae' think they'll be any mountain dwelling creatures comin' near this place. The eye of the storm is where it's calmest I reckon." Kruul said.

Kruul shifted his weight uncomfortably as he looked into the blackness. "Anyway, I've seen what came out'a that thing. Gives me the willies." He turned away with a look of disgust still smeared across his face.

It was true, they had not seen or heard any life at all since the gnarled trees they passed through before they arrived at Thronkah.

Vodius said contemplatively "Your logic is sound, Kruul. Besides, Kruul knows what dangers may arrest us out here. In there, however, is a different matter entirely. Better the devil you know I'd wager. I would certainly like a good night's rest before I venture in there." Vodius gave a small nod to the cave entrance which seemed to grimace back at their cowardice. He paused, then continued "Though I am intrigued by the black glass-like material which is around and in front of the cave opening, it looks almost liquid..." He trailed off into his own thoughts and started making notes in his notebook.

"From the report Kelregg gave me" he paused at the pang of grief, "he saw the mountain side explode violently leaving that opening. The stone turned to liquid as it belched out of the rock face, turning black and hardening into what ye see there. Look around ye, ye can see where it's hardened." Kruul pointed to a nearby dead tree, it was blackened as though burned but at the core of the tree husk was a hardened glob of black glass. "It vomited liquid rock even this far." Kruul shook his head.

Vodius dashed over to the tree to inspect the stone and returned, passing the stone from hand to hand like a hot potato.

"Incredible! The stone is still warm even now! The sheer amount of magical energy required to liquify stone in such a large area must have been immense..." Vodius sounded shocked and a little bit excited by the findings. He went back to making notes and sketching the stone.

"I trust your judgement on this one Kruul. Lets

rest here. I'll take the first watch." Kaln said.

The night was completely uneventful; there wasn't even any conversation or banter and no Corpsers or worse beset them in the night. They all slept surprisingly well having traversed the mountainside for most of the day, exhaustion set in as soon as they stopped moving. Lilly slept soundly knowing there was someone on watch, it also didn't hurt that she was sleeping in Kaln's tent with him. As ever, her rock.
What she didn't know was that he was equally thankful for her company to settle his nerves.

Morning came and the group gathered themselves, ready to delve into the unnatural cave. They climbed the slope up to the entrance, it was further than it seemed and the cave mouth was much larger when they finally did arrive. Everything at the cave mouth was covered in smooth, black shiny stone. A carpet of it trailed off down the hill, they were walking on it now. They paused at the entrance and glanced at each other. There were small nods and whispers of "Roku's" from each of them. They were ready for this. Vodius raised a hand, in it was the stone from the tree. His eyes closed for a moment and the stone began to twinkle in the morning light, the light grew and grew until it was too bright to look at, Vodius cupped his hand around it and pointed the light into the cave. From here the cave entrance looked like the gaping maw of the mountain itself. The interior was lined on all sides with uneven obsidian glass. The light from Vodius' spell refracted amongst the walls, floor and ceiling giving the cave an even more lurid atmosphere.

Vodius looked at Kaln with his freehand gesturing towards the cave "After you."
Kaln took a breath and looked into the darkness. The enhanced vision that had been gifted to him meant that he could see into the darkness without Vodius' light. He saw only a vast tunnel going directly into the mountain side. He cleared his throat, nodded and started walking, Emmental in hand. Kruul walked by his side.
Each of them braced themselves mentally, prayed to their gods, checked their weapons or ate one last glorious sausage and stepped into the glistening cave.

CHAPTER 29 - THE MAW OF DARKNESS

Each scuffed footstep echoed in the tunnel that seemed to stretch into endless darkness. What little light they had reflected, splintered and danced unnaturally in the black glass as they delved deeper. There were no other sounds, save for the now distant howls of wind warped and twisted by the strange tunnel from the cave entrance. They walked slowly at first, each step cautious and timid but after some time they grew more confident there was no immediate threat and began to pick up the pace, a little.

"At least it's not more bloody hill climbing, this tunnel is flat. Only thing keeping me going is knowing that the way home will be downhill!"

Kaln said to break the silence. The scoffs and sniggers of the others seemed to break the tension like a twig.

"I bet there *is* a dragon in 'ere, I told you he had one. Why else the cave so big? He only one man, I told you!" Gleb nattered as they delved deeper. The sound of wonder was evident in his voice.

"Gleb, that really isn't helpful." Lilly sniped. Her tone came out more harsh than she intended as she tried to cover the fear in her voice.

She put a hand on Glebs shoulder to let him know she was sorry for snapping.

Gleb screamed.

The others laughed as Lilly apologised, until she realised Gleb was laughing too.

Suddenly a gust of cool wind washed over them, so strong they staggered back. Kruul grabbed the scruff on Gleb's collar to keep him from tumbling back down the tunnel. It was coming from deeper in the cave. They all fell silent, crouched low and desperately scanned the darkness at the edge of the pale light of Vodius' spell. Though they frantically strained their ears for a clue of what was ahead, none of them heard anything.

After some time of watching, listening and waiting for some imagined monster to lunge out at them from the oppressive shadows, they plucked up the courage to begin picking their way deeper into the tunnel. Kaln was the first to see something ahead. He whispered and pointed ahead in the pale gloom, "Tunnel ends ahead, be ready. Vodius, the spell."

A moment later the light dimmed to a humble glow, illuminating only his palm, then faded completely and they were all left in utter darkness.

"Keep your hand on the person in front and follow me." Kaln continued as a large orcish hand groped at his shoulder from behind.

Slowly they ventured. First Gleb, then Kruul and Vodius and eventually Lilly all saw a pale blue light coming from up ahead. It wasn't the light source but something illuminating a cavern ahead. A short time after they came to a huge opening at the end of the tunnel, there was indeed a vast cavern. It was quite obviously natural as the obsidian stopped here. Here the cave walls were stone. There was a huge underground lake taking up half of the cavern floor. Its water was crystal clear and perfectly still. They could see even from here that the light in the cavern was from bioluminescent mushrooms growing under the surface of the water. Their eyes were initially drawn to the light but as they scanned the rest of the cavern for danger, they suddenly felt exposed and hunted. Then they noticed something quite wrong. Here in the depths of the mountains, by an underground lake was a house, a strange house with gothic architecture none of them recognised, gargoyles loomed over the great heavy wooden door at the front of the house like a cathedral to some dark god but it was nevertheless, a home. Its tall slender roof reached into the shadows of the cave above. It was covered in tall and thin windows framed in dark wood and built from murky grey bricks. It even had iron rails leading up to the front door.

Vodius gasped "How can this be-" His words were cut short as the shadow shrouding the roof of the house unfurled its wings. Wisps of black smoke rose off the massive figure perched on the house distorting its shape. A glimmer of the creature's eyes, like brilliant emeralds wreathed in shadow looked down at them before it lazily flapped its immense leathery wings, to test and stretch them. The group were blown from their feet, tumbling back in a spray of lake water. They scrambled to pick themselves up when the huge monster tore through the shadows above them. It was only an instant and it was gone. Down the tunnel they had just traversed.

The only sound after that, was that of the water dripping off the cave wall until Gleb screached, "I fuckin' told you! Dragon!" half terrified and half excited.

In horrified acknowledgement there was silence for a long moment before any of them moved.

Lilly whispered "...What do we do now?"

"Well, the thing's gone now and I ain't turning back. May as well keep goin'." Kruul grunted at the house looming in the corner of the cave.

"Ok, but nobody go near lake." Gleb said. The words had nearly left his lips when his eyes bulged as Kruul moved towards the house revealing Vodius some distance behind him, standing looking into the clear waters of the underground lake.

Vodius stood looking into the blue waters. They were so still and sereen, he could see every stone and plant bathed in the light of the mushrooms. Deeper into the waters was a dark cave that the light couldn't reach. It was hard to tell how deep it was, the water was so clear it looked like he could reach into the water and touch the bottom of the lake. He of course knew that wasn't possible. He was also quite content just looking at the beautiful mushrooms. He felt like he could sit here all day. Forgotten were the worries of he and his friends. Their task was unimportant now. He gazed upon two particular mushrooms paired together, they were glorious. He decided at that moment he would slip off his robes and shoes and wade into the water to collect those mushrooms, they would be brilliant additions to his collection, assuming he ever felt the need to leave this beautiful place. Something in his peripheral vision was moving, but that was unimportant. Though it was quite irritating and distracting.

Gleb sprinted with surprising speed to the

water's edge where Vodius stood motionless looking into the glass-like water. Without looking into the water, Gleb scooped a handful of cool water from the lake and threw it in Vodius' face. Even now the light from the mushrooms began to dim and the cavern was plunged into a weak blue light, something was moving down there. Vodius didn't react to the water, nor to Gleb swinging on his robes, trying to move him. The blue light dulled even more. It was here.

"Run Vodius!" Gleb screamed frantically.

The water's surface broke as something big lunged out of it, crashing down where Vodius and Gleb were standing. Kruul barrelled into them both and threw all three of them to the ground, just in time to look up at the monster that assaulted them.

It stood twice as tall as Kruul, had a snake-like body but instead of scales, it was covered in buckler sized crab-like plates covering its body. At its head was a hideous cluster of spider-like legs around savage looking mandibles. Tentacles drooped over the gnashing teeth hiding its true hideousness. Its face was covered in many shiny black eyes. Atop its head were the two glowing mushrooms, standing proud and casting eerie writhing shadows amongst the flailing claws and tentacles. Its armoured plates clattered and grinded against one another as it reared up like a snake ready to strike at the group. It lunged like a viper, its spindly legs outstretched ready to pluck a victim from the cave floor.

White light exploded out as Lilly managed to raise a shield over Kruul an instant before the strike landed. Water droplets from the monster reflected the light of her shield as silver light rained down. The force of the strike was transferred to Lilly and she was tossed weightlessly against the cave wall with a heavy thud.

Kruul stood defiantly between the monster and the others. It reared its ugly head back again to lunge. Gleb and Vodius threw themselves backwards. Kruul threw himself forward into a roll beneath the creature. He lashed out with his axe as he tumbled past and a few long severed spider legs flailed into the air. Streams of grey blood plumed from them as they fell into the water and sank into the darkness.

The monster recoiled and screeched in pain. It turned to loom over Kruul. He was still recovering from the leap. It raised its head ready to crush him against the cave floor but before it could, a deafening crack rang out in the cave and the monster jerked back violently as chunks of flesh covered plate armour exploded off its back and sploshed into the water, sending it a murky grey colour. The shot from Thunderbastard only seemed to enrage the creature and it lashed at them with this spiney armoured tail. All of them were knocked from their feet and Kruul was slapped over the water but was caught before he could plunge into its cool depths. At Kaln's command, vines from the cave floor and walls lashed out and caught the orc, pulling him to solid ground. Suddenly the cave was almost in complete darkness. Vodius harried the creature with purple bolts of magical fire, now the only light in the cave. It flinched back towards the water's edge as the flames splashed against its armour with horrific hissing sounds. The flurry of flames stopped as Vodius paused to gather his energy, leaving only blackness.

The cracking of the monster's carapice could be heard in the consuming darkness, something truly massive lurched from the water and grabbed it. A moment later the light returned from the water's depths, illuminating the cave once again. For an instant, Kruul saw something huge dragging the flailing monster deep into the dark depths of the underground lake leaving a trail of grey blood to settle between the glowing mushrooms.

Kruul wiped the water from his face with a meaty paw and looked at the others.
"Aye, let's keep away from the water, eh?"
He gave Kaln a small nod, "Nice catch lad." and patted Gleb on the shoulder as he passed him, walking towards the house. The others followed, keeping a wary eye on the water's edge.

CHAPTER 30- THE HOME OF A MONSTER

They approached the stone steps leading up to the house in a most incorrect place. A strange feeling washed over them, their skin crawled and every instinct told them to turn around. Just at that moment the shadows clinging to the iron rails, nearby stalagmites and doorway of the home coalesced into a form that was vaguely human, its willowey fingers dragged on the floor from lanky arms. Where the shadows face should have been was an eerie mask that was almost featureless bar two circular eye holes. It was expressionless and pale white. Behind the mask, glowing red eyes leered at them. The being stood as tall as Vodius and as the others slowed their pace to a halt, only

Vodius continued in his stride to stand in front of the shadow. The others glanced at each other nervously.

The shadow spoke, "Fenryr, romsku rassha." in a raspy voice that made their skin crawl.

Vodius straightened his back with his hands clasped in front of his waist. Like he was speaking to an old peer. "Raak'sha, you will speak the common tongue. You will address me as Vodius."

The mask twitched in the direction of the others and back to Vodius "Vodius…"

The shadow savoured the name, like knowing at least part of it had power.

"I sincerely hope you do not mean to threaten me Raak'sha." Vodius said calmly with a confident smile.

Raak'sha only stared at him silently from behind the mask, its shadowy form wavering like a flame.

Vodius took a step closer, to within arm's reach of the shade.

"You know precisely what happens next if you continue to look at me in that way." Vodius whispered dangerously.

"My lord sends me for the soul of Thaldur or the souls he owes. He is my quarry." Raak'sha said, somehow sounding less defiant.

Dark wisps of purple smoke began to rise from Vodius' form, the smell of almonds was thick in the air and the energy he emitted was palpable as

Vodius flexed unseen arcane muscles.
"Your lord has no right to claim any soul over me. In fact, I'd venture to say that your god knows I'm here and has sent you to be slain. Pray tell, have you failed him recently? Why else would he send you to challenge the Fenryr?"
The Shadow's form flickered and shrank at the implications of what Vodius was saying.
"Go back to your realm and tell your lord to speak with me himself if he sees fit to lay claim to any soul I hunt. Go now before you extinguish what little patience I still possess." Vodius continued.

A moment passed and the glowing red lights within the mask faded to blackness. The mask shattered into millions of grains of sand and the shadow disbursed to nothingness.
Vodius sneered and brushed away some flecks of sand from his robes, turned to the others and, gesturing to the house, he said with a smile "Shall we continue?"

"Are...Are we not going to talk about that, Fenryr?" Kaln said, scratching his head.
"Later, I will indulge your questions later but now we must make haste." Vodius said, ushering the others towards the heavy wooden door. He placed a hand on the goblin's shoulder as he trotted by "Gleb, would you do the honours and pick the lock? I assume that is well within your skillset. It would be prudent to check for traps too. Do not open the door until I have done my

own checks, ok?"

Gleb grinned and nodded enthusiastically. "Ok!" he chirped as he pulled out a leather bag that clinked with the sound of many delicate metal tools.

He stood before the large door, knelt and rolled out the leather bag revealing many intricately designed lengths of metals. Then he stood and slid his wiry fingers around the frame of the door with help from Kruul to reach the top. Once he was done he gave a small nod, and withdrew a tiny length of metal with a small mirror on its end. He slid the mirror between the door and the frame and inch by inch he checked for unseen traps. His tongue was sticking out to ensure everyone knew he was concentrating. He stopped, just below the handle of the door, scratched his chin for a moment and collected two more delicate instruments from his collection. One with a hook on a curved length and the other with a tiny cutting blade on its end. He hunched over the location where he had spotted something and with his tongue still out, got to work on disarming the trap. A few moments later there was a distant click and the sound of weight moving within the wall, only audible due to the total silence as the others watched in fascination as Gleb plied his trade. Next he moved onto the lock and with a similar impressive efficiency he unlocked the heavy lock. He turned to the group, gave an eccentric bow

with a huge grin and stepped aside.
They all flinched as Kruul let out a bark of laughter, it even surprised Kruul.
"Woops!" Kruul grinned "Nice work Gleb!" He whispered.

Vodius stepped up to the door, slid his hands across its surface and, like finding a loose thread, he plucked something invisible away from the door. As he did the string he was pulling on shimmered blue showing the arcane rune the fabric of the spell was hiding momentarily.
He pulled the string further, unbinding the spell in a silent but colourful explosion of light that bathed the cave in the smell of almonds.
Gleb cheered enthusiastically until Vodius glared him back into silence. He gave a nod to the group and delicately twisted the black iron handle. There was a light click as the group stood ready for anything. The door swung open. There was a distant tearing noise like the first time Kaln and Lilly met Vodius and the smell of magic renewed. What they saw through the doorway defied all logic. They stepped through the door to investigate. The entrance hallway was big enough to fit the entire house that they were just standing outside of, inside. Leading from the grand hallway were even more doorways. None of which could have fit within the strange house they just entered. There were expensive looking chairs and tables lining the hallway. The

walls were dotted with dark and eerie pieces of artwork that were difficult to understand and stained glass windows letting in lurid streaks of light that were an impossibility from the cave they just left. Large deep red drapes covered any other gaps in the decorations. The marble flooring covered in a well made rug led deeper into the house. It was all illuminated by pale white Everblaze torches bracketed the walls. An expensive incantation for folk without the gift of knowledge and magic. Almost every surface was covered in a thick layer of dust, obviously untouched for many years. There was no sound, only the quiet click of the door closing behind them. The air suddenly felt oppressive.

"Don't touch anything. Not all is as it seems." Vodius whispered to everyone but looked at Gleb to make sure he was listening.

Vodius closed his eyes, obviously trying to remember the details of something long since passed.

"Follow me." He said confidently and marched down the hallway.

The only sound was their boots scuffing on the dusty marble floor. Door after door they passed, eventually they reached a door that had a rose engraved on it. Dust covered the handle. At the next door, Vodius halted. His crooked finger pressed to his lips in thought. He was running through a list in his mind. This door handle was not covered in dust.

He nodded and looked to the others.

"In here is where the information I bartered for ends."

He turned the door knob and fire light crept through the doorway in stark contrast to the everblaze torches lining the hallway. They all stepped through. The room was immaculate, there was no dust or decay, instead there was a lit fire that popped and crackled. The warm light bathed the bedroom. It had a dark wood four-post bed with deep red silk sheets, a battered but well crafted chest at the end of the bed and a vanity table against the wall with pots of powders, creams, oils and a hairbrush laid upon its surface. As if the lady of the manor had just left the room. There was a chest of drawers at either side of the bed and an intricate rug covering most of the floor. It almost felt welcoming.

Vodius moved to the side of the bed and pulled the chest of drawers over with an almighty crash. Clothes spilled out across the floor. He knelt down and prodded a finger at something inconspicuous between the bedpost and where the drawers were. There was a click and a small portion of the wall swung open revealing a small hidden compartment. Vodius' eyes widened as he peered into the small recess. He reached in and turned to the others holding a small book.

"This is it." He said and started rummaging through his pouch for something.

"This is what?" Kaln said.

"What I traded for." Vodius said as he pulled a large scroll from his waist pouch, unrolled it on the floor and knelt on it.

"So, what is it?" Lilly asked.

"I'm about to find out." Vodius replied as he placed the book in the center of the scroll and waved his hand over several symbols on the parchment. Each illuminated a bright purple and once all were lit, the scroll ignited at its edge and burned rapidly towards its center. It was too fast for anyone to intervene but when the flames died out, the book was on the floor without any signs of damage. Vodius looked up at the group from the ground, the magical purple light was just leaving his eyes as he completed the spell and a tear rolled down his cheek.

"Poor bastard." Vodius cleared his throat and handed the book to Lilly.

"What did you just do?" Lilly snapped.

Vodius was visibly shaken, he shook his head and wiped the tear away.

"I used a spell to absorb the knowledge in that book. His diary." He said after a moment to compose himself.

Lilly looked down at the little book and flicked through its pages. He was correct. The first lines she read were '~~I must~~ I *will* find a way to bring them back! The pain is too great to bear. I must use my agony and rage as fuel to find an answer. To bring them back to me. It isn't too late.'

Followed by a list of medical, magical and alien procedures that Lilly did not understand. Each entry of the list had a strike through it. Each strikethrough was done more and more violently. The last almost tearing the page. Each strike also had a date written next to it. He had been doing this for years without success and the dates lined up with what the speaker had told them. Lilly continued to read, delving into the mind of a distraught, broken and raw father, husband and wizard.

"So, what now?" Kaln said expectantly.

Vodius moved over to the wall furthest the door and held out a hand that was still shaking from the knowledge he had just gained. He muttered an incantation and his fingers wavered like they were being viewed through a great heat. The wall before him silently disappeared revealing a stairway that led down, more everblaze candles lined the stone walls of the stairwell. These walls were plain walls, decidedly more functional and the temperature was notably cooler.

"Now we find his soul fragment." Vodius said and began to descend. The others followed, Lilly continued to flick through the pages of the diary as she joined them.

They came to a thick heavy set metal door. Vodius drew a key and slid it into the keyhole in the center of the door.

"It was with the diary." He said without looking back.

Slowly he turned the key. The sound of heavy metal sliding against metal came from multiple points around the big door. Gleb let out a quiet gasp of awe.

The was a distant clunk deep within the flanking walls and the door swung inwards weightlessly. Only darkness awaited.

Vodius took the stone he used to illuminate the tunnel from his pouch and held it up high. He uttered the same incantation and with an inaudible poof of magic the stone shone and a waft of magic filled the air. He looked at Kaln and Kaln gave him a nod. They all stepped through the doorway. They were left straining to see. There was, infact, a light in the room but it was not coming from Vodius, instead a small and distant light source some way in the vast room they had entered. Vodius' stone was not shedding any light. In the gloom they waited, listening. They could hear distant clinks of chains coming from multiple directions in the room. Only subtle and quiet clinks. The smell in this room was awful, a barrage of musk and decay.

Vodius whispered "There is magic in the room suppressing the light. Thaldur's notes mentioned this was his menagerie. Perhaps it's best I do not break that particular spell."

Kaln whispered back "I'd rather see what was going to tear me apart than to pass on to the afterlife having never known."

"Are you sure?" Vodius replied.

"We have to. Look for the exit everyone." Kaln said, reaching for Emmental.

"Ok, according to his notes, the doorway should be at the far side of the room. He had a fondness of visiting these creatures regularly. Be ready." Vodius whispered.

Vodius raised the stone high up and repeated the incantation as before, this time there were new words the others had never heard before that carried power. The light bloomed from the stone and illuminated most of the menagerie for an instant before the suppressing darkness of Thaldur's spell crushed the light again. It was enough time for them all to see the endless hanging cages all around and above them, thousands disappearing out of sight with all manner of creatures. The following cacophony of sound was incredible as cages swung and smashed. They heard the sounds of bellowing roars, piercing screeches, haunting warbles and harrowing barks. Nearby they felt some of the cages crash down around them and huge creatures in the dark began tearing each other to pieces. They didn't stay to find out if their assumptions were correct. They each followed Vodius' dim light as he sprinted towards the far end of the room cursing himself for not properly breaking the spell. As the dull light bobbed and weaved between the shadows of the hanging cages more unseen creatures growled and thrashed in their cages, more cages yielded to their rage. They passed the tiny candle in the center of the room barely illuminating its own pedestal.

They were halfway there.

Something grabbed Kruul's leg, he turned to lash out at the monster but realised in the last instant that it was Glab clinging to him as some sort of web was wrapped around the goblin's leg and was pulling him into the black abyss. Kruul slashed at the web with his axe. He pried the goblin off his leg, tucked him under one arm and pushed on to catch up with the others. He could see them at the door looking back at him. They were all through except Kruul and Gleb. Kruul ignored Gleb's screaming, ignored the deep grunting noises coming from his left, the hair raising chittering noises coming from behind and ran towards the elf with all the speed he could muster. Something massive squawked and flapped its wings above him, almost knocking him from his feet but he staggered and found his footing again.

As he closed in on the door he saw Vodius cast a spell and point directly at him. There was nothing he could do at that moment but keep running straight forward as fast as he could. A wash of purple light exploded behind him and heat washed over him. The spell illuminated long spindly spider legs to one side of him and the snout and fangs of an impossibly large wolf ahead of him. He dived and rolled under the beast and got to his feet in time to leap again through the door. It slammed behind him. The barrage of the sounds beastial combat continued beyond the tiny door.

They were all gasping for air.

"Roku." Kruul said with his hands on his knees.

"Roku." Gleb said, sprawled out on the floor looking up at him.

Vodius gave him a nod. "Perhaps it would have been better with the light out."

"Perhaps." Kaln agreed.

The colour had washed from all of their faces and it took them a while to even look ahead. When they did, they saw another stairwell similar to the previous one they traversed. It was illuminated with the same torches they had seen and sloped downwards as before. The stone steps were worn shiny through much use and at the bottom they saw another door.

CHAPTER 31 - BEHIND THE DOOR

They descended and gathered around a heavy metal door, there was no keyhole, no handle or latches.

"Huh." Vodius murmured, "No mention of this in the diary."

"Maybe it just needs a good push?" Kruul grunted as he put his weight into the door.

It didn't move.

He jerked his head at the door whilst looking at Kaln and Gleb. Kaln and Kruul pushed with all their might against the door whilst Gleb showed willing, no luck.

Gleb checked the door's edge but could find nothing obvious holding the door shut.

After some time they yielded, sat exhausted and

perplexed on the stone stairs leading to the door. Vodius stood up from his position next to Lilly, she was reading the diary.

"Perhaps there is a spell, binding the door. Though there was no mention in his diary… I suppose giving away access to every locked door would not have been an intelligent move."

He tapped his chin as he pondered at the great metal door.

"Lets see…"

He spread his hands wide and uttered arcane words that made the tapestry of the spell on the door bloom to light like a fluorescent spider's web of runes and symbols. The light quickly began to fade but it was long enough for Vodius to see what the spell was designed to do.

"I see. A spell that requires a specific spoken word to unlock the door. Quite ingenious." Vodius said thoughtfully, obviously impressed.

"And there's no mention of this word in the diary I guess?" Kaln nodded to Lilly reading the book.

Vodius shook his head, looked at the door and said the word, "Power."

Nothing.

The next hour or so was spent with each of them shouting words at the door, all of them except Lilly. She was engrossed by the diary.

'I have pleaded with wizards, doctors, witches and worse and none have the answers I seek. I have acquired a tome detailing the magical properties of

rare creatures which inhabit these lands. Maybe one of them has the means to bring back my family.'

Lilly flicked through the pages, each detailing the lengths Thaldur had gone to find some way of bringing his wife and child back to him. Each more sad, depraved and dangerous than the last. He detailed tracking down mythical beasts whose blood was rumoured to bring back the dead when made into a specific potion. This did not work. Nor did exposing the bodies of his loved ones to screams of a Shensai or burning the flesh of a Kazgol. Lilly flicked through more pages.

'I have spoken to some less reputable mages and have gleaned knowledge of spells not commonly known. Or atleast, not openly practised. They refer to it as "Necromancy" in their notes. This could be the key to bringing them back!'

The others continued, with less enthusiasm, to bark out random words at the door while Lilly read on.

'I seem to have the basics of necromancy down. Through trial and error I have created some wretched creatures. Though they did rise at my command, they were only tests and were destroyed. I will hone these skills as I search for more answers.'

The next few pages detailed what worked, what didn't work and what level of inhumanity

Thaldur had lowered himself to in the pursuit of knowledge. It showed how his value of any life, including his own, meant precious little in pursuit of finding a way to bring back his daughter and wife.
A fresh page, and Lilly could sense new enthusiasm in the notes that followed.

'Project P
I have sourced the best pieces of flesh I can find to create what I will be referring to as Project P. This creature is made up of many different body parts that I have gathered. Through my research into tethering souls to this plane which may be key to bringing back Rose and Mia-'

Lilly's head snapped up at the door, "Rose!"
The door didn't move. The others looked at her.
Vodius let out a small huff, and with a smile of understanding, said, "Ah yes, good try... Mia!"
Again, the door didn't move.
"Blast. Thought you had it Lilly." Vodius sighed as he and the others fell back into deep thought at what the word could be. All except Gleb, who was showing Kruul what he had retrieved from his nostril, having lost interest in the stubborn door.

Lilly continued to read;
'I have found that if a creature is raised through necromancy, they are significantly more potent if they have a soul tethered to part of the flesh. I have

chosen the eyes for this creature. After all, the eyes are the window to the soul, so they say.

The down side to this is that the spirit can keep some of their free will. Though useful for my end goals it is not a useful trait in a servant.

To that end, for Project P I have bound the soul of some baker, I believe his name was Peter Rollan - hence the name Project P. I have designed a spell that binds the flesh together, prevents it from rapid decay and tethers the soul to it. These things are arbitrary, the real key to the spell's success is that I have designed it in such a way that the soul in use is constantly between this realm and the afterlife, a constant state of agony.

I have harnessed this pain to use as a whip to control Project P.

If it behaves as I command, I lessen its state of pain by planting it soundly in this realm. If it defies me, then the soul is torn further and further until it inevitably falls back under my control.

After vigorous testing I have found Project P has made for an impressive weapon. Though the baker was not a warrior, it did attempt to fight against my control at first but eventually I wrangled the soul into obedience like a wild mare.

Given the specimen and the control I possess over Project P, I have fortified the creature with magical armour. This way I can use it to test future, lesser, creations from the comfort of my lab.

So far I am incredibly happy with progress. Project P does not even attempt to defy me now and has destroyed every other creation I have put before it with ease. I am so confident in the control I have over this creature I will use it as a guardian for my lab while I am away with studies with complete confidence it will be as I left it on my return.

I just wish I had the foresight to remove the voicebox before completing the spell work. Future versions will not have this. I cannot stand to listen to its pathetic droning any longer. I made it into so much more than the sum of its parts and yet it wont stop.

A worthwhile investment in time and energy and perhaps a stepping stone to bringing my family back together.'

"Family." Lilly said in a hollow voice lined with pain and sadness.

The door swung open silently. She looked up at the door through teary eyes.

The others looked at her with wide grins before seeing her sombre expression. Vodius tilted his head with raised eyebrows in acceptance of the power word and stood.

The room before them was a vast oval shape with everblaze torches high up on a large hanging metal plate. The way the room was lit casted dark looming shadows over the symbols engraved on the many archways lining the walls of the room. At the far end of the room there was no light, only darkness. Somewhere, distantly they could hear in a horse and muffled voice "aaaain...aaaain...aaaain" repeating over and over.

They walked through the doorway and the smell of decay, old blood and rusted metal hit them. The door closed behind them and from the darkness at the far end of the room a voice called out, "PAAAAAIN!"

Something huge shook the room as it stormed towards them. Bursting from the shadows was what looked vaguely like a man, monstrously large clad in full plate armour made of a strange dark metal that was covered in old blood stains and wielding a hideous sword that most men could barely hold with two hands, in one of its large gauntleted fists. It was terrifyingly fast as it barrelled straight at them from the swirling unnatural shadows.

Gleb was the first to react, firing off a shot with Thunderbastard as the thing bore down on them. The shot hit the creature square in the chest but instead of piercing its armour it exploded into a pale blue light which shimmered across the armour's surface and down its arm into the creature's hand. It raised the hand and pointed it at Gleb. There was a thick **-thwump-** noise and tiny flecks of debris around their assailant exploded away as a bolt of blue energy hit the goblin so hard he flew through the air and hit the door with a sickening crunch.

The monster paused long enough to bellow "PAAAAAAIIIIIN!!!!" at the group before starting to move again.

Kaln and Kruul ran to meet the creature with their own charge as Lilly ran to Gleb's aid and Vodius unleashed a torrent of dozens of bolts of purple fire that launched above him high into the air, illuminating the metal plate a glorious purple hue. The flames clustered like a swarm of fireflies for an instant then bombarded the charging hulk. There was thick smoke where the creature once stood.

Kaln and Kruul slowed their advance to see if the monster was slain. How could anything survive that?

The smoke began to clear. Suddenly there was a flicker of blue light and another **-thwump-** as the smoke around the creature was blown away revealing the creature looking quite unharmed. Vodius was not prepared for the bolt of energy that was much larger than the last hit his shoulder, sending him spiralling through the air. Luckily the bolt of energy glanced off the sorcerer's protective runes and vaporised a huge chunk of the wall leaving only a crater. Vodius was laying face down, he didn't move.

Kaln and Kruul glanced at each other and leapt at the colossal creature. Whilst in the air, Kaln swung Emmental with both hands in a spinning arc, turning all his momentum into a mighty cleave which he brought down on the creature's helm.

The weapon had sliced through armour as

though it was made from wheat in previous battles but this time it did not. It bit into the strange metal of the helm, splitting it at the mouthguard but that was all. Kaln, still holding the axe swung down and pushed off the monster's mass, prising the axe away as he leapt back.

Kruul was quick to spot the new weakness and instead of plunging in with his own axes, he used the momentum he had in the air to get as high as he could and swung off of the monstrous knight's paldron, landing on its shoulders. While it was still reeling from the mighty blow, he reached down and with both hands pulled against the split helmet with all his might. The magic binding the helmet screeched and cracked in protest, sending energy through the air as Kruul's muscles flexed and bulged. The spell broke and the metal helmet yielded to Kruul's strength and bent away. Kruul held onto the helm and leapt down off of the knight's shoulders, leaving it without a helmet.

The sweet smell of decay and magic washed over them as they looked up at the face of this monstrosity.

It was fragments of several faces all held together with dark magic. Different coloured lengths of hair were slick wet to its malformed scalp. The bloated and swollen mockery of face was pus ridden and peppered with stitches. Its mouth was unnaturally wide and there was simply a void where its nose should have been. Its eyes however looked incredibly human. Their blue colour shone out from the deep recess of its face. Even now, in this instant, they could see there was a deep sadness in them. It paused for a moment, as though assessing them.

Something washed over its hideous features as they screwed up in a grotesque wince. "PAAAAIN!" it screamed. It almost sounded pleading.

Lilly stepped between her friends and the goliath. Her staff was glimmering pale blue and at its tip was a blazing spear head. She wasn't holding it like a spear ready to thrust, but like a walking staff. She stood before the monster. Kaln and Kruul glanced at each other and prepared to help her.

Her voice rang out clearly in the vast room as she shouted, "Peter Rollan, I come to you as a cleric of Celuna. To offer you freedom from your prison, your pain and torment. Your soul will be guided to the afterlife. End this misery now."

She braced the spear on the ground with her foot and pointed the tip towards the knight and waited, resolute.

For a moment it looked like it was going to crush her until the word, "Pain." with a sense of finality to it, came from its crooked lips.

The huge sword clanged and clattered to the

ground and there was an almighty crash as it fell to its knees. There was a glimmer of something else in its sunken eyes now - hope. A tear trickled down its face and it calmly leaned its head into the tip of Lilly's spear. There was a brief hiss of meat on a blazing heat and instantly the magic was broken and the flesh within the armour fell to pieces and withered to blackened chunks. The armour fell limp and hollow. Lilly turned to the others, she was crying as she said the prayer of passage that Kaln had heard her recite to the old man at the roadside, what felt like a lifetime ago. She was looking directly at something the others couldn't see.

When the prayer was complete he held her. Vodius and Gleb joined the others and thanked Lilly for her healing touch. She gave them a short smile of recognition but her mind was elsewhere. Kaln held her tight and whispered "It's better this way. You did the right thing."
"I know." She whispered back softly "I just wish I could have done something sooner. That poor soul was trapped in there for years."
She stepped back, wiped the tears away and looked at the others.
"Let's finish this."

They were surrounded by portal runes, most were inert and a few that hissed with heat or popped occasionally with energy, sending sparks across the stone floor but none of them were active.

Lilly pointed to the unnatural cluster of shadows where the creature had emerged from.
"Thaldur's diary suggested that...Peter was guarding his lab."
Vodius stood with his hands on his hips frowning at the shadow "Indeed."
He took out a small stone from his pouch, illuminated it with an arcane word and force of will. Then he handed the bright stone to Kruul. It looked tiny in his grizzled hands as he tossed it lightly into the air a couple of times, making shadows rise and fall around them like waves of the tide.
"Right, let's see." Kruul said with a smirk and tossed the stone across the room, into the shadow.

At first the stone was engulfed entirely by the darkness but after a moment the shadows weakened and yielded to the light, like early sunlight burning away the night's mist.
Vodius let out a victorious bark of a laugh.
"Thought that might break your shadow spell. Not entirely perfect eh?" Vodius said to nobody.

The last of the shadow dissipated, revealing another ironbound door.
"His lab." Lilly sounded almost excited as she moved towards the door. The others followed.
This door had a handle, it was made of brass and

it was evident it had been well used as it shone in the stone's light.

CHAPTER 32 - WHERE HE HONES HIS CRAFT

"And what trick do we need to pass through this door?" Kaln said frustratedly.

"This one." Gleb said with a grin as he finished checking the door and turned the handle.

There was a light click and the door swung open revealing Thaldur's laboratory.

There were notes on every surface, there were large metal tables covered in flesh in varying stages of decay and bizarre looking hand tools. The room was lit by a single, shielded, everblaze torch which struggled to illuminate most of the lab. There were shelves stacked high with vials and jars filled with all manner of unidentifiable things, some still moving. The room reeked of sweat, metal, parchment, blood, decay, potent magic and some strange acrid chemical. In the corner opposite Thaldur's desk, which was also covered in notes, books and trinkets was a small stone table with an indent that was filled with a liquid. There were portal archways inlaid on two of the walls here too, though they were also inert. In the corner behind the door was a small bed that looked dishevelled but used. At the far end of the room was another door. From under it, a green light was rhythmically pulsing.

Vodius pointed to the door and said, "Through there."
He nodded to the book in Lilly's hand and said "About half way through, look for a mention of 'Soul shard'."

Lilly pawed through the diary, found the entry Vodius was referring to and read aloud.
"Not entirely intentionally, I appear to have found the key to immortality.
Through a process I have tested and subsequently perfected, I have splintered my own soul in two. I have then bound one half of my soul to a spell. The other half remains with my physical body. Should I be slain, my soul will naturally return to the anchored fragment of my soul to become whole again. At this point, under

normal conditions, the soul would then pass on to whichever creature beyond this realm sees fit to collect it. However, in this instance my soul is still bound to the spell. I believe it would take some time but if my soul were to be left uninterrupted for a long enough period of time, the spell could bind my soul to another vessel. To that end I have made preparations for such an event."

"Lets go." Kaln said as he marched towards the door, kicking tables, vials and chairs out of the way to get there.
The door opened as easily as the laboratory door. In the center of the tiny circular room was a lifeless body of a young man who did not look too dissimilar to Thaldur. He was naked and laid on a raised bed. Below him were many arcane symbols and shapes engraved into the stone floor. Each of them pulsed with dark arcane power flooding the room in green light. At the center of the room, in the center of the runes and directly below the body of the young man was a tiny bracelet looped around a wedding ring.

"Is this what we're here for?" Kaln said as he grabbed the bracelet. The room fell into darkness as the spell was broken. Kaln grinned. He handed the trinket over to Vodius who inspected it.
"It is." Vodius sounded lost in wonder as he rolled the bracelet around in his hands, seeing arcane elements of the spell that the others could not.

"Great." Lilly said, snatching it from his hands. She threw it on the floor, pointed the tip of her father's staff at it and closed her eyes. Light blazed into a spearhead that engulfed the tiny collection of jewellery and it shattered into a thousand tiny pieces. There was an explosion of magical energy that sent Thaldur's lab notes into the air with a deafening boom.

With her hands still covering her ears, Lilly smiled at the others and shouted "That felt good."

"Now what?" Kruul said as papers swirled and fell around him.

"Well," Vodius said as he stepped back through the doorway into the laboratory and walked over to the small stone table "I believe this is what he was using to find the Rehlk Stones. The spellwork definitely suggests so. Perhaps we can use it to see where he is heading or if he has the other stone, where he is now."

Vodius leaned over the tiny pool of liquid. "I just need to work out how to use his spell. It's designed quite differently to my own."

An hour passed as Vodius deciphered the spell work Thaldur had used. After being strongly advised not to touch anything by Vodius, they were all sitting waiting.

Kruul clipped Gleb round the ear to stop the goblin furiously shaking a tiny vial he found. It was bothering him that the two liquids inside had separated. Kruul's slap made Gleb drop the vial and something small and wet slithered away into a crack in the wall leaving a perfectly clean trail in the dirt on the worn stone floor. Gleb scowled at Kruul who was shaking his head in disappointment.

"Lilly, is there any mention of a Yassvyr in his diary?" Kaln asked.

"I'm not sure-" Lilly was interrupted by Vodius who was deep in concentration looking at the pool.

"Look for 'Creature research revisited' about half way through." He shouted and went back to the task at hand.

Lilly flicked through the book and after some time found it and began to read aloud,

"I have returned to some of my older research regarding rare and mythical creatures. Though it bore little fruit last time it was a means to an introduction with certain monster hunters. Through conversations with them I learned of some lesser known facts about dragons. It would appear they are not just savage brutes of the sky who breath fire. Indeed, depending on the colour of their skin, their age and their position in the dragon hierarchy, dragons have many varied abilities.

In particular, I learned that emerald dragons do not breath fire and reap destruction, instead they have an innate control over magic which brings about life.

If I can find one and harness this power, this

could be an interesting development."

Lilly skipped through the pages until she found a mention of Yassvyr and continued reading,
"After years I have finally tracked down an emerald dragon. Luckily I have used this time to devise a plan on how to trap and bind the creature to my will. I just need the beast's name for my spell to work.."
Lilly shook her head, skipped ahead and read on,
"Blasted thing! It should have worked! So much time, effort and energy wasted. Yassvyr, whilst having the abilities I had hoped for, will not yield entirely to my spell. I control the creature but not its magic. It is too stubborn for that! I can't even put the thing to practical use, all those claws and teeth and it refuses to kill anything I command it to!
Now I am forced to keep the beast in fear of reprisal if I set it free or try to kill it.
Perhaps it will live out its days in a cage in the menagerie with the other wonders I have collected if I cannot find a suitable use for it."

Kaln listened intently and when Lilly was finished reading he almost whispered "That thing on the roof of this place? Explains why it didn't incinerate us where we stood. That thing had green eyes but…"
"The shadows enveloping it is part of Thaldur's control spell." Vodius explained.
"Then what was it doing?" Kaln pondered.

"Who knows, the diary does not detail the level of control he managed to take from the dragon or if he was more successful later on. Perhaps it was going to warn him of our arrival. Perhaps he already knew from the second we entered the cave and it was flying to him to return here. Regardless, I believe I've cracked it." Vodius said as he looked intently into the light now being emitted from the pool in the stone table. The others gathered around to see.

Instead of their reflection, on the surface of the tiny pool of liquid they saw shapes beginning to form; it was undoubtedly the shape of a dragon wrapped in swirling shadows high up in the sky, its wings were outstretched as it glided through the clouds. The ruined forests of the Bleak Scar far below. On the dragon's back was a single being between the shadow flames that cocooned the dragon, he stood gripping a harness. He looked so tiny and fragile on the great creature's back. As they watched the shadow-wreathed Yassvyr soar over the land they saw it change from the dead forest to a savage mountainous land. The dragon gave two powerful beats of its huge wings and glided into the cave mouth, only darkness could be seen in the liquid's surface after that.

Vodius looked up at the others, pale faced. "This spell is designed to track the Rehlk stones. That means that not only has he conquered

Whitebluff and found the stone but that he is here, now."

The room stood still for a moment as they all looked at each other in silence. Kaln was the first to move.

"This is what we set out to do. Lets go." He said confidently as he walked through into the portal room they had entered through.

"Aye, let's do this!" Kruul said grinning and jerked his head over his shoulder at Gleb, who scrambled up his back with a nasty giggle and the two followed Kaln.

Lilly stared at Vodius, still stunned at the implications of what was happening, still scared she might freeze and submit to fear like she did in Crossay. A guilt she hadn't attempted to process yet.

He stared back, his features barely illuminated from the magic of the pool but Lilly could see he was battling with the same thoughts.

"It is now or never Lilly. For your father." He said calmly and followed the others.

Lilly walked through the doorway into the portal room. The empty armour still lay lifeless in the center of the room, much like the gateway runes along the room's walls. Suddenly a pale blue light filled the room as one of the portals opened up, through it they could see the cave waters and the illumination it brought. Two figures stepped through into the large room. One was wreathed in black flames that danced and flickered but it was no dragon, it was the same size as a human. The other was a human and from his scarred skin they could see it was Thaldur. He looked directly at them as he walked through the portal. "What have we here?" He said cooly.

Emmental in hand, Kaln replied "We're here to bring an end to the ruin you have brought to this land. Our homes."

"Is that so? And you plan on doing that how? By killing me? Do you think others have not tried? Do you think that things are not already in motion that cannot be undone?" Thaldur said with venom filling his every word, although the venom did not exactly feel aimed at them. As he spoke, his arms were outstretched, gesturing to all he had created.

"You took my father from me, my home!" Lilly found herself shouting back, invigorated that she did not fear him, she embraced the anger in her heart.

"If it helps, it wasn't personal. Merely a means to an end I'm afraid." Thaldur said with a stone-faced glare.

"You can stop this, right now, if you choose Thaldur. Would your wife and daughter want this for you? To see what you have become?"

Thaldur took what Lilly said as an almost physical blow. For the first time his expression changed to something that almost looked human, for an instant, before he recovered.

"It is far too late to stop, I have come so far. I must

continue with my work." he continued.

"I know about the deal you made with demons." Lilly pressed.

"Good, then you understand the importance of my collection of souls. Yours can add to it." He said drawing the small metal cube from his robes, the engraved runes shimmering excitedly in the fel light.

"It appears you have stolen at least one from me!" as he noticed the empty armour on the floor for the first time.

He raised his arms and shouted a cluster of arcane words. The room was awash with the smell of magic then something else, fire, blood, iron and sea air. New light filled the room as several portals opened. Immediately they could see the great white walls of Whitebluff as hundreds of Thaldur's creatures started to pour through the gateways. A group of cloaked ones burst through a portal behind Thaldur. Another portal opened and great swaths of undead were vomited into the chamber, shambling and clawing as they spread into the room. Through the same portal the large three legged creature they had seen at Cornwalk that night crouched and stepped through the portal, crushing several undead as it did.

"Leave these to me!" Vodius shouted as he pointed to the army of walking dead filling the room. He spoke arcane words and his eyes blazed with purple fire as he rose high into the air and launched a bombardment of fireballs down on the mindless horde. Hot blood, gore and bones showered the room but there were so many pouring through the portal continuing the rain of fire was all Vodius could do to try and keep them at bay. The room exploded into colours, the pale blue light of the lurid waters of the cave, the flickering purple and golden orange from Vodius' magic assault and the white of the walls of Whitebluff.

"We've got the big lad!" Kruul shouted, pointing at the three legged monster and smirking at Gleb. He crouched and lunged at one of its passing legs as it took a stride past him. He used his axes to bite into the monster's leg. Still on Kruul's back, Gleb grinned up at the creature, which didn't seem to notice them.
"We meet again, three legged donkey! Thunderbastard!" Gleb screamed and amongst the torrent of magical explosions there was the distinct cracking sound of Thunderbastard doing what it did best. Unfortunately the armour on the monster's legs was too thick and the round ricocheted into the blazing battery of Vodius' assault on the undead.

Kaln was being charged by five of the cloaked creatures. The first he cleaved down its center with Emmental but as he did, he saw that Kruul and Gleb were struggling to make an impact on the three legged monstrosity as they held onto one of its legs. He shouted over to Kruul, tossed Emmental and ducked under the scorpion tail that had struck out from within the darkness of the cloak of one of his assailants. He rolled and turned to face the creature. It lashed out again with its tail. This time Kaln was ready, he dodged to the side and grabbed the tail. As he did he transformed into the grey furred bear that had reaped so much havoc on the bandits. He used his strength to drag the cowled one to him, slammed it on the floor and placing his boot on where the creature's chest should have been, he pulled with all his strength. There was a tearing sound and fluids sloshed out as the creature writhed on the floor. He turned and threw the scorpion tail like a spear straight into the huge open, tooth-filled maw of another assailant. It halted its charge, shuddered violently for a moment and curled in on itself like a dying spider.

What was under their cloaks?! Kaln thought as he plunged his great claws into the center mass of another cloaked one and tore his arms outwards, showering himself and those around him in gore. The horrific sounds it made as it died were haunting.

Viscera still falling from his bloodsoaked claws, Kaln pointed to Thaldur through the battlefield.

Kruul leaped off the monster's leg laughing as he did and caught Emmental. He laughed harder as he descended back down, hacking at the monster's leg. Emmental cleaved through the monster's armour and flesh and bone. A clean cut. The creature stumbled as it tried to adjust its weight, not yet realising the leg was destroyed. The two halves slid apart under its weight and it came crashing down scrambling to find footing. Gleb didn't waste an instant and threw himself on top of the newly crippled creature. He placed the barrel of Thunderbastard up against the top of the creature's mass and pulled the trigger. There was a muted crack drowned out by the explosions around him and the monster's carapace burst open. Gleb lit the fuse on a small metal pipe and rammed it into the hole he had just made. The creature was still trying to stand and was lashing out wildly as Gleb threw himself off the monster. His goggles were on, his fingers in his ears and he grin was huge as he sailed through the air towards Kruul who caught him. An instant later there was a dull **-thwump-** sound that dwarfed all others as the three legged creature exploded sending flesh, bone and chitin in all directions.

Lilly watched as Kaln challenged Thaldur amongst the chaos. The Necromancer just glared at him as the cowled ones surrounded Kaln. She had to move. She burst into a sprint and her staff blazed into a silver fire-tipped spear. She plunged the righteous spear through the back of the creature that flanked Kaln. It screeched and others turned to see Lilly. She used the skewered creature's weight and her momentum to throw it into another that was preparing to pounce on Lilly. As she prised the spear, hissing, from the flesh of a fallen foe, the Rehlk stone around her wrist slid down into view. It glimmered brightly amongst the flood of lurid colours filling the room. The hairs on the back of her neck instantly stood on end and she turned back to Kaln to see Thaldur looking directly at her.

"The stone! Give it to me!" Thaldur shouted over the cacophony of battle, his hand outstretched. Around his wrist was the other, larger, Rehlk stone. It too danced in the lights, wanting to be seen. In his hand magic swirled and curled like writhing smoke and threw the energy at Lilly. It was too fast for her to dodge, all she could do was close her eyes as she saw the bolt of energy streak towards her through the battle. She winced and after a long moment she opened her eyes. She saw Kruul's back, he was hunched over and beyond him she could see the bodies of cowled ones being thrown into the air as she heard Kaln's bellowing roar. Kruul slumped to the ground and rolled onto his back at Lilly's feet. She could see now Kaln was furiously, savagely clawing, slashing and ripping his way through the masses to get to her and Kruul.

She felt like time had slowed and her senses seemed numbed. She couldn't understand what

had happened. *Did the spell hit me?*
Suddenly another wave of adrenaline washed over her as she looked down on the orc and understood. His right hand was withered, almost to the bone. The skin white and bloodless and the hand twisted into a claw. No muscle remained just the husk of an arm. Almost as though the arm alone had aged a hundred years. Kruul was alive but clutched his ruined arm with an expression of agony. He saved her.
"Kruul!" Lilly cried.

Kaln embraced the power of the savage beast of death within; he crushed and rended the flesh before him. His senses were alive as he heard and felt every enemy surrounding him. He smelled the magic as a bolt passed by him, he spun to follow its trajectory.
Lilly! The thought was sobering as his stomach sank.
He saw Lilly looking at him, she couldn't move in time. He slammed the Cowled one that he had just gutted to the ground and roared in frustration as more surrounded him, he couldn't see her. He barrelled into them, throwing them high into the air and finally he saw Kruul had leapt in front of her, holding out his huge arm trying to defend himself against the magical bolt. Thick battle-scarred orcish skin that could stop most blades was no defence against the necromancer's spell. The bolt soaked

into the orc's arm and almost instantly, his arm shrivelled and turned pale and bloodless. The orc's eyes bulged as he clutched his arm and roared in agony. Kaln saw Lilly, shaken but standing, looking down on Kruul. He saw a portal open behind her. He saw a huge monstrous hand made of arms imerge behind her. Each finger was an arm with a hand at its tip. Whatever huge monstrosity it belonged to loomed unseen beyond the flickering magical tear in this realm. It grabbed Lilly and there was only a moment as she locked eyes with Kaln before the grasping, grabbing claws of the hand that enveloped her snapped her neck mercilessly.
I failed her...
Kaln exploded into a tornado of violence, his claws crackled with energy that eviscerated anything before him.
His fur felt heavy, soaked with blood. The sounds were deafening and the enemies were endless.
Good. He thought as he channelled his pain into power. Lightening cracked and arched between the mass of enemies before him. The smell of burning flesh filled his nostrils. He could not see his allies.
If I die, so be it. I will take as many with me as I can!
Kaln roared as lightning arced from his claws into the sea of undead creatures.

Suddenly there was stillness.

The masses stopped advancing, the monsters

stopped lashing at him with tails, biting at him with fangs and swiping at him with claws. They simply stood, silently looking away from him. He felt a warmth wash over him, a familiar warmth. The way Lilly's smile made him feel. Even through his rage he felt this calmness, it pulled at him. He stopped ripping, stopped biting, stopped breaking and turned to the light which he realised was washing over the battlefield.

Lilly stood, blazing silver wings lifted her from the ground.

How could this be?!

"Stop this."Her voice was not Lilly's voice but it rang out over the stillness. A second wave of calmness and warmth washed over Kaln as he watched her fly higher.

She flew over Kruul, over Kaln and descended to stand before Thaldur. He too stared at her, stunned.

Thaldur blinked and stuttered "How...how are you alive?" genuine interest in his voice. The light of her wings making the scars on his skin shimmer.

She held out both of her hands, one hand empty, in the other hand was the Rehlk stone glimmering in the new light.

Her voice was calm and soothing "You have given so much to stand here before me. You have taken the life of Lilly and yet she forgives you. This must end now. I will give you one chance. One choice."

Thaldur's eyes darted to the Relk stone and back to Lilly's.

She gave a small smile and continued, "You can take the stone in my hand. You will have both stones and maybe even enough power to save yourself. Maybe even return your family."

She stepped closer.

"Or, you can give me your stone. Surrender all your power, your life to me. If you do this I can give you that which you seek most."

By her side, a shimmering silver light appeared in the shape of a woman, holding a child.

Thaldur gasped and his knees buckled. He looked up at the woman wreathed in light with tears down his face. He reached out with trembling hands. For the first time, he didn't appear to be the unfathomable darkness that had swept the land and laid ruin in his path. He looked like a desperate man at the end of a long road. Ready to rest his weary head.

"They...they are all I've ever wanted." he cried. His eyes moved back to Lilly's glowing form. "My soul is forfeit?" half question, half statement.

Lilly simply shook her head.

His shaking hand reached for the Relhk stone in hers. A flicker of sadness danced across her face. His trembling hand paused, then placed his Relhk stone with hers. The two stones snapped together to become one as a pulse of immense energy washed out from her form. In her other hand, he dropped the tiny metal box.

Her face softened to an emotion that resembled pride. She then placed the Relhk stones around her neck and the box trinket in a pocket.

She held Thaldur's face in her hands and kissed his forehead softly. The scars and runes flared brightly, then fell dull.

Suddenly, Thaldur's age changed. Wrinkles covered his face, his features became gaunt and his skin wrinkled. His eyes became sunken and glazed over, his lips became thin. An ancient man knelt before her. His eyes never left the lady holding the child until the last moment when he looked at Lilly and whispered "Thank you Celuna." in a weak raspy voice.

His eyes closed and his body slumped to the ground, an arm outstretched to the spirits of his loved ones. Thaldur was dead but his body continued to rapidly age and decay until only a skeleton and robes remained in a heap on the floor.

CHAPTER 33
- THE SCAR

As the life left Thaldur's eyes the portals around the room began to close, with violent gouts of energy they sputtered and cracked into nothingness. The everblaze torches high up in the large room flickered and dulled leaving the room with very little light. The undead legions stood motionless and directionless in the gloom, like they had the night of the attack on Crossay.

The spirits of Thaldur's family and the brilliant silver-white wings on Lilly's back faded away. She knelt before the skeletal remains of Thaldur. Slowly she lowered her head to the ground and the last of the divine light left her eyes as they closed. She was motionless in the murky light of the distant failing torches.

High up, in the darkness, a sudden and piercing

white light shone out; it was small, but bright. It slowly moved closer to Lilly and descended to her side. Vodius held the enchanted stone high in his hand. He was panting for breath, his face was pale and slick with sweat. He looked utterly exhausted from sustaining so much magical power. The air around him crackled with fading energy. Shortly after Kaln, Gleb and Kruul pushed through the crowd of undead around them, following his light.
The lifeless creatures didn't fight or even try to maintain their balance as they were barreled out of the way. They tumbled into the dark and didn't move.

All of them were exhausted and bathed in gore. Kruul was leaning heavily on Kaln. Kaln had returned to his human form and was desperately trying to keep Kruul on his feet while the great orc clutched his ruined arm to his chest. Kaln lowered Kruul to his knees and lifted the orcs' arm off his shoulder as he saw Lilly.
He ran to her. His vision of her swimming in tears, his blood soaked hands shaking. There was no anger now, only exhaustion. There was no sense of victory, only pain in his heart. He didn't dare to touch her. If he touched her and she was dead then it was real and not just a nightmare. That meant he had failed her. He forced himself to put his hands on her back. She felt so delicate. *Why hadn't I stopped her from coming on*

this foolhardy quest. She didn't deserve this! He thought bitterly.

His voice was weak, even in the stillness of the room, it was hard for any to hear him say, "I'm sorry Lilly, I failed you. I was supposed to protect you."

Lilly sat up, gasping as she took in a huge gulp of air like she had been submerged in water. Her eyes locked onto him immediately and narrowed. Her breathing calmed and she smiled at him warmly with tearfilled eyes and she shook her head. "You did everything you could Kaln." She choked through the tears.

The two held each other tight for what felt like a blissful eternity.

"How?" Kaln said as he pulled away from the embrace.

Lilly shook her head "Celuna blessed me with a second chance."

She held his face, her fingers delicately touching the scars as they moved up to the patch over his ruined eye. "We've been through so much-" she said before the entire room shook. From the laboratory they had left behind they heard vials smashing and metal containers falling. All around them, the undead fell to the ground. While they twitched violently occasionally, they were empty vessels now. Void of magic or purpose.

"While I am certain we are all very glad you are

ok Lilly, it would be prudent of us to leave this place immediately." Vodius said, helping them both to their feet.

"We must find our way back to the entrance before the entire spell collapses." He pointed to the far end of the large room.

"Wait, what about Yassvyr?" Kaln said, desperately scanning the room.

He spotted the form, stood still near the wall where the cave portal once was, still wreathed in shadow. Its eyes glimmered green in the light of Vodius' spell as they approached.

"Yassvyr?" Kaln called out as the room shuddered and the walls began to crumble.

The shadowy form didn't move or respond but the intelligent green eyes within the writhing shadow were watching them.

"I'm not certain we have time for this Kaln. This place is held together by Thaldur's magic. With him gone-" Vodius' warning was cut short by what sounded like the strings of a musical instrument snapping. Shimmers of blue light flared in the darkness for an instant.

"The magical tapestry Thaldur has weaved to create this place is coming apart with us inside!" Vodius shouted over the cacophany of the failing magic.

Lilly withdrew the Rehlk stone; its surface seemed to move and dance in the light of Vodius' spell and a light all its own.

"I hope you can use the power of this to break

Thaldur's spell over you, Yassvyr. I hope you are not a vengeful and spiteful dragon, Yassvyr." she said as she approached the shadowy form and lowered the stone over its neck.

The instant the stone touched the being the shadow wrapped around it exploded and dissipated. Before them stood a beautiful woman in green and golden robes. Her hair was a rich earthy brown. Her eyes were large, almost too large and a brilliant green. Her other features were delicate and slender similar to that of an elve's, but not entirely. There was a haunting beauty about her.

She blinked slowly and smiled softly.

"Thank yew, all of yew. I have been trapped h'yur in this awful place for so very long. I didn't think I would ever be free again." Her voice was as soft as her smile and she spoke with a strange thick accent.

Sympathy washed over her features as she looked at Kruul. Seemingly unaffected by the imminent collapse of the spells around them.

"Come h'yur won yew? Yew were so very brave. I saw but couldn't help any of yew."

Kruul limped over to her.

"Aye, we know of yer plight lass. Glad we could be of help teh ye. I think we best be goo'n now, eh?"

She placed a delicate hand on his crippled arm, softly. He winced but did not pull away. A rich green light blazed from her hand as she said.

"I won be able to make yew'r hand the way t'wos

before but I can make it even behttah. It feels so good to be able to use my magek again, I tell yew." She beamed as her magic wrapped his arm in emerald light that filled the room. It was only a moment before she stepped away and the light faded.

Kruul's arm was seemingly healed and looked similar to his other arm again. Only it was covered in scales which danced in the light of Vodius's spell that revealed the scales were not black as they appeared at first glance but in fact a deep dark green.

"I hope yew like et." She said as she turned to look around the room.

Kruul grinned a vicious toothy grin as he flexed his fingers and rolled his shoulder. "Oh, I like this!" He slammed a fist into one of the few still standing undead with such force that its head exploded.

He let out a barking laugh "I like this alot!"

He reached down and grabbed the skull of Thaldur, paused as he realised the others were watching him and said "Fer me clan, proof the bastards dead." gesturing with the rune-covered skull before hooking it on his belt.

Kaln shrugged, "Fair enough."

Yassvyr's inspection was complete, "Righy't, now we've to get out h'yur before it's too lay'te."

She waved her arm at the portal runes closest and the portal opened, flooding the room with the blue light of the cave again. She stepped through and the others quickly followed, the portal closed behind them.

"Look, I thought you should know, we helped because Aeathune asked me to." Kaln said as he jogged over to Yassvyr, keeping an eye on the water's edge.

There was a flash of recognition and a wry smile on the dragon's face as she said, "Oh really? Well I guess I owe *her* one now. I really must visit my sister some time...Don' worray abowt the beasties in that water. They won' bother us."

She eyed the cave entrance as the others caught up with them.

"Don't let this startle yew, will yew?" Yassvyr said as she stepped away and gave a little nod before anyone could reply.

The cave was filled with green light as she revealed her true form. She was truly glorious. Her scales were similar to those on Kruul's arm, she was a true ancient emerald dragon with huge wings tipped with gold and powerful legs with golden claws. Pearly white, sword sized teeth filled the maw of the great dragon and her green eyes were everbright.

They heard her voice but they couldn't see her lips move as she told them "Thank'yew again for setting me free but I must try and fix some of the damage that has been done h'yur."

"Wait, where are you goin'?" Kaln said, in a voice he intended to sound much more forceful.

"Whitebluff eventually. Got'ta see what I can do about the damage to the land first, yew see. See what I can do abowt repaying my debt to Aeathune."

"Can we.." He paused and Yassvyr turned to look at his tiny form. "Can we come with you? We owe it to Whitebluff to help whoever we can."

"Yew can speak to me in yewer mind if you sense my presence, and yes, on wan condition. You tell me all about how yew came to be my rescuers along the way? I haven' had any company or conversation in such a long why'el."

She lowered and spread one of her wings for them to climb up onto her back. The wing itself was not covered in dark scales like the rest of her body but black-green raven like feathers Kaln noticed as he watched Gleb scramble onto her back without hesitation. He was screeching like he did when he got excited. He already had his goggles pulled down and was gripping the harness ready to fly. The others gave each other a glance as the house behind them began to creak and crack with the sounds of the spell's death throes. There were brief nods all around and they scurred up the great dragon's back.

"Do make sure you have a tight grip on the reins, won' yew?" she said as she flexed her wings that shimmered in the pool light.

CHAPTER 34 - THEY ARRIVED ON DRAGON BACK

The great dragon thrust her wings and with shocking speed and power they lunged from the cave floor into the darkness of the tunnel. The light quickly faded behind them and the rush of wind drowned out the cries of panic and excitement as they clutched the reins.

"Hold on tight, the spell has collapsed" they heard Yassvyr say in their minds and glanced back to see a cloud of energy and debris barrelling down the tunnel behind them. The sparks of blue energy illuminated the tunnel and its obsidian walls. The wave of energy was gaining on them, quickly.

"We aren't going to make it!" Kaln thought to Yassvyr.

She dipped her head and thrust her wings again with another burst of speed.

Now they could see daylight ahead, the cave entrance was in sight but behind them the explosion of magical power made the tunnel collapse and crumble around them.

It was so close. They were helpless. They could only trust in the dragon as the blue light from the explosion enveloped them. An instant later they burst from the mountain side and jerked violently up into the air. Kaln managed to glance down as he held on for his life to see the side of the mountain explode and one entire half of it collapse below them. There was dust and stone for miles. The sound of the thunderous explosion hit them only after a few moments, once Yassvyr had halted her position high up in the air away from danger. Like a Kestrel that Kaln had watched as a child, she flexed her wings and hovered in the air for a moment. There were whoops and cries as a rush of exhilaration washed over them. Only then did they see the view in its entirety. They could see all of the land as no mortal had ever seen it, looking down they could see all the villages, all the forest, the bleak scar heading North and way off in the distance they could even see the white walls of Whitebluff from up here.

"Lets see what can be healed." Yassvyr's voice said in their minds.

She stopped beating her wings, tucked them by her sides and plunged nose first into the roiling clouds of smoke billowing from the ruined mountain. The sounds of screaming came to a halt as she spread her wings just before hitting the ground and began gliding at incredible speeds towards the forest below.

In what felt like an instant they were back at the forest, skimming the tops of the trees. Kaln could feel his sense return to him, could feel the forest again. Yassvyr closed her eyes and a shimmering green light danced between her dark scales. Then she breathed an ethereal cloud of swirling gold and green down on the dead trees of the bleak scar below. Kaln expected the dragon breath to ravage the dry dead wood like fire but instead the dead trees rotted instantly, and shoots sprouted through the earth in the hundreds. Kaln peered down behind them. There was a carpet of green shoots filling the forest floor where the scar had been.

"It's working!" Kaln thought to Yassvyr.
"Many of them won't survive the winter, but some will." she replied.

Kaln closed his eyes and used the sense that

Aeathune had given him. He could feel the wounded forest beginning to heal.

Yassvyr tended the forest's wound as they flew over the tops of the trees as Kaln and the others told her of their story. What they had lost and what they had gained.

It wasn't long before they had traversed the incredible distance from the mountain to Whitebluff. Where the forest ended and the open planes began. The land below now told a different story, of sieges and of heroism as they approached the great walls. The dead and undead were almost without number but Yassvyr continued to breathe her magical fire down on the land below. As with the trees, the dead and undead were both consumed by decay into nothingness as nature intended, their armour and weapons rusted and fell to dust in an instant and where their corpses were, now new life clawed at a chance to exist. Yassvyr circled around the huge city cleansing the streets with her dragon breath. The city laid in ruins, the walls had been breached and many had died. The streets were littered with corpses and motionless undead, waiting for commands that would not come. They were all reduced to nothing but nutrients for new life by Yassvyr's magic. But there was hope. The keep still stood, its gates battered and its walls cracked but it stood. The siege had ended before they could take the entire city. Some survived.

Yassvyr landed on top of the ruined wall as the sun began to set.
They climbed down from Yassvyr's back and thanked her for everything she had done.
Lilly looked out to the sunset and said to herself, "Here is as good as any place." She withdrew the strange metal box from her pocket, the strange runes that covered its surfaces made her feel uneasy. She directed some of her power into it. It opened.
The sound of thousands of ethereal voices sighed in relief as they plumed from the tiny trinket. Their clothes whipped and snapped like the wind was pulling at them. As they escaped, an unfathomable amount of energy washed out towards the sunset as she released the trapped souls and magical energy from Thaldur's binding.

Nobody spoke for a long moment after the last soul had left and the last of the magical energy had dispersed. Yassvyr gave Lilly a small nod.

Below them they saw the gates of the keep open and figures wearily emerging from its safety.

"I must go now. Hewmans don't take too kindly to dragons yew see." She looked towards the waning sun.
"Can I ask a favour of you Yassvyr?" Lilly

asked, watching the fading sunlight dance on the dragon's scales.

"Of course yew can." Yassvyr replied softly.

"Can you keep the Rehlk stone safe? So much strife seems to follow them in the hands of mortals."

Yassvyr gave a slow nod. "Of course child. It will be safe with me. If yew eva' need me, think hard on my name, imagine me in your mind's eye and I will come to yew with all haste. All of yew."

She leapt into the air and with three powerful thrusts of her huge wings she was up between the clouds disappearing into the sunset.

They lost vision of her just as voices from down below the wall from the survivors called out "Ho there, heroes! What be your names?"

CHAPTER 35 - INTO THE SUNSET

They were proclaimed the heroes of Whitebluff - 'The Whitebreakers'. Breakers of the siege on Whitebluff. From the survivors of Whitebluff and the aid that arrived shortly after from Mul'gur, they were given resources and manpower to help Crossay and begin rebuilding Cornwalk. Cornwalk was to be rebuilt as Whitebreak, in memory of those lost. The next twelve months were busy, a time of growth, healing, prosperity and importantly, change.

Kruul reclaimed the title of Clan lord after presenting them with Thaldur's skull. There was one minor amendment to the title - Kruul Blackhand, Clan Lord and Whitebreaker, as he became known. It made him smile when he had the opportunity to prompt officials who failed to recite his entire title when visiting.

For the first time, all races were welcome in Whitebreak and Kruul's clan became a staunch part of the community that prospered there.

Kaln kept his duties as Aeathune's warden and with her gifts he tended the forests and hunted bandits and slavers with the aid of Emmental, Kruul, Kally Gimmock and other survivors who were making a life in Whitebreak. They were so ruthless and efficient that the roads in the South became safer than they ever had been, bringing yet more prosperity to Whitebreak. He stayed by Lilly's side and the two escaped to his father's cabin when the need for a break was needed.

Gleb departed with Vodius as his laboratory assistant shortly after the building of a mage's tower in Whitebreak was completed, to sate his hunger for knowledge of both the world and magic. Each time they would return, Thunderbastard would have been refined, improved and additions made. Gleb eagerly showed off it with every visit, the weapon itself began to get its own reputation. They visited Whitebreak every few months and Gleb took great pleasure in telling them all of their escapades.

Lilly made Whitebreak a welcome home to any race, taking guidance from Kruul and other race representatives on her council. Whitebreak flourished and the forest began to heal.

Twelve months later and winter was upon them again, Vodius and Gleb had arrived via portal that morning as planned. The Whitebreakers, as they were now used to being called, sat in Lilly's house in the center of Whitebreak, the only house that had not been rebuilt. Each with a glass of Black Beck they sat by the hearth as the fire blazed.

"To what we have lost and what we have gained." Lilly said, raising her glass.

Kaln raised his glass and smiled at Lilly in agreement.

"Here, here!" Kruul raised his glass along with the others and they all took a sip.

There was a sombre moment of silence as they all stared into the dancing flames remembering what they had been through to get where they were now.

Vodius swirled the liquid around his glass, deep in thought until Gleb nudged him with an elbow in the ribs.

"Yes, I know Gleb. With an ounce of tact and timing we could have, perhaps, not ruined the moment." Vodius said irritatedly.

"If you won't tell em' I will." Gleb said, slapping his lips after necking the whole glass.

The two were like an old couple bickering having spent so much time together.

Vodius shook his head, sighed and stood before

the fireplace, "It appears." He placed the glass on the hearth, obviously choosing his words.

"The demon who was hunting Thaldur for his soul, or the souls owed… Well, he is a demon lord and is now after us." He said bluntly.